MAKING *Waves*

DK MARIE

To: Shanna and Rowena,

I know dedications are supposed to be for a single person, but I'm doing two because you ladies are essential to my writing and everyday life.

Shanna, yes, I dedicated my first book ever published, Fairy Tale Lies, to you, but you're as important to me today as back then—as a friend and now as a writer. I love that we can now talk about craft and our characters. Thank you for walking this path with me from the very start.

Ro, I'm forever thankful for the day we stumbled upon each other in the #WritingCommunity of Twitter, even more, when you suggested we meet in Detroit for dinner and to talk shop.

You two are the best! Both of you have helped me grow as a writer and person. Thank you for all the hours you've talked me through plot issues and rough days and for celebrating the good ones with me. Love you.

Contents

CHAPTER ONE

Lilith Brooks closed her laptop, cutting off the chipper voice of the plumber from the how-to video. She set the computer on the side table, then picked up the travel-size toolbox she'd purchased yesterday. Time to tackle the sink.

The clay-like scent of fresh paint followed her from the living room to the kitchen, where the pleasant smell was replaced by stagnant water and yesterday's dinner of perch. The stench wouldn't last. She'd googled enough tutorials on sinks with their clogs and P-traps that she was practically an expert.

Scooting under the kitchen sink, she turned off the water valves. Pride and satisfaction washed over her. Contrary to Marshall's belief, she could take care of herself and their daughter.

Wrapping her hand around the slip joint nuts, she twisted. Bits of rust from the ancient pipe fell on her, but it didn't budge. She tried again, grunting as it shifted a fraction of a millimeter.

"You okay, Mom?" Chloe asked from somewhere around Lilith's legs.

She slid out from under the sink. "I'm great. Just fixing a clog."

"When you're done, can we go next door? To the white house."

Lilith wiped her forehead with her arm. "Why?"

"I saw a girl my age. I want to meet her."

"They might be weekend renters," Lilith hedged, not excited to make idle chit-chat with strangers.

"But maybe not."

"We'll see. I have to get a few things off my to-do list."

Chloe rolled her eyes, tightening her ponytail. "That thing's longer than Santa's naughty list."

Lilith eyed her daughter. Did she still believe? She was ten now, about the age when kids let go of childhood magic.

"How about tomorrow?" Chloe bounced on her tip-toes. "Please."

Lilith wanted to put it off all summer. There was so much work to be done to get the house ready for weekend renters. Plus, meeting new people was never fun.

"Mom..." A little whine crept into Chloe's voice.

"What? Should we march over there right now, demanding to know if they're permanent residents and if the girl will be your friend?" Lilith joked.

"Works for me." Her daughter wasn't kidding. "And, of course she'd want to be my friend."

Lilith would love to have even an ounce of Chloe's confidence.

She accepted defeat. "Fine. If they're home when I'm done, we'll stop by," Lilith said, looking inside the toolbox.

"Yah!" Chloe yelled as the doorbell rang.

"Will you answer that? It's probably Uncle Tate. Why he wouldn't just walk in is beyond me," Lilith muttered, selecting something the person at the hardware store had called tongue-and-groove pliers.

She returned under the sink and twisted hard on the valve. All thoughts of her brother and new neighbors were drowned as the part snapped from the wall, water spraying everywhere.

"No!" She tried blocking the rushing water with her palm, and it burst through her fingers, hitting her in the face. "Crap! Shit!"

"Do you need help?" came a deep voice that wasn't Tate's.

Scrambling from under the sink, she stood, facing a tall man around her age—which was dangerously close to thirty—in a gray T-shirt and dark shorts.

"Who—" she began, but the splash of water hitting the kitchen floor stole all her questions. He could be the neighborhood serial killer for all she cared. What mattered was his offer. "Yes, please. Help me. The water valve broke."

"Where's the main shut-off?"

She held up trembling hands, the need to cry pressing against her throat. "I don't know."

He took off, calling over his shoulder, "I'll find it."

She didn't have it in her tight budget for a flood. Sprinting to a nearby drawer, she yanked it open, pulling it clear off its tracks, dumping towels everywhere. She dropped it, pushing the pile toward the rapidly growing puddle. As she debated about grabbing more from the bathroom, the water cut off.

Heavy footsteps grew louder as the stranger returned from the basement. He appeared in her kitchen a few seconds later, filling up the archway with his broad shoulders.

His hazel gaze caught hers, and her heart jumped. Whoa. The man could have stepped off the cover of one of her favorite romance novels. Longish dark blonde hair, a stubble beard that couldn't hide a strong, angular jaw. And his lips—

Who cares? Definitely not her.

"How did you find the valve so quickly?" she asked.

"I got lucky. I looked where mine is. Yours is in the same place."

His explanation held no censure, but humiliation flooded her, washing away her earlier pride. She straightened. "I'm an idiot. I should have located it before I started this project."

What was I thinking? I can't do this on my own.

He waved away her mistake. "Most people don't bother. I work in construction and built my house. That's why I know where mine is." He offered his hand. "Anyway, I'm Asher Crowley. I live next door. My daughter Raven has wanted to race over since seeing a girl around her age here."

Lilith laughed, shaking his hand. "That's my daughter, Chloe. I'm Lilith Brooks. You must be the neighbor with the white house. Chloe is also eager to meet your daughter."

"I hope you don't mind that Raven went off with yours." He let go of her hand, his gaze following the downward motion of her arm. Around chest level, his eyes widened, then snapped toward her kitchen disaster. He rubbed the back of his neck and asked, "What's wrong with your sink?"

Wondering what caused such an odd reaction, she glanced down and choked on a gasp. The front of her cream tank-top was soaked. And she wasn't wearing a bra.

Her cheeks flamed hot as she crossed her arms over her chest. "It was clogged. I was trying to clean the P-trap." She pointed with her chin at the lower cabinet.

"I have a replacement valve at my house," he said. "I'll grab it and fix it for you."

Lilith rocked on the balls of her feet. He'd already rescued her once, and she didn't want to take advantage of his neighborly hospitality. However, she was afraid to touch the sink after the current disaster, and hiring a plumber was out of her budget.

As if sensing her hesitation, he said, "I've put them in and replaced a ton. It will take me less than ten minutes. Then you won't have to go without water while waiting on a plumber."

"Are you sure you don't mind?"

"Not at all." He nodded toward the stairs. "Do you mind if Raven stays here while I run to my house to get the valve? She went downstairs with your daughter."

"That's fine," Lilith replied, pointing to the hallway. "I'm just, um, going to change into dry clothes."

After he left, she trudged to her bedroom. She slouched on the edge of the bed, kneading a kink in her shoulder. Everything in her wanted to crawl under her comfy blue quilt and let its softness soothe her embarrassment.

Instead, she changed, and this time she made sure to put on a bra. Then made a quick stop in the bathroom to wash her face and brush out the wet tangles. She glanced in the mirror. Her red, chin-length hair stuck to the sides of her head, the wetness making it look almost brown. She poked at the faint circles under her eyes. They highlighted her sleepless nights—the worry, but also the excitement of being free.

Almost free.

Shutting off the light, she returned to the kitchen, stopping at the entrance. Asher was scooting out from under her sink, holding the P-trap. When he saw her, he held it up and said, "I hope you don't mind. Fixing the valve was quick, so I took this off."

She was impressed. "I don't, and thank you."

"Something's stuck in it. It's probably why your drain was clogged." He rose from the floor and shook the curved pipe over the sink.

A bright pink object made of hard rubber or silicone, shaped like a large acorn on a stand, rolled across the counter, stopping next to the drying rack.

"I think someone was playing a practical joke on the previous owner," Asher said, sounding like he was trying not to laugh. "Seems fitting."

"What do you mean?" Her chest tightened, feeling exposed but not sure why.

"Well, this couldn't have accidentally ended up in the pipe. The strainer body would have to be removed, then this dropped into it. And," he scratched his cheek. "The guy you bought this place from, was um, on the wild side. I could see a disgruntled guest doing this."

Bought the place from? It was her vacation home. Before that, it had been her dad's. He'd given it to her as a wedding gift. Who the hell had been squatting here?

"What did this man look like?"

"The owner? A white guy. Tall with black hair. Lean. Why?"

He was describing her soon-to-be ex-husband, Marshall. So, this was where he was during some of those supposed 'business trips.' There was no shock, only dull disappointment. He'd sullied her childhood summer home with his many affairs.

Not wanting to admit who the man was to her, she said, "I don't see the point of dumping this kitchen tool in the sink's pipes."

Asher snorted, and she looked at him. "What?"

His smile slipped a little. "It's not anything you'd use in a kitchen…"

Her brows furrowed, unease running alongside her confusion. "What is it?"

"Um." He shifted from side to side as if his feet ached to leave.

It made her more curious and anxious. Was it dangerous? Something to do with drugs? She repeated her question, needing to know. If it was hazardous and there were more in the house. She'd have to find them before Chloe.

"Please tell me."

He stared at the sink, and she held in the urge to ask again. Clearing his throat, he said, "It's, umm, a sex toy."

Double fists of embarrassment and humiliation sucker-punched her hard enough to make tears well in her eye."

"Oh," was all she could manage.

The desire to be alone rocked through her. This was why she didn't like to be around people. She was the last to get the joke. Or was the joke.

Inhaling her mortification, she exhaled sadness. She was supposed to stay at her vacation home for the summer while she figured out what to do with her disintegrating life. Now she'd see her shame and inadequacies reflected in her neighbor's eyes every time they spoke. The fastest way to get rid of him was through the truth. No one wanted to hang around in her messy life.

"This house has been in my family since I was a kid." She met his eyes. "That guy is my husband."

Asher groaned, the color draining from his handsome face. "I'm such an asshole."

"Hardly, and believe me, I'm an expert. I've been married to one for a decade."

Grabbing the dishtowel hanging on the stove, she picked up the offending item and tossed it into the garbage next to the sink's cabinet door. She wrapped the towel around her fist, staring at it.

The quiet became heavy. Oppressive.

He drummed his fingers on the counter. "My daughter. She's with yours. Is it okay if I get her?"

Her mortification deepened. He had at least one kid and was probably happily married with a perfect family. The poor man had just wanted to introduce his daughter, not get pulled into her mess.

"I'll see if they are in Chloe's room," she said.

"If you'd rather put your sink back together, I can find her," he offered.

"Sure. Sure." *Please anything. Just leave.* Remembering her manners, she added, "Thanks for your help."

"Anytime," he said, backtracking from the kitchen.

Reaching for her phone on the counter, she knew it was a bad idea, but perverse curiosity held her tight. She googled 'sex toys', then clicked 'images.' "Christ." She slumped against the fridge. "A butt plug."

It was official. She was going to hide in her house until the end of summer.

CHAPTER TWO

"**M**om?" Chloe shouted, her feet drumming up the stairs.

Lilith set her paint roller on the tray as her daughter ran into the living room with a smile bright as the sun. She took Lilith's hand, pulling her to the glass sliding door.

On the balcony, she pointed toward the lake, where a woman and a child were swimming. "Can we go over there? I want to see Raven again!"

No. Two days had passed since Asher and his daughter had stopped by. Lilith had no desire to look him in the eye or speak a word to him all summer.

"She's busy swimming with her mom. And I'm in the middle of painting."

"Hey, why didn't you wait for me?" came Asher's deep voice.

He appeared from around the side of his house. The homes around their large lake weren't piled on top of each other, as was common in the area. However, they were close enough to give her a good view of him moving toward the water.

Wow. He was shirtless today. Broad shoulders met with beautiful back muscles that flexed and bunched as his long strides ate the distance between grass and lake. He ran a hand through his sun-tousled hair before taking off at a full sprint. Reaching the dock, he cannon-balled into the water.

His wife screamed, sounding delighted. He popped up next to her. She took off, swimming at a fast pace with him right behind her, Raven clinging to his strong shoulders. His deep rumbling laughter carried across the lake, settling hot in Lilith's veins.

She blinked, shame oozing into her. The man was enjoying a lovely afternoon with his family, and she was eyeing him like dessert.

I'm no better than Marshall.

She puffed out an annoyed breath, anger playing with her self-reproach. Thoughts were one thing. Marshall was a man of action.

"Mom, you okay?"

Lilith plastered on a smile. "I'm fine. Why do you think something's wrong?"

"You have that angry line between your eyebrows."

She rubbed the spot. "I'm good, just mentally going over the things I need to get done today."

"I'll help, Mommy."

Mommy. Lilith cherished the name. Nowadays, Chloe rarely used it, only when trying to get out of trouble or for comfort. She pulled Chloe into a hug. She should be like the girl in the lake, carefree and not a worry in the world.

"Lil," called her brother from in the house. "Where are you?"

"On the balcony," she yelled.

A few seconds later, Tate joined them.

"Why are you two standing out here instead of in the water? It's freaking hot."

He had a point. June was turning out to be a scorcher of a month.

"Yes! Let's go swimming," Chloe shouted.

There was no way Lilith was getting into the lake with Asher there. He probably wanted to talk to her as much as she did him.

"Would you mind going with Chloe while I finish painting the living room?" she asked Tate.

He shrugged. "Sure."

"Will you come out after?" Chloe asked.

"Maybe."

"Mom, you have to. All you do is work, and I want to do something fun with you."

How could she argue with that reasoning? Or the joyful pleading in her daughter's eyes.

"Fine. In a little bit." Like when their neighbors are no longer in the lake.

Being the wuss she was, Lilith hid inside. She finished painting, then removed some of the outdated wallpaper in the main bathroom.

When she figured it was safe to go outside, she set three lemonades on a tray and made her way to the shoreline. Chloe was swimming, and Tate was lounging in an Adirondack, his feet buried in the sand of the tiny beach. After handing him a drink, Lilith took a seat that had her back to Asher's house.

"How's the water?" she asked.

"Not too bad for early June," Tate said.

"Mom," Chloe called from the floating dock ten feet from shore. "You coming?"

"Give me five minutes," Lilith replied before turning to Tate. "Hey, thanks for helping me put in the docks. I think we'll get a lot of use out of both."

He waved away her gratitude as laughter from the next yard snagged his attention.

"I'm going to like you living here," he muttered.

Damn. Guess they hadn't gone inside.

"Are you seriously checking out Asher's wife?"

Tate cocked a brow. "You know his name?" After a slight pause, he added, "Also, she could be his sister."

"Ha." Lilith took a sip of her lemonade. "What are the chances?"

"It could happen. Some siblings do hang out." He pointed between them, then tipped his chin at the neighbors. "Her *brother* is the sort of dude you used to drool over in high school." He winked. "He could be your rebound."

Lilith shook her head. "No way. I'm hoping to avoid him for the rest of the summer."

Tate sat straight, his spine stiff. "Why? What happened?"

"Whoa, untie the overprotective super-brother cape. He's fine. A nice guy. I'm the idiot." She told him the whole embarrassing encounter.

For about ten seconds, they just stared at each other, then Tate snort-laughed. "I'm sorry. I am pissed at that asshole Marshall, but, shit—"

"I know. How am I supposed to look my neighbor in the eye when our first encounter had him removing a butt plug from my—"

Tate wiggled his eyebrows.

"Oh-my-God! You are the worst." She kicked sand at his legs. "From my *sink*."

Now her jerk-of-a-brother did a full-out belly laugh. Leaning closer, he said, "And I bet you had to google what it was."

Her face flamed as she nodded, making him laugh harder. Wiping the mirth from his eyes, he said, "The guy recognized what it was, so I reaffirm he might be a good rebound. He might be able to teach you a few things."

"Shut up, Tate." Lilith covered her face with her hands, peeking between them. "Will you let me at least get divorced before you start worrying about my sex life?"

He rolled his eyes. "You've been living separate lives for the past two years, and Marshall left the marriage way before the separation. I don't see why a little piece of paper from the courts should matter."

All he said was true, but it didn't change reality.

She dropped her hands to her thighs. "He did. Not me. I need time to adjust. And I don't want a rebound. I want a damn divorce. To be free."

"When does the court's waiting period end?"

"Soon. The end of July."

"Thank Christ," Tate said before taking a sip of his lemonade.

The date didn't soothe Lilith. Marshall *would* contest it. He'd made it clear the day he was served.

"Mom," Chloe yelled. "You coming?"

"Yeah." Pulling herself from her worries, she stood and took off her coverup.

Tate stopped her from leaving, wrapping a finger around her wrist. "Lil, I'm glad you're trying to get free of Marshall, but you're still hiding from life."

She sighed, looking skyward, before returning her gaze to him. "Why? Because I want to avoid my neighbor after looking like a total fool in front of him."

"One. Marshall is the fool, not you. Two. Chloe chattered about this guy's daughter non-stop. She seems hell-bent on making her new best friend, so your plan might not be possible. Three. He knew exactly what was in that sink, so he's no prude. I'm sure he can move past it, if you can."

She wasn't sure she could, but she might have to for Chloe.

Crap. This was supposed to be her fresh start, but so far, it felt rotten.

CHAPTER THREE

Flipping the steaks with one hand, Asher took a sip of scotch with the other, drinking in the sight of Lilith striding down her dock. The sun kissed her elegant legs and arms and shimmered against her strawberry blonde bob. Were her loose waves soft as they looked? Same with her curves?

Rising on the tips of her toes, she executed a perfect dive into the lake.

"Who's she?" Jackson asked, an inch from Asher's ear, making him jolt.

He pushed his friend's shoulder, laughing. "Asshole. I almost dropped my drink."

"Hey, it's not my fault you were too busy ogling the hot lady next door to notice me." He handed Asher a plate.

"I wasn't ogling. We met 'em a few days ago." He switched his glass for a spatula and used it to point at Raven before removing the steaks from the grill. "I was thinking of inviting them over."

Thankfully, his daughter was deep in conversation with her Aunt Hope and didn't hear his lie. He had no intention of doing that, which made him a shitty dad. All Raven could talk about since meeting Chloe was, well, Chloe. Yet, he wouldn't encourage the friendship.

Not because of his little attraction to Lilith, he could crush a crush. No, it was that he couldn't stand her husband.

During his stays, he and Asher tossed insults at each other from their yards. And last year, they'd almost gotten into a fistfight. If Lilith's husband planned on spending any time at the lake, Asher was keeping his distance.

With his past, shit like that could cause him huge problems. And he didn't want his daughter near that asshole.

"You should invite them," said Raven. "Chloe's my best friend."

"Already?" Asher asked. *Damn it.*

"Uh-huh." She pointed toward Chloe. She and Lilith were doing backflips into the water. "She's fun, and I need a friend. Since Alex moved, I don't have anyone around here."

Jackson leaned closer to Asher and said quietly, "I bet you wouldn't mind getting close with the new neighbors. Especially the mom."

"Dude. She's married," Asher said flatly, reminding himself as much as informing Jackson.

"Is that her husband?" his sister, Hope asked, pointing at the man relaxing on Lilith's beach.

"No. I don't know who he is. Remember the guy who was in the house the last few summers?"

Hope wrinkled her nose. "How could I forget?"

"I don't remember him. What happened?" Raven asked.

She wouldn't know him. After the near-fight with the dickhead, Raven stayed at her grandparents on the weekends he was at the lake.

"Nothing big," he said. "Playing his music too loud and other annoying stuff."

"Oh," Raven said, grabbing a slice of watermelon, seeming to lose interest.

"Anyway, why are you moping about not having friends? You have a ton at Grandma and Grandpa's."

"That's great when I'm *there*," Raven huffed, "but I need friends here too."

"Aren't you a demanding princess?"

"Daaad. I hate when you call me that."

Which is why he did it. "What about that kid at the end of the street? What's his name? Chase?"

"He's boring. Chloe is way more fun. The only thing he wants to do is play video games. And his mom looks at you weird. She always asks me if you have a girlfriend. Gross."

Hope and Jackson howled with laughter.

"Shut it. All of you." He sat next to Raven, ruffling her ink-black hair. "Run inside and grab us plates and forks."

When she left, he took a sip of his drink, scanning the lake. Lilith was now on the floating dock with her daughter. Her simple one-piece was way sexier than the porn suits he'd seen her husband's other women wear during past summers. Hers was a dark blue halter; the front dipping between a set of marvelous breasts.

"You're doing it again," his sister sang from the picnic table.

"He is," Jackson agreed.

Asher scoffed. "You two know me well enough to know I'd never go after a married woman."

"Especially one with a douche-bag husband who you nearly punched last summer. His wife is probably as much trouble as him," Hope said.

Jackson's eyes widened. "Whoa. You? I can't remember the last time you hit some—" Guilt that didn't belong bloomed on his face. "Sorry, man."

The three stared at each other as regret and remorse passed between them.

After a beat, Hope filled the haunted silence, pointing at Lilith. "Her husband was practically screwing a woman on his dock in the middle of the afternoon. Asher told him he had a little kid and would appreciate it if they'd take it inside."

"The fucker told me this lake wasn't a daycare and to go inside if we didn't like the show," Asher said. "Then he winked at Hope and told her she was welcome to join them."

Jackson's jaw flexed and his nose flared. "I hope you punched him. In the dick."

"Nah," Asher laughed. "The woman he was with said something, and they'd went inside, with him saluting me goodbye with his middle finger as they left."

"I take it that"—Jackson tilted his head in Lilith's direction—"wasn't the same woman."

"Nope."

"Hmm. They could have an open marriage. The guy sure acts like it," Jackson said.

"Why? Do you want to play with them?" Asher joked.

"Maybe with his wife. She's hot." Jackson volleyed back, earning him a pinch from Hope.

He jumped away from her. "Ouch, woman. I'm kidding."

Asher eyed them. Sometimes, they acted like they were still dating.

Hope glanced next door. "Whatever they've got going on is messed up. That family is nothing but trouble. You and Raven should stay away."

Even though he'd been thinking the same thing moments ago, he argued, "What, because the husband is an ass, that means so are his wife and kid? It isn't fair to judge them for his actions."

His words rang true. Keeping Raven from Chloe was wrong.

"Maybe, but I've been watching you watch her. You're defending her because you *like her*," Hope said in a sing-song teasing voice that she knew drove him nuts.

He refused to bite.

Fine. He tried not to bite.

"I don't *like* her. I feel bad. She didn't know he'd been here these past summers. I might've been the one to clue her in that her husband was a cheating asshole."

"Ow," Jackson grunted, gripping his short dreadlocks before running a palm along one of his shaved sides. "That must have been awkward."

"You have no idea." Asher chuckled, recalling the butt plug rolling across the counter.

Less funny had been the emotions that shifted and fell from Lilith's face. The sweet naivety about the toy to the dull embarrassment about her husband was heartbreaking to witness.

Asher's gaze moved to the lake. Lilith was getting out, talking animatedly with her daughter. Easy joy radiated off her, warm as summer. The way the water trailed down her curves was mesmerizing.

Hope tapped the picnic table, snagging Asher's attention. "What?" he asked.

"Don't deny it. You want her. You're my twin. I know you. We practically share a brain." Hope shuddered, her wicked smirk returning. "And let me tell you, brother, you have a dirty mind."

Asher laughed loud and deep, more than happy to steer the conversation toward his sister's perversions. "If I recall, mom found 'Playgirl' stuffed in your mattress, not mine."

Jackson guffawed, "Do tell more."

Hope's cheeks turned bright red. "Don't let him fool you. He had his dirty stash hidden in a cubby in the back of his closet."

Plates clattered onto the table, followed by Raven asking, "What's 'Playgirl?'"

Asher choked on a swallow of scotch. Oops. After ten years, he should be better at PG-ing his talk around his daughter.

"It's a magazine I better never catch you with."

"You told me I need to read more."

He ran a hand over his mouth, swallowing a laugh. "Well, it's more of a picture magazine..."

"Like a graphic novel?"

"Oh, it's graphic alright," Hope giggled.

Asher knocked on the picnic table. "Speaking of reading, we need to go to the library to get your summer reading list."

"Can we go tomorrow?" Raven asked.

"Sure."

"And bring Chloe?"

"Um..."

"If we do, I promise to stop asking about 'Playgirl.'" She grinned. "Or google it later."

"I think you just gave me my first gray hair." Grabbing a corn-on-the-cob, he said, "Fine. After dinner you can run over and ask her."

Raven kissed his cheek. "Thanks, Dad."

"Yeah, yeah. Eat your food."

Hope rested her chin on his shoulder. "You should have told Raven, no. You're playing with fire."

Possibly, but for Raven, he'd dance in the flames.

CHAPTER FOUR

Lilith pointed to a medium-sized boulder. "Chloe, are you able to push that in line with the others?"

She nodded.

"It's a little late in the season to start a garden," said Asher.

Lilith startled, nearly dropping the hoe. Twisting around, she found him and Raven standing less than a foot away.

Two thoughts raced inside her. The first, quieter one asked why he was back. He'd stopped by yesterday, inviting them to the library, and she'd refused with an excuse so lame he had to know she was rejecting his olive branch.

The second, louder thought demanded to know why he had such incredible arms—muscular biceps and sexy, veiny forearms. They begged to be licked.

Following the path to his hands, she noticed he was holding a tiller. She'd seen the exact one at the local hardware store and had wanted to buy it, but had resisted and got the bargain version.

Pointing, she asked, "Why do you have that?"

"I saw you and Chloe working over here. We,"—he indicated himself and Raven— "had to stop at my parents earlier. My dad's a big gardener, so I asked to borrow a few of his tools he uses to get his ready in the spring. He loaned me this and a few other things. The rest is in my Jeep. I figured I'd check with you first to see if you wanted to use them before dragging over everything."

Stress slid from her body, replaced with gratitude. Her paltry and cheap selection of gardening equipment was adequate but barely better than digging with her bare hands. Meanwhile, the fancy tiller would save her hours. She'd love to see what he had in his vehicle.

Raven held up her arms. She was holding a pitcher that contained dark purple juice with fruit floating in it. "Do you want a sangria?"

The whole scene was a tad surreal. Chloe had spent the morning trying to escape garden duty. Now, two people show up offering help, with the ten-year-old playing bartender.

Lilith squinted her eyes, smiling. "So, um, where did you learn to make alcoholic drinks? I didn't realize bartending classes were available in the public schools."

Asher's eyes shined with humor. "Sorry to disappoint. There's no wine in it. She uses sparkling water. Last year, in her Spanish class, each kid had to bring in something to eat or drink from a Spanish-speaking country. Her pick was sangria."

"Good choice. It is one of my favorites. Chloe, would you run to the kitchen and grab us glasses?" Lilith asked, rubbing the back of her neck, trying to ease the tension that had dug its fingers into her.

"Can I go?" Raven asked.

"Sure," Asher said. The two girls took off for the house. Awkwardness filled the space between them, but before she could think of an excuse to follow and escape her embarrassment, he spoke. "Listen, I'm sorry about the other day—for running my mouth without thinking. I'd seen the moving truck and assumed you were a new owner. I hope my stupid comments didn't cause problems between you and your husband."

His apology surprised her, and since he was making an effort, she could do the same.

"Don't worry about it." Lilith picked up her discarded hoe. "You didn't tell me anything I didn't already know about my husband's faithfulness. But the party is definitely over. I hope the local ladies he used to entertain aren't too upset they're now stuck with his dull, doormat wife."

"I—"

She gripped the handle and slammed the blade into the dirt as anger overtook embarrassment. "That isn't true. My doormat days ended when I walked out on him."

Her gaze whipped to Asher, daring him to say different. He raised his arms as if in surrender. His face was plastered with confusion. "So... you're not married?"

She took a deep, calming breath. So much for trying to make things normal between them. Asher must think she was unstable.

Returning to her task with more gentleness, she said, "On paper, I am, but the marriage has been dead for years. In the spring, I made it official and filed for divorce. For reasons unknown to me, he refuses to sign the papers. I'd hoped moving out had made it clear... I'm not sure it has." She waved a hand. "Anyway, sorry. My heavy baggage just popped open and spilled onto you. Again. It seems I'm destined to look like a fool in front of you."

Asher gripped her elbow. She stilled as his light touch sent goosebumps along her skin. As did the soft intensity of his eyes.

"Your husband is the fool, not you. He's an asshole, and I'm sorry he's putting you through this. And you're not dull," he said with such certainty she wanted to hug him.

Instead, she moved from his comforting hold. Was she so starved for touch that the first man who said something nice to her, a married man at that, made her weak in the knees?

Resting a hand on the top of the hoe, she placed the other on her hip and joked, "Oh, you know I'm not dull after spending ten minutes under my sink cleaning my pipes."

Why did that sound suggestive to her? His gaze flickered to her shorts, then returned to her face. He swallowed hard, his Adam's apple bobbing.

Hmm. Maybe not just her ears.

Then, because she was socially awkward and obviously unfit to be around people, she continued. "And remember, what you found in the kitchen wasn't mine. Though I now know, with the help of Google, it's not what you use to plug a sink."

Before she could melt with mortification, Asher laughed. "That's good. If those are the sorts of tools you'd try to use for any other DIY projects, I'd be worried."

"Or you might offer to help, just to have a front-row seat at the dumpster-fire." A lightness blooming in her chest. It had been a while since she joked and teased with someone.

"Yeah," he agreed, bumping the front of his foot against the base of her tool. "The conversation about garden hoes could have been interesting."

"Or stopcocks." She snorted. It wasn't lady-like but felt great.

He chuckled. "How do you even know what that is?"

"After the water disaster, I learned everything I could about how to turn off any and all valves in my house."

"Smart." He looked around. "How can I help?"

"Why would you want to? You have nothing better to do on this gorgeous Sunday?"

Like spending it with your wife.

Lilith glanced at his house. She hadn't seen the pretty blonde since the barbecue.

"Nope. No plans until this evening." He volleyed the tiller, hitting it with his palms. "Raven's happy to be here, and I like working with my hands."

An image of his big hands working on her flashed quick, hot, and dirty in her mind. She inhaled at the sudden ache pooling low in her. *Stop.* She didn't want these urges for another woman's husband.

She would never sink that low. However, it might be time to take her mother's incredibly embarrassing advice and buy BOB—a Battery Operated Boyfriend.

"You okay?" Asher asked, dragging her from her musings.

"I'm fine. I think the heat is getting to me," she fibbed.

He pointed to the chair. "Rest. I'll see where the girls got off to with the cups and ice."

Before she could answer, he was striding toward the house, calling out his daughter's name.

Instead of taking a break, she worked harder, attacking her garden with renewed force, trying to get her runaway desires in order. She gave a final shove to a boulder that had slipped, settling it next to the natural border she was repairing. Straightening, she gripped the bottom of her top and wiped her forehead.

She dropped it and saw the three of them had returned. And that Asher was checking her out. Hot excitement rushed over her, but she quickly shoved it aside, replacing it with annoyance.

He was married. He shouldn't be looking. And her pleasure was equally disgusting. She didn't want another Marshall in her life, not even as a friend.

"You want water or sangria?" he asked.

She pressed her lips into a thin line, giving him an icy stare. Picking up her cup, she turned to Raven. "Let's try what you made."

Taking a sip, Lilith sighed. The drink was cool and tasty.

"Why are you bothering with a garden so late in the season?" Asher asked.

"Because I love it—"

"It's boring," Chloe grumbled.

"Hey," Lilith laughed, "Gardening isn't boring. Growing and eating fresh food is rewarding."

"It's lame," Chloe muttered to Raven.

"Anyway," Lilith said, choosing to ignore her daughter's complaining, "I'll be in my new place when it's time to harvest, but I can check on it when I come here to clean up after renters."

He tilted his head. "You two aren't staying?"

"Just until school starts." She took another sip of her sangria. "Then we're moving to a condo by my brother. I'll be renting out this place. After I saw how much I could charge, I couldn't pass up the income." Her stomach tightened at the hurdle of how she was going to support herself and Chloe.

Setting down his half-empty cup, Asher grabbed a shovel, asking, "What can I do?"

"*You're* going to help dig up this garden?" Disbelief was etched in Raven's every word.

"Why are you surprised?" He sounded mildly offended. "Manual labor is my job."

"Building houses, making cabinets and decks is what you do," she retorted, widening her eyes, said, "Not a landscaper who works in the dirt, where there might be *centipedes*."

"Shut it, daughter," he grinned, scanning the ground.

Lilith laughed. "Are you scared of them?"

"Scared might be too strong of a word..."

"More like terrified," Raven said with glee.

Asher shrugged. "Those fu—bugs move way too fast. And you're no help. The last one I asked you to kill, you screamed and ran away."

"I'm a kid. And a girl." As if that was all the reason Raven needed.

"I'm a girl, and I get rid of them," Lilith said.

"Thank God," Chloe muttered, making everyone laugh.

"Yeah, Raven, don't be sexist," Asher teased. "Also, Aunt Hope never had an issue taking care of them when we were kids."

"Then call her next time one's crawling up the wall." She pointed at herself. "And not me." The girls took off toward the lake before he could reply.

Asher shuddered, and Lilith laughed.

"You have a sister?" she asked, sitting on a nearby boulder. "Are you from a big family?"

He sat on the one next to her. "No. It's just Hope and me. What about you? Do you have any siblings?"

"I have a brother, Tate. You might have seen him here the other day."

Asher nodded, pointing at his head. "He had the same color of hair as you, so I'd wondered if you two are related."

She couldn't explain why, but she liked that he'd been watching and wondering about her. "I also have a half-sister. Miley. She is seven years younger than me and super smart. She's getting her bachelor's and thinking of going to law school," Lilith said proudly. "She lives in Florida with my mom and stepdad, Ted."

"Are you originally from Florida?"

She shook her head. "No. My parents divorced when I was four. My mom remarried a few years later, then had to move there for Ted's job. Tate and I didn't want to go, so we moved in with my dad. We lived about an hour south of here—Dad still lives in the same house. It's been nice for Chloe to be closer to her grandfather."

"But not you?" He dug a heel into the dirt and glanced at her. "Let me know if I'm being nosy."

"It's fine." That was the truth. Talking with Asher was almost therapeutic. "And no, not easier for me. My dad thinks I'm wrong for leaving my husband. And he has to tell me this *every* time we see each other."

Asher scoffed. Opened his mouth like he had a lot to say, then promptly shut it, shaking his head. She understood his befuddlement—what kind of father would want his daughter to stay with a cheating, narcissistic asshole? But her dad didn't believe in divorce, no matter the reason. If he'd had a say, he and Mom never would have split, and they would still be together, making each other miserable.

Taking a sip of her sangria and setting it in the grass, she asked, "What about you? Are your parents still married? Are you and your sister close? Does she live nearby?"

"Yup, my parents are still married. This year will be their thirty-fifth anniversary. We're a close family. We work together and all have houses on this lake. My sister hates to cook so she's at my place all the time." He tapped his chin. "She and my friend Jackson were over the other day for dinner. They're coming over today too."

Lilith startled, as something like delight fluttered in her stomach. "She's your sister?"

"Mom," Chloe called from their small beach. "Can we go swimming?"

Lilith nodded and waved that it was fine.

"You two should come over," Asher said. "I'm throwing ribs on the grill and taking everyone out to waterski. It'll be fun."

"Who's everyone?"

"My sister, my friends Jackson, Max, and Wyatt. Oh, and probably his wife."

Yikes. That was a lot of people. Spending more time with him was appealing, but being thrown in with a group of new people was her idea of torture.

"No, thanks. I don't want to intrude. Also, I told Chloe we'd try that sushi place on Fifth Street."

"Did you hear the part about how my sister and I are together too much?" He tapped her knee with his glass. "Also, I wouldn't bother with that restaurant. It's an overpriced hangout for the summer tourists. The best place for sushi is in Novi. I'm working on a house there. If you'd like, I could get an order to go this week."

"Would you? Please." Her taste buds could have cheered.

"Sure. But now you don't have dinner plans, so you'll have to come over."

She shuffled at the dirt with her beat-up sneakers. Unable to find another excuse, she asked, "Are you sure your sister and friends won't mind?"

"If there's food and beer, Max and Jackson are happy. As for Hope... getting the chance to have a new member for her coven,"—he winked— "I mean circle of friends, would make her day."

Lilith twisted the threads on her cut-offs, her stomach in knots. "I'm not much for covens or big groups. Most of the time, I find them overwhelming and exhausting."

"Even better. She'll keep you from her friends and have you all for herself."

Lilith's head fell back as she laughed. "Now that sounds creepy."

He chuckled. "I guess it did. I meant she loves being in groups or hanging out one-on-one. She and I have that in common."

Lilith sucked on her lips and then released them as warmth filled her cheeks. "I thought she was your wife."

Asher had been mid sip of his drink and choked on it. She rubbed his back until the coughing fit passed and switched to laughter.

His cup dangled from his loose grasp. "Nope. She's my twin. I'm not married."

"Were you ever?" Lilith's gaze traveled to their girls before finding his again. "I'm sorry. Feel free to change the subject if you don't want to talk about it."

"It's fine." Asher stared at the water as if his story was floating in the calm waves. "Raven's mother Eden and I never married. We met the summer I'd graduated high school. She was attending UMich, heading to Stanford the following year. We hadn't been together long when she found out she was pregnant. She had no plans to stay, and I couldn't leave, so after giving birth to Raven, Eden signed off her guardianship and left, only recently returning."

Lilith had so many questions. If Eden had given up guardianship, why had she come back? Was it for Asher? Had they picked up where they'd left off? However, she had already been too intrusive. She took the conversation in another direction.

"Are you Crowley Construction?" she asked.

He nodded.

"I've seen your signs around," she said. "You guys do beautiful work."

"Thanks. My grandfather started the business, and construction seems to run in the family. My father loves it, and when Hope and I were kids, we used to beg him to take us to work so we could play with the tools. He did and taught us so much. Now, we've taken over for him. I do mostly carpentry, and my sister manages the office—deciding in high school she liked numbers more than tools," he said, pride in his smile. "What about you? Do you work outside of the home? Have other homes you rent?"

She ran her finger around the rim of her glass. "Before my life imploded, I kept myself busy with Chloe and hobbies. As for renting, this is my first and only one."

"What sort of hobbies do you like?" he asked.

She waved a hand. "Nothing exciting. Reading, gardening, canning. Marshall used to tease me, told me I belonged in the early nineteen-hundreds."

Asher scoffed, but she felt like his annoyance wasn't directed at her.

"Why," he said, "because you're interested in calmer things that use your mind?"

His lack of judgement, his understanding, was a balm to her bruised ego, but he couldn't honestly be interested in her boring life.

"You don't have to humor me," she said, pointing toward his dock. "I see your speedboat. Also, isn't there a dirt bike parked in your driveway? I get the feeling books and canning aren't what you'd do with your free time."

"I love to read," he argued. "I'm a huge John Sandford and Gillian Flynn fan. Anything they write, I'll read. And, although I've never tried canning, I wouldn't mind learning. My dad loves his garden but gives away or composts most of it. It is such a waste. I could learn and do it for him."

Her eyes narrowed. Was he humoring her? If so, she would call his bluff. "Fine. I'll teach you. You can help me with whatever I get from this garden."

"Sounds good to me." After a moment, he clapped his hands and stood. "Let's finish lining up the rock border so we can get in the water with the girls."

"That's a perfect plan." Crouching in front of a large gray stone, she peeked up at him, catching his gaze. "Let me know if you need me to rescue you from any bugs."

"Smartass," he chuckled, bumping her with his leg. "Tell you what. I'll get that big rock for you, and you stay by my side and protect me from anything that might crawl from under it."

She laughed. "Deal. We make a great team."

"That we do, Lilith." He squatted next to her, close enough that she could smell summer on his skin. The scent of freedom and adventure wrapped around her, becoming her favorite season.

CHAPTER FIVE

Lilith grabbed the potato salad she'd managed to whip together for dinner at Asher's place. "Are you ready, Chloe?"

"Yup." She was already at the front door.

Lilith smiled, amused. "Eager to visit?"

"Um, yeah. There'll be ribs. And Raven said we might go out on their boat. It looks fast." Chloe clapped. "Do you think he'll let me ski?"

"I don't even know if we'll stay long enough to join them on the water. I'm tired," Lilith said, leaving the kitchen.

In truth, she hoped to be home right after dinner. The possibility of spending an entire evening with strangers had her heart hammering as if she was clicking up that first terrifying rollercoaster hill.

Chloe's shoulders slumped, then perked up again as she opened the front door. "Oh well, at least there'll be ribs."

Her girl loved them. Hopefully, she wouldn't try to eat an entire rack. If she did, she could have Lilith's portion. Her appetite had disappeared, replaced with old anxieties.

What if her mind went blank, and she had nothing interesting to say? Everyone would find her dull. It would embarrass Asher to have her as that socially inept friend, and he'd never invite her over again.

If it weren't for Chloe's cheerful chatter and the skip in her step as they walked from their house to his, Lilith would have canceled. She wanted to hide amongst her books and beautiful solitude.

Needing a distraction, she studied Asher's home as they walked to it. It was a beautiful farmhouse style with white siding that ran vertically instead of the usual horizontally—topped off with a neat, black slate roof. Even homier was the wide front porch. She loved the dark wood floors and beams and the well-used outdoor furniture that spoke of treasured memories.

Her finger trembled slightly as she rang the bell. Before it even finished dinging, the door swung open, and Asher's sister stood on the other side. Lilith almost laughed. How could she have mistaken her for his wife? It was obvious they were related. She had the same kaleidoscope of blonde and brown hair, big hazel eyes, and a smile that was impossible not to return.

"Wow. Asher would have made a beautiful woman," Lilith blurted, then grimaced as her stomach pinched.

Way to play it smooth and cool. I'm such a dork.

"You must be the new neighbor," Hope said, pulling Lilith into a surprise hug. "And my new best friend."

Asher came from around the corner, carrying a bright green water bottle. His brows shot up. "Why are you accosting Lilith?"

"It's all good. We're best friends," his sister replied, stepping to her brother and tweaking his cheek.

"Why? Did she bring your favorite vodka?" he joked.

"I don't think so," Hope replied, eyeing the bowl Lilith had shifted to her side during the hug.

Her playful nature loosened the stiff knot of anxiety in Lilith, and she smiled. "Sorry, I don't have a bottle hidden. It's only potato salad."

The other woman shrugged, taking the bowl from Lilith and handing it to Asher. "I don't mind drinking my brother's top-shelf scotch."

He groaned, and his sister laughed. "Anyway, I love your neighbor because she said you're a pretty girl."

His lips twitched as he glanced at Lilith. "What's that now?"

"I'd said, *if* you were a girl, you'd be stunning. Big difference." Her cheeks were scalding. They were probably red as her linen shorts. She peeked at Hope. "You're beautiful."

Asher rested against the sage-colored foyer wall. "Ah, I see. No wonder my sister loves you. She is pretty vain."

"All I heard in that sentence was you saying I'm pretty," Hope sang, winking at Lilith.

Their teasing was like what passed between her and Tate. It made her feel at home. Maybe she shouldn't leave right after dinner.

Hope's gaze shifted to Chloe. "You must be Raven's new best friend. My niece talks about you so much I feel like I already know you." She pointed toward the stairs. "She is waiting for you on the downstairs patio."

Chloe thanked Hope and took off to find her friend. "Are you going to steal her from my daughter, like you're trying to take Lilith from me?" Asher asked.

He was clearly teasing, but it chased away a few of the shadows in Lilith's heart. It was nice knowing he valued their new friendship.

"Can I have you both? Have the complete set," Lilith joked.

Hope handed Asher the bowl of potato salad, then linked an arm through Lilith's. "Chloe is safe, but you, brother, look out." She turned them around so they were facing the door. "Everyone's in the boat."

Crap. That's right. There were more people to meet. As Hope led Lilith around to the lakeside, she gazed at her own home. Its silent comforts reaching out to her.

"Wait up," Asher called, hurrying toward them.

"Why? She's mine now. Go play with the boys," Hope teased.

"No way." He slipped his arm through Lilith's free one. "She likes me more. I'm way cooler."

They both seemed great to her. However, she had to admit, if only to herself, Asher's warm skin against hers was lovely. Fantastic, really.

Hope snorted as they reached the water. "We should take a vote. Ask the guys."

A touch of Lilith's shy nervousness returned as she eyed two very handsome and nicely built men sitting on the dock with their feet in the lake. Asher was her favorite, but damn, what the hell was in the water here that made everyone so good-looking?

As they got closer, she recognized one of the men. He'd helped her at the hardware store. He smiled at her, and said, "I know you. You bought the starter toolkit at my store."

"I did. I've been using it a lot." She pointed with her thumb over her shoulder toward her house.

He stood, offering his hand. "I'm Jackson Harris." He was tall, had an inch or two on Asher, who had to be at least six feet. He had flawless dark skin, short dreadlocks, and arms that could bench-press a car.

She told him her name; then he introduced the other man, Max London. He was pale, the sort of person who sunburned if he stepped outside without sunblock for more than a minute or two. In fact, the bridge of his nose and cheeks was already reddening, as were his shoulders.

"Nice to meet you," Max said. His playful blue gaze jumped from Hope to Lilith. "I heard you two talking. What do you need us to vote on?"

"Who's cooler? Me"—Hope pointed at herself, then Asher— "or him?"

"I abstain," Max said, holding his hands in an *I surrender* gesture.

"Me too," agreed Jackson.

Hope huffed. "Why?"

"Because if we pick, we're screwed." Jackson chuckled. "Asher will run me onto a beach when I'm skiing. And you'll try drowning me next time we're in the water together."

"That's true." Asher smirked, grabbing and pulling the boat's ropes, bringing it closer to the dock.

"He isn't lying." Hope's smile was all devil and fun.

"Remind me to never get on the Crowleys' bad side." Lilith laughed as Jackson and then Max jumped into the boat.

Asher cupped his hands around his mouth and called to the girls. They came running from the walkout basement, then pounded down the dock to them, shouting about skiing and tubing.

"What happened to dinner?" Lilith asked.

"Everything is done. We're just waiting for Wyatt and his wife. They're running behind. I figured we'd go out while we wait for them." Asher's brows knitted. "Why, are you hungry?"

No, but it meant she'd be staying much longer than she'd planned. However, his friends were welcoming, and memories of boat rides on this lake had her yearning to stay. So, perhaps she should relax and enjoy the possibility of fun.

She shook her head. "Just curious."

"You sure?" he asked. "I could grab you a snack."

When she shook her head again, he nodded, then said in a louder voice. "Plus, I wanted to go out on the boat before everyone started drinking." His impish gaze fell on Max. "I don't want anyone puking over the side. Again."

"Hey, I wasn't drunk." The other man flushed darker than his sunburn but was smiling. "I got sick from your driving. Remember, you kept going in tight circles, trying to throw Jackson from his skis?"

"For the record, he wasn't able to," Jackson said, flexing those rather impressive biceps and smiling widely.

Lilith bit her lip. "You aren't going to do that today, are you?" She had visions of losing her lunch.

"No." Asher ran a palm down her arm, squeezing her hand briefly before letting go and hopping onto the boat with graceful ease. "It's your first time with all of us, so we'll be gentle."

"Are you going to ski?" Hope asked Lilith, stepping onto the boat.

Asher followed, offering her his hand. She took it and got on, stumbling a little. He steadied her, gripping her waist. Ignoring how much she liked his hand there, she stepped away from him.

"No. As a kid I tried. I could never get out of the water and stand in the skis. I'm happy to watch." *And not look like a fool.*

"They might've been too big. That makes it difficult to stand," Asher said.

She nodded. "Could be. My dad only had one set, and they worked for him and Tate."

"Try Raven's skis. They should work."

"You should," said Chloe, jumping onto the boat behind Raven.

"We'll see." She had no plans to try it and look like an incompetent idiot in front of everyone.

"Take a seat here," Max said to her, patting the empty spot next to him. "I'll give you tips on getting and staying up."

"Are you sure you're the best man for that?" Jackson asked with a chuckle. "I heard you have issues with keeping it up."

Everyone broke into raucous laughter as Lilith took her seat next to Max. He tossed a life jacket at Jackson, saying. "You heard wrong." He looked at her, humor in his eyes. "Don't listen to that dumb ass. He's bitter because the ladies like me more than him."

"Bullshit," Jackson called out.

As Asher eased the boat from the dock, the two men continued to tease each other good-naturedly. Hope sat on the other side of Lilith, giving suggestions on how to get up on skis, then peppered her with questions about summer plans.

Her inquiries didn't tie up Lilith's tongue or make her uneasy, as it usually did; instead, it was like being welcomed into the fold. Happy warmth filled her as her gaze traveled from Hope to the lake where Jackson was in the water, getting ready.

Gripping the ski rope with one hand, he held up his thumb with the other. She looked at Asher to see if he'd caught the gesture. He hadn't because he was watching her. Heat washed over her as he grinned, and the heat had nothing to do with the summer sun. Though, when he shifted his focus to Jackson, it was as if a cloud had passed over her.

She groaned. *Please. No.* Leaving Marshall was supposed to be her chance to change, to find the strong woman she'd abandoned when getting married. She wasn't supposed to become enamored with the first man who smiled at her, even if he was equal parts sweet and sexy.

Thankfully, he wanted only her friendship. Anything more might be impossible for her weak, pathetic heart to resist.

CHAPTER SIX

Asher cut the boat's engine. "Moment of truth, Lilith. Your daughter did it. Are you going to let her own you or will you get in those skis?"

Thankfully, she laughed. He didn't want her to take his joking for pressure to do something she didn't want to try. However, the way she watched everyone who went out on the water made him think she was interested but might need a gentle push.

"Mom, you have to try it. It's so fun," Chloe shouted, bouncing on her bare feet and wrapping a towel around her bony shoulders.

Lilith glanced at the water, then toward land. "I'm sure everyone's hungry and wants to head back to eat."

"I don't mind waiting," Hope said. The rest of the group agreed with her.

"What if I can't stand?" Lilith said to the hem of her bathing suit cover.

"Then you get to cool off in the water, and we get to spend more time enjoying a great summer afternoon. There are worse ways to waste time." Asher leaned over, resting a hand on her bouncing leg. "But if you really don't want to, I'm cool with heading to the house. You let me know what to do."

She bit at her bottom lip. The sudden visual of her doing that to him, scraping her teeth across his naked flesh before kissing or nibbling, had all his clean thoughts and good intentions diving south. He removed his hand from her knee and sucked in a breath, trying to drive out the swift and intense ache for her.

"Let's do it," she said.

"Huh? What?" His gaze shot to her bottomless blue eyes. Had she read his mind? Seen a few things he wanted to *do* to her?

She stood. "I want to try to ski."

"Oh." Freaking idiot. Skiing. "Good. Great. Hope, will you help Lilith get set up in the skis?"

She had them on and in the water in a few minutes. After a couple of tries, she was up, her whoop of triumph echoing over the lake.

Max took the empty seat across from Asher. "Is Lilith divorced?"

"Nope," Asher said, tight-lipped, hating how the question had him drowning in jealousy.

"Shit. Really? She hasn't mentioned a husband once, and from the things she's said, it sounded like it was just her and her daughter," Max said.

"They're separated," Asher admitted.

Max's gaze returned to Lilith. "Does she want to get back with her husband or divorce him?"

"Divorce."

Why had that been so hard to share? And why did it piss him off the way Max was watching Lilith?

"So...she's basically single."

"Dude, do you really want to be her rebound?"

Max winked. "Have you seen her? Heard that husky voice? I'll be whatever she wants me to be."

"I don't think she's interested in being anybody's anything," Asher replied, working to keep his tone level.

He was telling the truth. Maybe. Probably.

Max shifted his gaze from the lake to Asher. "Are you and Paloma together, or do you have something with Lilith? I'm getting mixed signals."

"Lilith? No, we're friends." He hated the way those words tasted a little bitter. "I meant any man. I get the feeling her marriage wasn't great, and she isn't in a hurry to hook up with another guy. And Paloma and I aren't dating. We're just friends, sometimes with benefits."

Max opened his mouth to reply, but Hope leaned into him, asking, "Did you bring your cell?"

He nodded.

"Will you let Jackson borrow it? He asked for mine, but I left it at the house. He wants to text Wyatt."

"Sure." Max got up, moving to the rear of the boat with Jackson.

Hope slid into his spot, asking Asher, "You okay?"

"Yeah, I'm fine." Had his annoyance at Max's questions shown on his face?

"Then why do you look like someone stole your best friend?"

Guess it did.

She lifted her chin, smirking. "Oh, wait. That was me."

Asher rolled his eyes and groaned. "You're such a dork. Plus, weren't you the one who told me to stay away from her?"

"She's not what I expected," Hope confessed. "She's sweet and funny, in an honest, no-filter way. However, I still think *you* should stay away. I can be her friend, but not you, because I don't want to see her naked."

"I don't want that either."

"Sure. I believe you," she said in that know-it-all tone that drove him nuts. "Her divorce—if she gets one—will be messy. Stick with Paloma. What you two have is simple."

What they had was fun and fucking. Nothing more or nothing less. It was what they both wanted from the other. Paloma was focused on her career, building her interior design business. Raven didn't need people coming and going from her life. Her relationship with her mother was confusing enough.

"My mom fell," Chloe shouted.

Asher turned the boat and cut the engine. "Here, take over," he said to Hope, determined to be the one to help Lilith out of the water.

Because we are friends. It had nothing to do with not wanting Max touching her.

On his way to the back, Jackson said Wyatt had texted him. He and his wife had arrived, and they were threatening to eat all the food.

The thought made Asher's stomach rumble with hunger. Pulling in the towrope, he called to Lilith, asking if she was good. She gave a thumbs-up.

Already out of the skis, she had them under her arms and was swimming toward him. She was beaming. "That was fantastic. Such a thrill! I wish I had a boat."

He took the skis and stored them as she climbed the side ladder. He held out a hand to steady her. "No need. I'll take you out on mine whenever you want."

"You might regret your offer," she surprised him with a tight hug. "Thank you. I haven't had that much fun in a long time."

"Ready to eat?" he asked, stepping away. Her wet, soft skin was paradise against him and was doing the opposite of cooling him off.

Turning the boat toward his home, he considered what his sister had said and thought she might be right. He was way too attracted to Lilith and needed to stay away. It was obvious she wasn't ready to be with a man. And even if she was, he was certain she wouldn't want one who had a record.

However, as neighbors and with their daughter's friendship, he and Lilith would see a lot of each other this summer. So, Hope's other suggestion was a good one.

Paloma *had* phoned him this afternoon, asking if he was free. On his way over to Lilith's, he'd automatically declined but now reconsidered calling her back.

Forget thinking about it. He would call. This little infatuation with Lilith had to end, and Paloma was great at making him forget everything.

CHAPTER SEVEN

Only two weeks had passed, but Lilith was amazed at the changes in herself. She actually had a social life. Last weekend, she and Chloe had biked the nearby trails with Asher and Raven. Tonight, she was out for drinks and dinner with Hope.

"I'm so glad you suggested this," Lilith said.

The two of them were sitting at a worn wooden table on The Hill's outdoor patio, sipping drinks and reading the menu. The restaurant was aptly named as it sat on a high hill overlooking a sparkling lake. It was one of many in the quaint community, though this one had fewer homes nestled amongst trees than hers.

Hope pointed inside to where a band was setting up on a stage in the corner. "I'm also suggesting a little dancing after dinner."

"It's been so long. I'm not sure I remember how."

"Are we talking months or years?"

"Well, I was pregnant and married before I could legally drink or get into clubs..."

"What about after you were married?"

"It was never Marshall's thing." *At least not with me.* Lilith ran a fingernail along a gouge on the table. "You dance. I'll stay out here. Go hang out by the water."

Hope snapped her fingers. "Aw, darn, it's private land. Restaurant patrons aren't allowed." She pointed to the bottom of the hill, where land met water. "Plus, I'm not sure you'd want to. Do you see the two houses?"

Lilith's gaze traveled down the steep gravel private road. It split off with a home on each side when it reached the water. They backed into the trees that grew up the hill. All she could tell was that one was two stories and red brick, and the other was a cute log cabin. It might even have a large covered front porch that faced that lake.

"Raven's mom lives there." Hope indicated the smaller home. "I don't know why she didn't just get a place in Ann Arbor."

"Why Ann Arbor?"

"That's where she's doing her fellowship."

"Fellowship?" Lilith hated sounding like a parrot but hated being confused more."

"It's some kind of extra training after a residency."

"Eden's a doctor?"

"A surgeon."

Hope nodded and waved a hand. "She'll probably leave again when it ends."

"Wow. A surgeon. That's impressive." Lilith couldn't help feeling smaller. Eden was making a difference in the world. Lilith was taking up space.

"I guess," Hope said with a lackluster drawl that made Lilith laugh.

"Well, maybe I'd rather meet the mysterious Eden than get my butt on the dance floor," she lied. The woman sounded incredibly intimidating.

"Damn." Hope leaned into her chair. "You must really hate dancing."

"I used to enjoy it when I was a teenager. I went out a few times after getting married. But, as I said, it wasn't Marshall's thing, and I got tired of begging him to take me.

"You never went with friends?"

Lilith returned her thumb to the gouge on the table. "We moved far away from where I grew up, so I lost touch with my friends. It wasn't easy making new ones."

"Well, that's changed." Hope rapped her knuckles on the table. "You have friends now. Everyone you met at Asher's loves you. *And* they all love to dance."

"Does your brother dance?" She had to admit that the image intrigued her.

"Yup. He comes here most weekends that Raven's at our parents'. He meets up with a *friend.*" She made air quotes with the last word, her gaze focusing on something behind Lilith. Hope leaned to the side a little and waved, saying, "Speaking of his most recent friend..."

Lilith twisted in her seat. A woman about her height was walking toward them, carrying a takeout container. She had shiny black hair, with a slight wave, nearly to her curvy waist, and wore a summer dress Lilith wished she had the confidence to pull off. The bohemian maxi had a dangerous dip in the front and a high slit up the leg. She looked sensual and self-assured.

When she reached the table, Hope stood and hugged the woman, introducing her as Paloma before pointing to one of the empty chairs. "Sit with us."

"I wish I could, but I need to drop this off at my parents." She tapped the take-out box. "Then I'm going over your brother's. He's making me dinner tonight."

The way she said it made it sound like Asher was going to be her dessert. Lilith told herself the burning sensation in her stomach was from her drink and not because Paloma was spending the evening—and probably night—with Asher.

"Anyway," Paloma continued, "it was nice meeting you, Lilith. I'm sure I'll see you at one of Hope's pontoon parties." She hugged Hope again, then headed for the main doors of the restaurant.

Trying to extinguish the unpleasant emotions surfacing, Lilith asked, "What's a pontoon party?"

"I have all my girlfriends over for a sunset toast on my boat." Hope tapped her chin. "However, maybe at the next one, I'll invite the guys too." Hope winked. "I'm positive Max will want to be there if you are."

"Oh." Lilith scratched her temple, her heart fluttering. "I'm, um, married."

"On paper or in your heart too?" asked Hope. "I don't mean to be nosy, but you've been living here a few weeks, and I've never seen him. And Chloe mentioned going to his place every other weekend."

"On paper—and I wish he'd sign the ones he's been served. I filed for a divorce and I don't know what kind of trouble he'll start, so I have to be on my best behavior." Lilith sighed. "Not that I'm ready to get tangled up with another man. I've had enough headaches and drama for a lifetime with my husband."

Mentally, anyway. Physically, her body was ready. The last couple of years her sex drive had been in a dead sleep. Yet lately, it was wide awake. And Asher was feeding it espresso shots and steroids.

But her life needed decaf. Not seduction, but sedation.

"No rush," Hope said, dragging Lilith back into their conversation. "Although, when you're ready, keep Max in mind. He's a nice guy."

"I will." Wanting to change the subject, Lilith scanned the menu. "What do you recommend I order?"

"I wouldn't get anything fancy. Stick to a burger or the whitefish. The food isn't terrible nor spectacular."

Lilith squinted, her mouth pulling into a smile. "Um, why did we come here, if the meals are mediocre?"

"Because on Friday and Saturday nights, the best local bands play here, turning this restaurant into a club. Also, Sam,"—Hope pointed inside the restaurant at the bar— "makes spectacular vodka gimlets. Here, try mine."

Taking a sip from the offered drink, Lilith moaned in appreciation. It was delicious.

"Okay, how about this?" Hope asked, tapping her glass on the table. "We eat and have a drink or two. If the band doesn't make you want to dance, we'll leave. Does that work for you?"

Lilith appreciated Hope wasn't pushy, but it didn't stop guilt from leaking into her veins. "Sorry I'm so boring."

"Are you kidding me? Great drinks, mediocre food, and laughter are as fun as dancing."

Giggling, Lilith lifted her bourbon sour. "Cheers to that!"

A while later, a violent but brief thunderstorm brought them inside. They sat at the bar. The band's music was intoxicating, and Lilith tapped her foot against her stool.

"Are you ready to go out there?" Hope pointed with her drink toward the area now cleared of tables to make room for dancing.

It was a little after nine, and the makeshift dance floor was already crowded. There were couples, groups of friends, and along the outer edges, men and women eyeing the dancers.

She remembered those people. The faces changed, but not the intent. Some were deciding if they'd join the group. Others were people watching, and many were picking who they'd try to dance with and maybe take home.

Lilith missed the rush. The way her pulse raced to the beat and her hips swayed to the rhythm. However, she was no longer the carefree and confident girl of her youth. Her body felt stiff and old, unable to find a tempo, let alone move to one.

"Let me buy a drink for you and your friend," said a man who seemed to materialize from nowhere.

He looked to be in his late thirties, medium height, with his head shaved bald. He was not unattractive, but he had a cocky stance, and the way he was invading her personal space was not appealing.

"We're good, Mick," Hope said, tired annoyance slipping into her voice.

"I was talking to the pretty little redhead."

"No, thank you," Lilith muttered, staring at her nearly empty glass and wishing he'd leave.

"Aw, come on. Don't be like that. A sweet thing like yourself deserves another nice drink, and after, I'll take you out on the dance floor." He slid closer, his heavy hand pressing into her shoulder.

She hunched, making herself smaller, longing to be invisible. Shifting closer to Hope, Lilith tried again. "I'm here with my friend tonight..."

He squeezed her shoulder. "I'm sure she won't mind."

"Christ, Mick, get a freaking clue," Hope said. "She isn't interested. Piss. Off."

Lilith's admiration for her friend shot through the damn clouds even as her own self-worth crawled around in the dirt. She should be like Hope. Strong and assertive, not this mouse, squeaking at the man's unwanted advances.

"Don't listen to your friend, gorgeous," Mick drawled. "She's a bitter spinster."

Hope snorted, clearly unfazed, but Lilith's blood began to boil. It melted some of her timidity. "That was rude."

"And untrue. I'm totally not bitter about being a spinster." Hope added, her gaze sweeping over Mick. "Especially when my pickings are so...unimpressive."

"Please, leave me alone," Lilith finished.

"Fuck this shit." Mick pushed away from the bar. "No pussy is worth this crap. If you ditch this bitch, come find me."

"Don't count on it, jackass," Hope taunted to his retreating back.

"What a dick," Lilith muttered before taking a heavy swallow of her drink, and finishing it. "But, listen, if I ever do decide to date, I want you as my wing-woman."

Hope rubbed her hands together. "Oh, that will be so much fun."

A light buzz ran through Lilith's veins. Some was from the alcohol. More from realizing she'd found another good friend in her new temporary hometown.

Finishing her drink, she looped an arm through Hope's. "Let's go shake our butts on the dance floor."

She stood, bringing Lilith with her. "Yes! We're going to have so much fun, *right now!*"

Lilith was starting to believe that was possible, not just for the night, but for the entire summer.

CHAPTER EIGHT

Lilith sank her toes deep in the sand, relishing the coolness beneath the hotter grains. The sun was setting, and a light breeze wafted from the lake. It was pure heaven but also hell because it wouldn't last. Tomorrow the calendar would flip to July, and no matter how badly she wanted to stop the clock, it kept ticking. Summer was passing by too quickly.

Which looped around to the unpleasant reminder she'd have to face Marshall. When she and Chloe didn't return home in the fall like his arrogant ass believed, he was going to make life difficult.

Sighing, she twisted to look at Chloe—eyes closed, shoulders relaxed, a small smile playing on the corner of her lips. There. Right there was her joy. Her peaceful, content daughter. As long as Chloe was with her, Lilith was home.

"Do you want to visit Grandpa, then go to the mall near his house?" she asked.

Chloe peeked through slit lids. "Ooh, shopping. What kind of shopping?"

"We could pick out your wall-hangings and a new bedspread for your bedroom at our new condo before your dad picks you up for the weekend."

Chloe's smile faded, causing a cloud in Lilith's sunshine mood. "What's wrong?" she asked.

Her daughter loved decorating. If allowed, she'd redesign her bedroom every six months. "Are we really not going home with Dad at the end of summer? I love

Uncle Tate. Being close to him will be cool, but I miss Dad. And my friends from school. I won't know anyone at my new one."

Lilith closed her eyes, wishing she didn't have to uproot Chloe's life. But homes were too expensive where she and Marshall lived, and being near Tate for comfort and help had seemed a reasonable choice. Now she wondered if it had been a selfish one.

"No, sweetie, we won't live with your dad anymore, but you can see him whenever possible." She took Chloe's hand. "Your dad and I love you, but he and I aren't happy together."

Chloe's brows pulled together. "Does someone else make you happy? You smile more now."

Lilith's mind flashed to Asher. But that was ridiculous. He was just a summer friend. "I am happier, but it doesn't have to do with anyone. It's more…."

Ugh, it was hard to explain without making her father, the man she adored, look like a jerk.

"You're happier without Dad," Chloe finished, sounding lost and sad.

Lilith sighed. Leaning forward, she took her daughter's hand. "Yes, but that's on me and him. Our mistakes. None of it is because of you."

She's the only thing right and good between Marshall and me.

Chloe nodded, but her face remained solemn.

"Would you rather stay home tomorrow?" Lilith asked. It might be better not to remind her of their move. "We can take our bikes out on that trail you like."

"No. I want to shop for my room. Can we go early? Dad said he has a surprise for me. I don't want to miss it." Chloe's returning grin sparkled with excitement.

It should have loosened the tightness in Lilith's neck and shoulders, but a new worry dug into the kinks and knots. Should she call Marshall and double-check what he had planned?

The idea of talking to him soured her stomach. Nearly every discussion ended with the same demand; that she return home, using Chloe as a tool of guilt.

"I'm sure you won't miss it. He won't leave if you aren't here when he arrives."

Chloe nodded, seeming to agree.

Lilith hoped that, throughout all of her and Marshall's mistakes, their daughter didn't doubt their love for her.

"Where do you want to go? The mall or—" She turned to the sound of approaching footsteps.

Raven waved, skipping closer and taking one of the empty Adirondacks.

"How was the climbing park?" Chloe asked.

Bouncing in her seat, Raven said, "It was so cool. I did the second highest course. My mom did the one below me because she's afraid of heights. And at the end, when she had to go on the zipline, she closed her eyes and made Dad push her off the platform." She broke into giggles, shaking her head. "Want to come over, and I'll show you the pictures? Oh! We can watch that new X-Men movie too."

"Can I, Mom?" Chloe asked.

"Yes, but be home right after the show. Remember, we have lots to do tomorrow before your father arrives."

"Okay."

When the girls were halfway between their houses, Lilith called out, and they stopped. "Raven, tell your dad if he isn't busy to come by. I'll be sitting here for a while stargazing."

"I will," she said before sprinting to her house with Chloe close on her heels. Their laughter bounced and echoed across the lake.

Smiling, Lilith closed her eyes and listened to the waves, crickets, and katydids sing their summer song. Sometime later, a rustle of the lavender bushes between her and Asher's yard told her he'd arrived.

"Didn't want to watch the movie?" Lilith asked, opening her eyes.

"Pfft. I refuse to sit through another X-Men movie until Gambit joins the team."

From his cargo shorts, he pulled two bottles. On the arm of the Adirondack, he popped off the caps, handing her one.

"Don't you hate beer?" She wiggled her bottle. She did, and hoped he didn't notice she wouldn't be drinking hers.

"I didn't want to try crossing the yard in the dark with my hands full of snifters. It'd be embarrassing if I'd tripped and my face broke the fall." He settled into the chair next to her.

"Funny though," Lilith giggled.

He tapped her knee with his cold bottle. "Nice friend you are," he said with laughter in his voice. "Anyway, this Belgium brand is decent. And I brought you a hard cider. You like those, right?"

She twisted the bottle in her hand, reading the label. Warmth bloomed in her chest.

"I do," she answered, taking a quick swallow, hoping he didn't notice the slight quiver in her voice.

He'd not only remembered her unimportant comment on drink preferences but had bought her favorite kind. Knowing men like him existed, who were thoughtful instead of selfish takers, made the world feel a little less mean.

Once she had her silly emotions under control, she peppered him with questions about the climbing park. It sounded fun, and she planned to take Chloe before summer ended.

After most of her cider was gone and the moon was high in the sky, she asked, "How do you and Eden do it, hang out together? I'm happy speaking three sentences or less when Marshall picks up Chloe."

Asher took a deep swallow of his beer, then twisted the bottle in the sand. "It wasn't always that way. When she first left, I couldn't even talk to her. When she'd call to check on Raven, I made my parents answer." He faced Lilith, offering a crooked smile. "Real mature, I know, but it'd stung. She'd gone to California to become a surgeon. Meanwhile, I was a nineteen-year-old who had to move back home and learn to be a father. I was pissed at her for my inadequacies as a parent."

"That's understandable," Lilith replied. "I was young too when I had Chloe. Twenty and clueless. I'd felt the same when Marshall was gone more than home."

"You had more of a reason than me to be upset. He made a commitment—to marry you, raise your kid together—then didn't honor it."

He had a point. She'd seen her husband's glaring red flags but had been scared and let him and her dad sway her. They'd convinced her that getting married was the best for the baby. And while Marshall provided for Chloe and clearly loved her, he treated Lilith more like hired help than his wife. Hell, she hoped he was nicer to those who worked for him.

Asher picked up his beer but didn't take a sip. He rolled the bottle between his palms. "Eden was clear about her intentions. She wanted to give the baby up for adoption. I couldn't let that happen and told her I'd raise her. So why blame Eden for my choice?"

"It's odd," Lilith said. "She kept in contact, even after giving up her daughter and moving to the other side of the country."

Asher nodded. "It is, but she seems to genuinely care about Raven. She'd call nearly every week when living out of state, and when on break, she'd visit Raven before heading to her home state. Eden is originally from New Mexico, so Michigan isn't exactly on the way. I figured if she wanted to be in her daughter's life, I wasn't going to stand in the way."

"Will she stay when her fellowship ends?"

"I don't know. Honestly, I'm afraid to ask. It'll hurt Raven if her mom leaves." He stared toward the inky night water. "She's still hands-off. I make all parenting decisions, but she's around, and Raven seems to love it. So, that's what I focus on."

Curiosity ate at Lilith. Was that really why he wanted her to stay, or was it because he had lingering feelings for his old girlfriend? They had a child together and got along really well.

Before she could think of a way to ask a question she had no business asking, he had one of his own. "What's Marshall like as a dad? Is he hands-off?"

"This might shock you, but no—when he's home. It's one reason I stayed with him well past when I should have left. He was never devoted to me, but he is to his daughter."

"Do you think he'll fight for custody?"

She rubbed her brow as a prickle of unease ran along her spine. "I don't know. He works long hours and travels a ton. He made it clear when we were together that he didn't want a nanny to raise Chloe. I think that's the reason he won't divorce me. Well, that's not the only reason. I figure the other has to do with his enormous ego, and me being the one to leave him."

"Wow. That surprises me," Asher said.

"What? That I left him?" Pinpricks of heat infused her cheeks. She wasn't sure if they were embarrassment or anger.

Asher sat straight. "Shit. No. Not at all. I meant about him being concerned how his daughter's raised, not about refusing to divorce you. Only a fool would want to leave you."

His kind words soothed her, even as her practical side told her he was offering platitudes because he was a compassionate guy, not because she was some great catch.

"I get it," she said with a wave of her hand. "I'm sure what you saw of him during his weekends here didn't paint him in the best light. Plus, he *is* a selfish prick. Just one who happens to be a decent dad."

"I wonder what it'll be like for him when Chloe starts dating and brings around a guy that reminds him of himself," Asher mused, chuckling.

Lilith tried to laugh, but fear seeped into her. "I'm so afraid that will happen, and it will be my fault. I was the one who taught her to put up with men who don't respect her."

"Shit," he muttered. His warm palm covered the top of her hand. "I was kidding. Thinking along the lines of karma biting your ex in the ass, but it won't happen. Chloe is smart and strong. Like her mom."

She snorted. "I wish. My daughter, yes. Me, no. Smart isn't someone who gets pregnant right out of high school. Lets her father talk her into marrying a man clearly wrong for her. Then stays with him for a decade."

"It's true," Asher insisted. "First off, you left him. Second, I'm sure the next man lucky enough to have your heart comes along, you'll demand the respect the gift deserves, and Chloe will see that." He squeezed her hand before letting go.

She missed his warmth, proving his words false. A strong woman wouldn't be so affected by the simple touch of a man showing kindness.

"Me leaving will have to be enough of a lesson for her," Lilith said with a smile she hoped didn't look as broken as it felt. "Because I'm done with the love and marriage crap. It makes me a doormat, and I'm tired of being walked on."

"I wish I could argue that, tell you love is out there, but I'm twenty-eight and a single dad. My last serious relationship was two years ago, and the way it ended didn't give me confidence in happily ever after either. Which is too bad. I'd always wanted the whole white picket dream. A home with lots of kids."

She felt his loss because it was her own. "Me too."

In the quiet pause, a fish jumped and splashed in the lake. They turned in the direction of the sound, and by the light of the moon, Lilith saw ripples in the water.

A deep chuckle rumbled from Asher. "Damn, so much for a light, fun talk under the stars." He scratched his cheek. "Sorry, I didn't mean to spill my personal shit on you, but you're easy to talk to."

"As are you," Lilith replied, delighted and a little unsettled at how comfortable she was around him.

She didn't want the connection to end. Which told her she should probably call it a night.

Before she could come up with an excuse to get away from him and the enticing way he made her feel, he asked, "Want to go to my place, check on the girls? If I'm gone too long, mine might decide to raid the snack cupboard."

There was her perfect out. But she couldn't find the willpower to take it.

"Works for me," she said, hating herself for being weak, even as her insides danced at the chance to spend more time with him. "I'd like to see what snacks they might have already found. And I wouldn't mind catching what is left of the movie. Unlike you, I like watching the X-Men. Especially Wolverine."

He offered his hand. She took it, and he pulled her up, asking, "What is it with everyone and that guy?"

Clutching her heart, she sighed dramatically. "All those muscles and angst."

Asher groaned. "Gambit is way cooler."

Lilith laughed, even as her brain shouted to turn around and go home.

A baser need had her following Asher. If she wasn't careful, whatever this was with him would ignite and burn to ash the life she was trying to build.

CHAPTER NINE

"Mom, hurry. Raven's back from her grandparents. I want to talk to her before Dad gets here," Chloe called from her kayak. She was a few strokes ahead of Lilith and picking up speed.

"Go ahead. I'll meet you there," Lilith replied.

They'd finished their shopping in record time, returning home in the early afternoon. After a quick lunch, they'd come out on the water.

Dipping her paddle into the clear lake, Lilith breathed deeply. The summer sun warming her skin was peace. The scent of water, lake weeds, and grass was a fragrance of bliss.

Last year at this time, she'd been drowning in misery, trying to keep busy with Chloe's summer activities. Marshall was never home and not even bothering to give excuses for his whereabouts. She'd been contemplating divorce but hadn't worked up the courage to file for it.

Now, she was nearly free, and it was damn liberating.

Sure, she was tethered to Marshall by his refusal to sign the papers, but at this moment, everything was perfect.

She paddled slowly toward Asher's dock. He'd rolled his worn jeans to his knees and was sitting with his feet in the water, sipping on a drink. Hope sat in a chair behind him with a beer.

Lilith would forever be thankful for him pushing her to meet his sister. She was as easy to be around as Asher. Hell, easier because she didn't have naughty dreams about Hope.

Last night had been rough or good, depending on how she looked at it. After the girls finished the X-Men movie, all four of them watched another superhero movie. Sitting close to Asher, his masculine scent teased and tantalized her, followed her home into her fantasies.

Unable to resist, she stopped paddling and closed her eyes, revisiting a taste of that recent dream, where the heavy press of Asher's body covered every inch of her. Him, using his knee to spread her legs while kissing her breathless. Then, when he slid inside—

"Lilith, did you fall asleep out there?" His deep voice boomed across the lake.

She startled, and the kayak wobbled, nearly tipping. Her cheeks flushed hot, but her voice was steady. "I was relaxing. Thanks for the near heart attack."

She was close enough to his dock to see the white of his teeth as he smiled. He held up a glass that had been sitting next to him. "Your Friday drink is getting all hot-and-bothered waiting for you." He smirked. "Look how wet it is."

"It's not the only one," Lilith muttered.

"What'd you say?" he asked.

Hope shoved his shoulder with her foot. "She's probably calling you a pervert."

He twisted to face her. "What? I was talking about her sangria. You, my sister, need to go in the lake to clean your dirty mind." He made a grab for her ankle. She was faster, jumping from her chair.

"I'll kill you. Murder you," Hope warned, pointing a perfectly manicured finger at him.

She hadn't changed from her impeccable work clothes. She'd shed her heels and suit jacket, but the pencil skirt and silk sleeveless shirt were definitely not meant for lake water.

"I'd listen to her," Lilith said, gliding to his dock. "Last weekend, when we were at The Hill, this guy wouldn't leave her alone when we were dancing. He made the mistake of grabbing her by the waist. She nearly broke him in half. It was pretty bad-ass."

Asher beamed at his sister. "I'm so glad you started taking those self-defense classes in college."

"Me too," Hope replied.

Something passed between them—unhappiness, anger, a secret? Maybe a combination of the three. It was gone before Lilith could name it.

"I never asked, how was your night out?" Asher stood, helping Lilith from her kayak.

Once she was on the dock, he grabbed the ropes crisscrossing the front of the little boat and dragged it to shore. He was shirtless, giving her a marvelous view of his jeans hanging low on his waist. Watching him bend and flex was a delicious treat.

"We had fun," Hope replied. "Although my ego took a hit."

Asher's brows furrowed. "How?"

"Besides that one slime ball, all the attention was on Lilith."

Heat returned to her cheeks, and she glanced at Asher. He was scowling.

She brushed aside Hope's remark. "I'm new. A novelty, that's all. Plus, after you nearly castrated that jerk, the other guys probably didn't want to risk your wrath."

Lilith still couldn't believe Hope had talked her into dancing half the night away. Well, once she was out on the floor, it didn't take any convincing to stay. It had been a fantastic evening.

"Also, this guy," Hope pointed to Asher, "and Jackson are a problem."

"How so?" Lilith asked.

"Because of them, half the guys in town are afraid they'll end up in a ditch or a shallow grave if they hit on me."

Lilith shook her head. "Brothers. Tate used to do the same thing. Probably will again when I move to my condo in his complex." Her smile widened. "But, right now, this summer, he lives too far away."

"Lucky," Hope muttered.

"I could take Tate's place when he's not around," Asher rumbled. He grinned, but his eyes had a sharp glint to them. "I'm sure I could get Jackson to help too."

"I'm good." She patted his arm. "No sense scaring off possibilities for if and when the day of me dating ever arrives."

The thought of possibly giving her heart away tied her stomach in knots. However, with her near-constant, steamy dreams featuring the man before her, meeting a guy for sexy times could be a good thing. No emotions, just sex— like what Asher had with the gorgeous woman who warmed his bed: Pam, no, Paloma.

"Don't forget, you promised I could be your wing-woman," Hope said, raising her hand.

Slapping her palm, Lilith laughed. "Of course. Together, we will find the perfect... Well, I don't think I'll ever want another husband. Even a boyfriend sounds like too much work."

"How about a boycycle?" Hope suggested.

"What the hell is that?" Asher asked.

"A man whose only use is to be ridden like a bike."

Asher's jaw flexed, and he stood. "I'm going to check on the girls."

"Did our talk offend him?" Lilith asked when the screen door shut.

"Him? I doubt it. Who knows what crawled up his ass." Hope shrugged. "Maybe it's the heat. He had to work outside and all week it's been hotter than Satan's balls."

Lilith nearly choked on her sangria. "Thanks for that lovely visual."

"My pleasure," Hope giggled.

"I finally had to give in and turn on the A/C." Lilith frowned. The expected relief had been dismal. "I hear the fan running, but the house isn't cooling off much. I swear, it's always something with my place."

They bitched about homeowner issues until Asher returned with the girls. He'd changed into swim trunks and seemed a little more relaxed.

Chloe was already in her swimsuit from kayaking, and she headed for the lake with Raven. Before she got in, Lilith stopped her, asking if she was packed and ready for her dad's.

He usually arrived around five. The last thing she wanted was to make small talk with him.

"Yeah, I packed this morning," Chloe said. "So, can I go in?"

"What time is it?" Lilith asked Hope.

Glancing at a silver watch on her delicate wrist, she said, "Ten after three."

"Yes, you can go in," Lilith said to Chloe. "But I want you out and in the shower by four."

The two girls nodded, running to the end of the dock and cannonballing into the water.

"What about you?" Asher asked.

"Definitely. Between the scorching summer sun and the paddling, I'm melting," she said, removing her coverup.

"Oh, my, I love your bathing suit," Hope said.

"Thank you." It was one of her favorites, a retro style with black and white polka dot bottoms and a red halter top.

"Doesn't she look adorable, Asher?" his sister asked, wearing a devilish smirk.

His gaze flickered over Lilith briefly, then away. "Yeah. Cute."

She deflated a little. Was she so dull he'd dismissed her in two seconds flat?

Ugh. His opinion or anyone else's shouldn't matter.

She shook it off, asking Hope, "Are you going to change and go in with us?"

"No. I'm meeting a few friends for drinks and darts at The Hill. Hey, why don't you come with me?"

"No, thanks. I had a great time, but I'll pass. I have big plans tonight."

Hope leaned forward in her chair. "Oh, do tell. Do you have a hot date?"

Asher turned from the water, his focus one hundred percent on her. Was he surprised that his homebody neighbor might have a date? It made her wish she did.

"Yes," she laughed. "With my book-boyfriend. The story is fantastic, but Chloe and I've been binge-watching a series in the evenings. By the time she's in bed, I'm too tired to read."

"Come on, the book will be there tomorrow." Hope placed a hand on Lilith's shoulder. "I've noticed you aren't a fan of crowds, but it will probably be just two other ladies and me. They're both super sweet. Also, the rumor is the owners of The Hill are going to sell and retire to the west coast. Whoever buys it may not keep Sam the bartender or get such great bands. We have to enjoy it before it's gone."

Hope had a point. The last time they'd gone out had been fun, even if the attention from the men had been a tad unsettling. And again, it could be what she needed. Dancing herself into exhaustion might help rid her of the nightly erotic dreams where Asher did very naughty things to her.

"I'll go," she said

"I'll join you two," Asher smiled at Lilith. "We can drive together."

Hope crossed her arms over her chest. "Who invited you?"

"Myself. I was thinking of going before you even mentioned it. Mom called this morning, asking if Raven could stay the night. I was going to text Jackson. See if he wanted to meet there for drinks. Hell, I have to, if the rumor is true that they might sell the place."

"Great," Hope muttered.

"What, you don't like hanging out with your brother?" Asher teased.

"Not there," his sister huffed. "You and Jackson are cockblockers."

Asher's laughter sounded strangled. "Oh, I thought you wanted darts and friends, not a booty-call."

"Are those only for you?" Hope retorted.

"Whatever," he scoffed, facing the water and giving her his back.

An unpleasant burning sensation flared in Lilith's chest. Turning, she dived into the lake, letting its coolness wash it away. She swam underwater toward the girls sunning on the floating dock. She stayed under until her lungs were nearly bursting. Breaking to the surface, she was surprised to find Asher a few paces behind her.

"Last one there's a rotten fish," he yelled, taking off, churning small waves in his wake.

Competitiveness shot through her, and she reached the dock in record time. The splashing behind said he was close.

Panting, she grabbed the half-submerged ladder and hoisted herself onto the raft. His hand snaked around her foot. Startled, she let go and he pulled her into the water.

"No fair!" she shouted, her heart pounding with exhilaration and delight.

"Oh, and your massive head start was?" he laughed, pulling her behind him.

She shot forward, clinging to his broad shoulders. There was no way he could climb up with her dead weight on him. The dock tipped dangerously as he grabbed the ladder. Laughing, the girls shifted to the other side, helping to level it out a little.

Then, holy shit, he did it. He lumbered up onto the raft with her hanging on him like a freaking monkey. Even more incredible was his wet skin against hers and his scent of male and summer. She wanted to lick him.

Once in the middle of the dock, he raised his hands in a Rocky pose with her still clinging to him. "I'm the winner!" he shouted.

"Nope. Not true!" She slid off him. "I touched the ladder first, and I got on here at the same time as you."

"By cheating." Asher reached around, probably planning to throw her in the water. She tried to jump away, but he caught her around the waist.

"Lilith," called a man, immediately popping her fun mood. *Marshall.*

He stood on the balcony of her house, his arms held in a what-gives gesture. Damn it. There was no way it was already five.

"Be right there," she yelled to him, then said to Chloe, "Make your shower quick, please."

She agreed, saying goodbye to Raven and Asher before diving into the water and heading home.

"Guess I should go too," Lilith sighed.

Asher looked toward her house. "You could stay here until he leaves."

"Tempting, but I want to say bye to Chloe and double-check her packing."

He nodded. "I'll pick you up after I drop Raven off at my parent's."

"Sounds good." She waved and then dove into the water.

At her beach, she dried off and went inside. Entering the walkout basement, she heard Chloe's shower. Lilith went into her bedroom to check her packing. She noticed pajamas and underwear were missing. After putting them in her weekend bag, Lilith dragged herself upstairs.

Marshall lounged in his perfectly cut suit on her couch like he belonged there. His haughty blue eyes were busy surveying the changes to what was once their summer home.

"You're early," she said, stating the obvious.

"I got Chloe tickets for that awful boy-band she loves. The show's tonight, and the venue is closer to you. There was no sense going home after work." He lifted his cell. "I tried to call. You didn't answer."

He could have told her earlier in the week, but not wanting to argue, she kept the remark to herself and said, "We went out on the kayaks, so I left my phone here."

"Funny, I didn't see the boats anywhere. Just you hanging on some guy."

She stared at him, not saying a word. She didn't owe him an explanation.

His lips quirked in an arrogant smile, and he gazed around the room. Thankfully, he dropped the subject. "Nice paint choices. Lightens up the place. We really should spend more time here as a family."

"Instead of using this as your place to bring your other women?" Her boldness at calling him out sent rivulets of shock through her.

Going by Marshall's slack-jawed expression, it had him too. After recovering, he scoffed. "I don't know what you're talking about. I brought no one here."

Wow. The lie rolled off his tongue with such ease.

"I'm friends with the neighbor. He remembers you."

"*He*? Was that the guy you were climbing all over on the lake, shoving your tits in his face?"

Lilith's body warmed from head to toe. She couldn't tell if it was from embarrassment or anger.

"Dad," Chloe called, her feet pounding up the stairs. "You didn't tell me where we're going. What should I wear?"

"Something comfortable. It will be a long night. That's all I'm going to tell you. The rest is a surprise."

Chloe nodded, returning to her room.

Lilith crossed her arms over her chest, taking deep breaths. She didn't want to fight with Marshall. Not with their daughter so close, possibly listening.

"Would you like a drink while you wait?" she asked.

"With the concert I'm about to endure, I'm tempted to have a few shots of your strongest stuff." He shuddered.

She didn't blame him. The band was awful.

"But since I'm Chloe's driver, I'll have a water. Do you have Fiji?"

"I have tap."

"Fine," he sniffed. "With ice, please."

Snob.

She went to the kitchen, filling a glass. The temptation to spit in it was fierce. Returning, she handed him the cup.

Right before taking a sip, he eyed her. "Did you spit in it?"

She burst into surprised laughter. The teasing was as unlike him as her reaction. They'd been a serious couple.

"It crossed my mind, but no."

She settled into the armchair across from him, and he studied her.

"What?" she asked.

"You seem different. Less uptight. Are you sleeping with that guy?"

Her splash of hilarity died. "That's none of your business."

"Since I'm your husband, I'd say it is."

"Sign the papers so we can change that."

Marshall let out a harsh exhale through his nose. "No."

"Why? You don't love me."

Before he could reply, Chloe bounded up the stairs again, sing-shouting, "I'm ready, Dad."

Marshall's eyes softened in a way they never had for Lilith. Although she no longer loved him, it made her ache. Her heart wanted someone to look at her that way. She longed to be someone's whole world.

Once they were gone, she slumped into the couch. On the lake with Asher she was a happy, self-assured woman, ready to face Marshall. By the time he'd exited, she'd become a pathetic, lonely woman chasing after her neighbor while still under the power of a man who could barely stand her, let alone love her.

Digging her palms into her eyes, she forced back tears. She'd already given him too many, but she couldn't go out tonight and fake happiness. It would be like sliding into the false woman she'd been while married to Marshall.

A few tears escaped when she texted Hope, canceling.

CHAPTER TEN

Asher opened the screen door to his sunroom and found Hope in one of the wicker rockers, his current read, a cop thriller he was halfway through, in her hand.

"You've been reading this guy since high school. Same series. Don't his stories ever get old?"

"No," he said, taking the novel from her. "And don't give me shit. You've been reading Nora Roberts since middle school. Don't her happily-ever-afters get boring?"

"Nope. She's the queen of romance." Hope smirked, squinting at him. "Also, don't lie. You like her. I remember when we were in middle school, I caught you more than once flipping through them."

"I was looking for the sex."

"Ah, well, if that's what you want, I'll have to loan you a couple of books from this new author I've started reading." She fanned herself. "Hot. Hot. They'll be great for your spank bank."

"Shit. Stop." He pretended like he was going to swat her with his paperback.

She made to punch this thigh, and he jumped out of range.

"Oh, that reminds me. Do you want to know what Raven talked with me about yesterday when she made you leave the room?"

"Yes—" He swallowed. "Maybe. If masturbation reminded you of the conversation then I'm not sure I do."

"You should be nervous. She asked what a player was. She said one of her friend's mothers called you one."

"I'm not a player," Asher sputtered.

"You don't have a girlfriend yet get laid on a regular basis."

Asher's cheeks warmed. Not that he'd been with anyone in a while. Including Paloma.

They'd met last weekend for dinner, which usually ended up in her bed. However, when she'd suggested it, he'd given her a lame excuse. They always enjoyed themselves, but for reasons he didn't want to examine, he was no longer interested.

"Why do you know so much about my sex life?"

"It's a small town, and I'm friends with a few of the women you've slept with, including the current one." She waved a hand. "Anyway, I'm not judging. Just telling you what Raven asked."

"Damn it." He rubbed his face. "What am I supposed to do, be celibate?"

"Here's a crazy idea." She paused as if for effect. "You could have a girlfriend."

Not happening. "No. Raven needs stability. I won't risk her growing attached to someone who's going to leave eventually."

"The one who's meant to stay will."

"Or there isn't 'the one' for me. And that's fine. I have Raven, family, and friends. I'm fine with the way things are."

He meant it. Or he had, until meeting his new neighbor...

Hope crossed her arms. "You mean no relationships, only meaningless sex."

"Yup. It works for me and them."

Except it wasn't any longer. Now he found himself craving more with women—a particular woman.

Shit. That was a path he couldn't take. Lilith was married, and it didn't matter that the marriage was dead. His young daughter wouldn't understand.

Not to mention, even if Lilith was single, she was leaving in the fall. She'd be almost two hours away. Why start when there was an end date? He might have preferred that in the past, but not now. Not with her.

Focusing on Hope and trying to forget about Lilith, he said, "Anyway, why are you still here? I thought you'd left when I was swimming." He had to get in the shower, but he took the seat next to his sister. "Don't you need to get ready?"

"Why bother?" she sighed. "If you and Jackson are going to be there, no man's going to come near."

"Oh, is that your reason for going out tonight? What happened to 'chicks before dicks'?" he teased. "I thought you wanted a night with friends?"

"Both would be nice. I was hoping if I gave you a hard time, you'd lay off."

"Fat chance."

"Asher, I'm a big girl. I can take care of myself." She looked him straight in the eyes. "I'm not your responsibility. You can quit hovering."

"No, I can't. You're my twin. I want to protect you." Guilt dragged his mind through mud and memories of their junior year in high school when he'd been more concerned about partying than looking after his sister. He deserved every damn thing that had happened after; from the nightmares of that asshole's eyes as his life left him, people's scorn and fear, to his time in juvie—all of it.

"Stop. I see that look in your eyes. It wasn't your fault. I shouldn't have gotten so high and gone off on my own." Her chin trembled, and it made tears well in his eyes.

"No." Asher chopped the air with an open palm. "Don't take responsibility for *his* actions. He's to blame. Not you. You could have danced naked at the party, drinking and smoking everything offered and it still wouldn't have given him the right. Dumb choices don't equal consent."

"Yeah, but my dumb choices ended with you spending a year in juvie and a record."

"It was *his* choices that landed me there. Not you." He squeezed Hope's hand, desperately wishing she'd believe his words.

She took a deep breath and straightened. "Enough. That night has taken up too much real estate in our lives. Let's leave the past in the past."

He wanted to argue, but if she needed to pretend they could forget, he'd play along. So, he nodded in agreement and closed his eyes, concentrating on the sound of the gentle waves kissing the shore. It pushed him into the present, his anger and self-reproach washing away.

She tapped his knee, and he looked at her. "And I don't believe for a second you're only following me to our local hole-in-the-wall out of a sense of duty or because its doors might close soon," she said as her phone dinged. She glanced at it and huffed out a laugh. "Oh look, your reason for going is texting me."

"Reason for going?" he muttered, scratching his temple, playing dumb. "Who is it?"

"Lilith. And she wants to cancel."

He frowned. "Why?"

"Wasn't her dick-of-a-husband over? He probably upset her."

"He needs his ass kicked."

She texted something, then said, "I'm sure you wouldn't mind being the man to do it."

"So? You don't want to kick him in the balls?"

"Yes, I do, but..." Her phone dinged again, and she wrote a message before continuing. "But I think your reasons have nothing to do with him being scum, or that Lilith is your friend."

"Hope, stop being cryptic. Say what you want to say." Though he already had an idea.

She held up a finger, reading a new message, then smiled. "I talked her back into going with us."

His mood lifted. He told himself it was because Hope had made Lilith feel better, not because he wanted to see her tonight.

Hope set her phone on a side table. "I saw the way you reacted when she talked about dating. You want her."

"You don't know anything. Lilith and I are friends." Asher stood. "Now, I need to rinse the lake off me before dropping off Raven at our parents."

"Oh, that's really why I'm here. I told Raven I'd drop her off on my way home. I'm waiting for her to finish packing." Hope stretched her legs out, crossing them at the ankles. "Busting your balls was an added bonus."

He laughed. "Lucky me."

"Oh." Hope reached for her phone. "I'll ask if Lilith wants to ride to The Hill with me."

Asher tapped on the screen door's frame. *He we go again.* "I already asked her. She and I are going together."

Hope snorted. "Of course you are."

"She is my neighbor."

His sister tipped her chin and looked at him in a way that said who-are-you-trying-to-kid? "Be careful. She's going through a lot."

"Which is why we'll only be friends. I won't risk causing her more stress or pain."

"Asher, she might hurt you. Not intentionally, but she's coming out of a terrible relationship. One she was in for a decade. I don't want you to pay for her husband's mistakes."

He padded the flimsy door. "Don't worry about me. I'll be fine." Not interested in continuing the conversation, he left the sunroom, heading for his shower.

Tonight would be fine. Even if Lilith was interested in him, she'd never shown a desire to act on it. As for him, he had control of his attraction toward her.

Tonight would be fine.

CHAPTER ELEVEN

Lilith blinked, adjusting to the darker interior of The Hill. Asher pressed his large palm against her back, leaning close to her ear. "I see them. They're at the corner table."

"Lead the way," she told him.

He slipped past her, smelling and looking like a dream. She'd been running late and rushed to get ready, so focused on not making him wait, she hadn't really looked at him. Now she did, and she liked what she saw.

He'd kept it casual but was mouthwatering as ever in fitted, gray cotton slacks and a tight black t-shirt. It stretched over his physique in the most enticing way.

Following him, she glanced lower. *Wow.*

His loose boardshorts hadn't done that part of his body justice. Fit and firm. Perfect.

She forced her gaze away from his ass. Her talk with Marshall, then Hope, had put Lilith in a reckless mood, but that didn't mean she wanted Asher's friends to notice her ogling him.

In the far corner, past the dance floor she and Hope had spent hours on last week, sat their group. She spotted Jackson and Max at a large table near the back of the restaurant. Next to him were Wyatt and his wife, Emma. Hope and two women Lilith hadn't met were on the opposite side of the horseshoe-shaped bench.

That was a lot of people.

Asher put a reassuring hand on her shoulder. "Looks like everyone invited someone. You going to be okay?"

"Will you sit by me?" she asked, hating herself for her weakness.

"Sure. If you want me to."

He said it like it wasn't a big deal and she wasn't acting ridiculous, yet she felt the need to defend herself. "It's stupid. I've met most of them, but—"

"Lilith, you never have to explain yourself to me. If you need me, I'm here. It's that simple."

Her heart constricted, and she gripped his arm. "Thank you. You're a good man."

"Not always," he said, something like unease or shame flickered over his face. Then it vanished, and his gaze fell to her lips, then slowly moved to her eyes. "But I will try with you."

She couldn't move, only stare at him. He wasn't looking at her like a friend, more like a dessert to devour. And she wanted him to taste her.

Hope called to them, breaking the sweet spell. Asher turned to his sister and waved. To Lilith, he said, "Come on, we'd better get over there before Jackson orders the pizza. He always tries to put pineapple on it."

Asher shuddered and Lilith laughed. "What's wrong with pineapples?"

He groaned, steering them toward their group. "Ugh, not another one for Team Pineapple."

Reaching the table, he introduced Lilith to those who hadn't yet met her. The waitress arrived seconds behind them, and they ordered drinks.

The group fell into easy conversation, joking, and teasing. It was apparent they'd been friends for years, but it didn't make Lilith feel excluded. Instead, she had that wonderful sense of belonging again, and by the time the Friday band arrived, she was relaxed and comfortable. Although part of it might have been her third drink.

Jackson set his beer on the table and rubbed his hands together. "Who's up for team darts?"

Nearly everyone at the table shook their heads, and Asher said, "No way. Wyatt, how many drinks have you had?"

He held up three fingers. His smile said they were strong ones.

"Last time, he was sober and managed to miss the dartboard and hit a wall socket." Hope shuddered.

Lilith glanced toward the people playing and laughed. She pointed. "Is that why they all have childproof covers on them?"

Emma snorted. "Yup. Given his poor aim, I bet no one will be surprised that he's in charge of cleaning all the toilets in our house."

"Hey, that's not me. It's our little demon boys. I swear they pee with their eyes closed."

Emma didn't say a word, just quirked a brow. Wyatt took a healthy swallow of his drink and shrugged. "Mostly them."

The opening chords of an old summer tune rang out, and he scooted out of his seat, holding out his hand to his wife. "My aim might suck, but I've got moves."

She smiled, and a little heat entered her eyes. "That you do, my dear."

They left for the dance floor.

Lilith was a little envious of their teasing and obvious closeness. She'd never had that with Marshall.

"Come on," said Hope, tapping Lilith's hand resting on the table.

She nodded. They were soon swallowed up in the crowd of dancers. The band was fantastic, and Lilith lost herself in the rhythm. Well, until they switched to a slow song. Then, she floundered as everyone paired with partners.

Max smiled at her, moving closer. Before she could decide what to do, Asher stepped in front of her, taking her hand and playfully spinning her. "Do you want to dance?" he asked.

She nodded. For the evening she wouldn't think about her problems or what could go wrong. She'd enjoy the moment. And, oh, she was enjoying every moment in his arms. The man could dance; he was all grace and sensuality.

When the slow ballad ended, she didn't step away. Neither did he. A fast, sexy beat pulsed around her. She let it move her hips. He slid a leg between her thighs, rocking with her. A light sheen of sweat had his shirt clinging to him. If she ran her tongue along his neck, would he taste like summer and desire?

The band called for a break. As he took her hand and suggested a drink, a woman tapped him on the shoulder. After a second, Lilith recognized Paloma. Her hair was braided, showing off her heart-shaped face, and she wore a sexy red dress. Her gaze bounced between Asher and Lilith.

He hesitated mid-step, cleared his throat and let go of Lilith's hand. He draped a loose arm around Paloma. "Meet my new neighbor, Lilith," he said.

"We met last week when she was here with Hope." Paloma smiled. It was almost friendly. "How are you settling in?"

"Good. I'm lucky to live next door to Asher," Lilith said evenly, trying to pretend her good mood wasn't crumbling.

"Oh, how so?" Paloma's tone held an unmistakable edge.

"Raven is my daughter's favorite person in the world, and he introduced me to Hope. Both she and Asher are great *friends*. I couldn't ask for better lake *buddies*." She edged away from them. "Anyway, Hope ordered another pitcher of Long Islands, and I'm going to get a drink. Nice seeing you again, Paloma."

"Same," she replied, turning into Asher's body.

Lilith scooted into the booth next to Hope, trying to squash the jealousy and annoyance fighting within her.

"I figured Paloma would show up sooner or later," Hope said, refilling Lilith's glass and handing it to her.

She took a large sip, relishing the cold sliding down her throat, followed by the burn of the different liquors. "Why, does she come here a lot?"

"I have no idea, but I called her to tell her I was here with Asher."

"Ah, yes. She would want to see her boyfriend." Labeling Asher as someone else's hurt way more than it should.

"Like I said before, Asher doesn't date. They, um…" Hope made a sour face as if she'd bit into a lemon. "Sorry, I just had a teenage flashback. In those days, he used to have actual girlfriends. I'd walked in on him with one. Thank God it was winter, and covers were involved."

Lilith burst out laughing, even though picturing Asher naked with another woman stabbed her with uncomfortable envy.

"Same happened to me with Tate. But it was summertime. I wanted to bleach my eyes." She shuddered, taking a sip of her Long Island. After setting it on the table, she asked, "Why doesn't he have girlfriends now?"

"Mainly because of Raven. He says most relationships don't last, and women coming and going from his daughter's life isn't good for her." Hope paused, swirling her drink with a straw. "Once he broke his rule and got pretty serious with a woman. Julie. In the end, she left. Said she wasn't ready for an instant family. Bitch."

Lilith tilted her head. "I'm not sure that's fair. Not every woman wants to be a parent. At least she was honest."

"No. I get that. Hell, the world is a damn scary place. I'm not sure I want to bring children into it either, but Raven was already here. And Asher doesn't hide the fact he has a daughter. If him being a parent was a problem, she should've broken things off when first learning he had a kid."

Lilith nodded. She should be like Asher. Find a man who could pleasure her body, leaving her heart out of it. What did Hope call this kind of man? Ah, yes, a boycycle. The image made Lilith giggle.

"What are you thinking about?" Hope asked.

"Meaningless, hot, sweaty sex," Lilith replied.

Hope's loud laughter caused a few heads to swivel in their direction. Including Asher.

A drink of him would be sweet.

Damn vodka. And gin. And tequila. And rum. Perhaps it was time to cool it with the Long Islands.

"Sorry. My mind went off track, straight into the gutter. I was thinking I have the same issue as Asher and maybe should do the same as him." She traced the rim of her glass. "Hell, it's been so damn long since I've had sex. I'm practically a virgin again. Forget dating and love. I just want a toe-curling orgasm or two."

Laughter burst from Hope, pushing her into the cushioned bench. "I love how drinking makes you blunt," she gasped.

Lilith grinned. "Yes, it's how I know when to stop refilling my cup."

"Hell, no. This side of you is awesome."

Hope picked up the pitcher of Long Islands, but Lilith covered her glass. "No way, lady. I have to hold on to the last few shreds of common sense the alcohol hasn't burned away."

"Common sense and Friday don't belong together," Hope countered.

"They do if regrets have a chance of following me into Saturday," Lilith said, pushing away her near-empty glass and catching sight of Asher in the crowd of dancers. There wasn't a sliver of space between him and Paloma. "I'm getting tired. Do you know anyone who will be leaving soon?"

"Max mentioned he's thinking of going," Hope replied, snagging his attention and waving him over.

Sliding into the booth across from them, he filled his glass with water. "What's up?"

"If you're leaving soon, would you mind giving me a ride home?" Lilith asked, unable to keep from dancing in her seat. The band was playing one of her favorite songs.

"I am, and I don't mind, but," he smiled, tilting his head toward the band, "would you like to dance first?"

Her gaze jumped to Asher and Paloma, then back to Max.

"Yes, I'd love to dance with you."

She danced a few songs with him, waiting for the high to return like when she'd been with Asher. And while Max had good rhythm and a wicked, fun sense of humor, her excitement for the night had waned. So when the band called for a break, she asked if he was ready to leave.

Waving goodbye to their friends, they pushed through the double door. Lilith tipped her face to the moon and sighed.

"It's a perfect summer night," Max said. "Reminds me why I love Michigan."

She nodded, taking in his strong profile. He seemed like such a nice, uncomplicated man. Part of her wished she felt some spark for him.

A cool gust of wind, smelling of rain, pushed at her. It crept over her exposed skin. She crossed her chilled, bare arms.

"Damn. I'll be right back. I forgot my jacket in the booth." She turned to go inside at the same time Asher pushed through the main door.

His sharp gaze pinned her. "Where are you going?"

CHAPTER TWELVE

The main door swung shut as Asher stalked outside. Paloma was probably pissed with the way he'd taken off, but he had to make sure Lilith was okay. They'd driven into together, they'd leave together.

What he wasn't doing was checking up on her to see if she was going home with Max.

A small, quiet part of him whispered he was a liar. This was more than him watching over a friend.

"Where are you going?" Asher repeated, sounding way too harsh.

"I'm going home."

"With Max?" His hands curled into fists.

Lilith pointed to the bar, her blue eyes flashing with anger. "Go back inside. Enjoy your evening."

"We drove in together. I'll take you home."

"Don't worry about it. I'm taking her," Max said.

A burning sensation flamed in Asher's chest. "No," he said with such force, the other man took a quick step back.

Paloma moved in front of Asher. "What's going on?"

Good question. Why did he suddenly want to punch one of his closest friends?

"Go, Asher. Enjoy your evening." Lilith turned to Max. "Ready?"

"I said, I'll take you," Asher growled. "You came with me, so I'll make sure you get home safely—"

"Dude," Max bared his teeth. "Are you saying she isn't safe with me?"

"No." *Shit*. What the hell was wrong with him? "I didn't mean it that way," Asher said.

Max took a deep breath. "Then what do you mean? What do you want?."

"Good question," Paloma seethed.

Fuck. He was making a colossal mess.

Lilith pointed to The Hill. "I'm going to get my jacket. When I come out, I hope this weird pissing match is over, and one of you will take me home."

Soon as the door to the bar slammed shut, Paloma whirled on Asher. "Are you sleeping with her?"

"No."

Max and Paloma didn't look like they'd believed him. She slammed her hands on her hips. "Then what the hell is going on with you two?"

"Nothing, we're friends. I'm worried about her."

"With me?" Max spat. He was obviously angry and with good reason.

"Fuck," Asher sighed, shoving his hands in his pockets. "Listen, I'm sorry. You know how I get with crowds and drinking. I saw her leave, and I panicked. I wasn't thinking clearly."

"No shit," Max groused, but there was understanding in his eyes. He hadn't been at the high school party, but he heard about it and the fallout. Hell, everyone had—violence and the death of a teenager was big news anywhere, but especially in a small town. "If it'll ease your mind and she doesn't mind, take her home."

He should drop it and go back inside, but he couldn't. "It would, but swear, it's nothing against you."

Max nodded, then headed toward The Hill's main doors. When it closed behind him, Paloma said, "This isn't about your normal controlling tendencies—"

Offended, Asher said, "I'm not controlling." Protecting those he cared about was different.

She waved a hand. "Fine. We'll call it your hero complex."

He scoffed. He didn't have either and was about to say so, but Paloma continued talking. "I see the way you watch her. You don't look at her like she's a friend." She took a small step away from him. "Don't be that guy who wants to fuck someone else but is too much of a ball-sack to 'fess up."

"I swear that's not what I'm doing." He ran his fingers through his hair, pulling at the ends before letting his hand fall to his side. "But we should take a break."

She crossed her arms in front of her chest. "And this has nothing to do with your neighbor?" Disbelief dripped from her.

Yes and no. Lilith would remain only his friend, but thinking of her when Paloma was in his bed seemed wrong. Plus, she was acting like they were a couple, like she had a claim to him.

"It has to do with you wanting more than I can give you. Like I said before, I'm not in a position to be in a relationship."

"You use your daughter as a shield. An excuse not to get close to any woman because you're afraid of getting hurt." She waved a hand when he opened his mouth to argue. "It's true. I do feel more than simple lust for you, so it's better to break it off now if you don't feel the same. I'm not interested in being with a guy who can't give me what I need."

Silence fell heavy between them as if she was waiting for him to fill it with commitment. "You deserve more than I can give you." His words sounded like a cop-out but were the truth.

"Fine." She straightened her shoulders, seeming to gather her poise and pride, then kissed his cheek. "I'll see you around."

She sauntered inside the bar without a backward glance, and he expected nothing less. Paloma wasn't the type of woman to share her pain with those that hurt her. Plus, he was positive she'd be over him quickly. She might have wanted more, but they'd never had more—just shallow fun.

Still, he should regret a good thing ending. Instead, his mind chewed on images of Lilith with Max, laughing and dancing, hardening his gut. He unclenched his jaw, shaking out his shoulders.

He could *not* hook up with a married woman. If she even wanted him. Raven wouldn't understand, and raising her came before his wants and needs.

Asher leaned on the nearest street lamp, crossing his legs at the ankles. Lilith pushed through the bar's main door. She glanced around, spotted Asher, and walked toward him.

"I take it you're the one driving me home." She sounded irritated.

He straightened. "Is that a problem? Would you rather it be Max?"

She stepped past him, heading in the direction of his Jeep. "I don't care who does it, just as long as I leave now."

Before she could open her door, he hooked a finger around her wrist, nudging her to face him.

She halted and swung around. "What, Asher?"

She was close. Too close. He could smell the peppermint and liquor on her breath and wanted to taste it.

"Why are you angry?" he asked.

"Because I can take care of myself. I don't need another man bossing me around," she nearly shouted.

He dropped his hand from her, ashamed at the way he was behaving. "I'm sorry. I didn't mean to be an overbearing dick. If you want to go home with Max, I'll get him."

Fuck, that hurt.

"Christ, Asher, he was *taking* me home, not *coming* home with me. I'm upset because you're treating me like a child. I have a brother. I don't need another one."

"Lilith, the last thing I see you as is a sister." He bit his lip.

Their gazes collided, and he caught a spark of... something.

"What do you mean?" As if in a dream, she brought her hand to his lips, brushing her fingers over them.

His eyes closed, a soft moan escaping him. When he opened them, the desire reflected in hers nearly burned him. He bent toward her, needing to taste her kiss.

Laughter and loud conversation from an approaching group cut into the night air, bringing him back to reality. He stepped away, needing to clear his head before he could think about anything but the press of her mouth against his.

CHAPTER THIRTEEN

"Let's go," Asher said, opening the passenger door for Lilith.

Humiliation choked her as she nodded and climbed inside. She stared resolutely out the open side window. There was no way she'd let him see the conflicted tears welling in her eyes.

She focused on the scenery, dark as her mood, flying past them as he drove. It helped a little with burying the millions of emotions trying to burst from her.

When they parked in his garage fifteen minutes later, she grabbed the handle, planning on sprinting to her house. "Thanks for the ride," she said.

"Lilith, wait."

She kept going. "I'm tired. We'll talk later."

Like in a month. Or three. When her pride wasn't swarming and stinging for nearly mauling him and then being shoved back into the friend zone.

Coming around the side, she found him waiting for her. *Damn it.* "Let it go, Asher. I got the message loud and clear."

His brows furrowed, causing a deep line between his brows. "What was the message?"

"You're interested in me as a friend. Nothing more."

He stepped closer. "Is that what you think?"

She tilted to look into his eyes and found his mouth an inch from hers. Her brain screamed to move. Her body refused to listen.

With a groan that echoed with defeat and desire, his lips met hers. He tasted even better than in her dreams. His kiss was tentative as if he was trying to keep it chaste. She teased him with her tongue, and his virtue burned away with the heat of her need.

He pressed her against the Jeep, deepening the kiss. She arched and his arousal pressed into her. Pleasure hummed through her as she ground against him. The desire to hike up her skirt and wrap her legs around him was nearly overpowering.

With her last thread of willpower, she grabbed onto the reality of her life, even though this fantasy was so much better. She pushed gently on his chest and whispered against his lips, "Asher."

He stepped away. "Sorry, I shouldn't have done that."

"Don't apologize. I wanted it as much as you." *Still want it. Desperately*. Her hands shook with the desire to reach for him, to bring him back against her body. Instead, she focused on smoothing her skirt. As if fixing her outward appearance would do the same for her rioting insides. "But you're right. We shouldn't have done it. I can't take these kinds of risks. If Marshall found out, and I wouldn't put it past him to hire someone to follow me around looking for dirt, he'd use it as blackmail, or worse, to take Chloe from me."

"I understand." His hands went up as if to touch her. He seemed to reconsider and shoved them into his pockets.

"Also." She pressed a palm against his racing heart. "I'm emotional chaos. Starting anything with you would end up destroying our friendship. I can't lose you."

The words were true, though her deprived body hated them.

"I wouldn't do anything to complicate your divorce." He took her hand, sliding his fingers through hers. "But I could handle your chaos. As a friend or lover. Protect you from it."

She didn't want a protector, but the strength within herself to heal and handle her life.

"What I need now is a friend."

He cupped her cheek. "That I will always be."

"Thank you." She hugged him, and it took herculean willpower to let go.

Walking away with her regrets and desires was equally difficult. Between her lust and longing, it was impossible to know if she'd made the right decision.

CHAPTER FOURTEEN

Lilith locked the door and deadbolt. Not because she was worried about her safety, more because every cell in her body screamed to run back into Asher's arms. She slumped against its solid frame, pulling her phone from her jean jacket, thankful Florida was in the same time zone as Michigan. She needed her mom, hoping she could talk her off the ledge of desire. Lilith messaged her so she wouldn't risk waking her early-to-bed stepdad and half-sister.

A few seconds later her phone rang.

"Is everything okay?" Her mom asked, sounding frantic.

Lilith pulled her cell from her ear to check the time. Yikes, it was after midnight. "Sorry. I thought it was around ten. I should have checked before texting you."

"It's fine. I was worried because you're normally asleep at this hour. I'm up, you know I'm a night owl."

Lilith heard shuffling in the background. Her mom was probably sitting on her couch with a lap desk, sketching.

"Funny," her mom continued, "I was thinking of you right before you called."

Lilith walked to the kitchen, opened the fridge, and grabbed a pitcher of lemon water. "Were you thinking about anything in particular?"

"Birthdays. Chloe's and yours. And yours is the big three-oh. I'd like to visit."

Tears prickled along Lilith's bottom lashes. She'd never put much importance in her birthday. Which was good since there was always a fifty-fifty chance Marshall would forget it. However, turning thirty and starting over both thrilled and depressed her. Fine, if she were being honest, letting the day pass without celebrating tipped more on the sad side.

"We could have a small party," Mom said. "Me, Tate, Chloe, and your new friends."

The mention of her friends had Lilith recalling Asher's kiss. His *hard* body against hers.

"Does that sound good?" Her mother asked.

Oops. She'd missed some of the conversation. Trying to cover, she said, "Um, sure?"

Her mom chuckled. "I asked if coming in two weeks is too soon, and if you wanted me to come alone or bring Ted and Miley?"

Lilith slid into the kitchen chair, resting her forehead on the table. "Sorry, I'm a little scattered this evening. Anytime you want to come, works for me. And, yes, I'd love to see Miley and Ted."

Last winter, when she and Chloe had flown out, she'd barely talked to her step-father and half-sister. The trip had been brief and depressing. She'd been teetering on the edge of seeing a divorce lawyer and had wanted to talk to her mom about it. It'd be nice to see them now, when she wasn't in such a low place.

After they finished discussing travel plans, her mother said, "Did you call to talk about anything in particular? You're never up this late."

Lilith sat straight. "Then you'll be shocked to learn I just got home when I called you."

She was a little embarrassed at how proud she sounded.

"Really? Where were you?" She heard delight in her mom's voice.

"I went out for drinks and dancing with a few friends."

"Did you dance?"

"Yes."

"With a guy?"

"Actually, two." Lilith grinned.

"Look at you, breaking from your shell," her mom crooned. "Who'd you kiss?"

Lilith nearly fell out of her chair. "What makes you so sure I kissed someone?"

"Call it motherly intuition."

"You remember how I told you Chloe made a new friend pretty much the first day we arrived here?"

"Yup, and if I didn't remember you telling me, I wouldn't have forgotten—when Chloe and I chat, she mentions her new best friend a lot. Raven's her name, right?"

"Right."

"She also mentions you get along well with the father. That you all hang out frequently…"

"Yeah, his name's Asher." Slouching, she blurted, "And, well, I kissed him."

She heard her mom clapping. "Good for you."

"Not good," Lilith groaned. "Ugh, I called because you were supposed to tell me it was stupid and impulsive and to never do it again."

Her mom snorted. "Really, me?"

"Yeah, in hindsight, I see my mistake," Lilith laughed.

"Of course I'd say go for it. You wasted too many years on a man who doesn't deserve you. All he cared about was himself. You must have been braindead bored."

"Chloe made it easier. Kept me busy."

"Sure, as a mother, but not as a woman. It's time for a little excitement in your life."

She had a point. Chloe had been the highlight of her marriage. The rest was lonely. Marshall had never been home, and when he was, she'd felt even more alone.

"True, but that doesn't change the fact that kissing Asher was a mistake."

"Why? Was he bad at it?"

"Not. At. All." More like the best kiss she'd ever had. The mere memory of it had heat pooling between her legs.

"Oh. Uh-oh. Did he reject you? If so, one, he's an idiot. Two, yeah, that'd be awkward."

Lilith recalled how Asher had responded. The way his hungry moans had swallowed hers. The way his erection had pressed against her stomach said the attraction wasn't one-sided.

"No, the kiss was reciprocated and really, really nice. It's the million other reasons that made it wrong."

"Such as."

"One. I'm still married. I can't risk starting anything with a man until I'm divorced. Two, he's Raven's dad. The chances of this not ending are slim. I don't want it to mess with my kid's friendship. Three, I'm not ready to date. And I've heard he doesn't anyway. Plus, even if either of us were, I'm moving two hours away at the end of the summer. Most importantly, I like him a lot. I don't want to lose his friendship because of a silly attraction."

The line went quiet, but Lilith didn't break the silence. Her mother liked to consider her words before speaking.

Finally, she said, "Those are some good reasons. Does he also agree friends is better than lovers?"

"Yes. He's worried about our daughters and that it could complicate my divorce."

"I get it. You and Marshall were over years ago, but Chloe doesn't know this. Plus, the girls are too young to understand the messiness of love." Her mom paused, then said, "A guy who can see beyond his immediate wants and desires is a good man. I like Asher better the more I learn about him."

"Me too," muttered Lilith.

"But it sounds like you've both made up your minds. So, tell me..." Her mother's mischievousness couldn't be seen but was heard. "Was it a quick peck, something easy to forget in the morning light?"

"There was nothing chaste about it," Lilith admitted.

Her mother laughed quietly. "Aaaand his approval rating shot up again."

Figuring she'd confessed so much already, why stop now? "His kiss was the best I've ever had."

"Damn. Complicated, indeed."

"True, but it doesn't matter, my life's complicated enough. I won't add to it. His friendship is too important to throw away because of a little lust."

"Seems like more than a little…"

No lie there.

"It'll fade," Lilith insisted. "By the time you arrive here, he and I will be back to normal. You'll see." Standing, she shut off the kitchen light, heading to her bedroom. "Anyway, it's late, and I should try to get some sleep."

"Will that be possible?" Her teasing tone had Lilith blushing before her mother even finished. "With all this tension, you should take my advi—"

"Mother! Please don't bring up BOB," Lilith said, choking on embarrassment and amusement.

"Fine. Fine," her mom said through her laughter.

Lilith rested her head in her palm. "I'm hanging up and pretending this part of the conversation never happened. Love you."

"Love you too."

Smiling, Lilith disconnected, tossing her cell on the bed and falling next to it.

Having her mom's support was settling but didn't quiet all the turmoil.

She didn't want to make responsible, wise choices. Not when the reckless taste of Asher's lips was damn delicious.

After that kiss, could she see him as only a friend?

CHAPTER FIFTEEN

"You weren't kidding about finding a big vehicle." Lilith took in the SUV from the comfort of the passenger seat. Three rows of beautiful leather and chrome. Before leaving for the airport, she'd checked out the cargo area. It was massive. "Where did you find it?"

"I have a friend from work who has four kids, and each is in a ton of activities," Asher answered. "He's hoping they don't join anything else, or they're going to have to get a full-size van. Or a bus."

"Well, I appreciate you going through the trouble of getting this and sacrificing your Sunday to drive an hour and a half each way to pick up my family from the airport."

He waved a hand like it was no big deal. The man had such a kind heart. It made her want to hug him and never let go.

Not that she would touch him. They'd managed to stay friends after that panty-melting kiss from three weeks ago. She wouldn't rock their fragile boat.

So, no hugging. Or looking at him too long, noticing his firm lips, penetrating eyes. Or staring at his big hands gripping the steering wheel, remembering how they felt on her body.

Asher parked at the curb of Arrivals at Detroit Metro Airport. Lilith told him, "My mom texted me ten minutes ago. They were heading to the baggage claim. They shouldn't be much longer."

"No worries. I don't have other plans today, and I'm sure Raven and Chloe are having a great time at Hope's house."

"I owe you both. Let me take you two out for dinner once my family is gone. Chloe was bummed she couldn't come with me until learning she'd be spending the afternoon with Raven and your sister."

Guilt tugged at Lilith. She worried Hope and Asher would tire of helping her, or worse, they'd think that was why she was friends with them.

As if reading her thoughts and wanting to calm them, Asher said, "Hope was happy to have them. It got her out of gardening with Dad. She's going to take them to the state park down the road. They have a huge beach and a few slides. One in the water, and another off a floating dock."

"Really? Sounds cool. I'll have to check it out."

He patted her knee briefly. The warmth of his big palm stayed long after he removed his hand. "We'll go this week with your family. Maybe have a barbeque at my sister's place after."

"That would be nice."

She loved the way he made easy plans with her. It was almost like they were a couple, except without the expectations and minefields that come with a relationship.

The downfall was, she couldn't kiss him. Or do any of the things that happened in her late-night fantasies.

Since that evening at The Hill, those had amped up to nearly every night. Somedays it was difficult to look Asher in the eye. The things they'd done in her dreams were downright naughty.

Stuff she'd never experienced in real life but wished she had the courage to try—Asher tied to an old four-poster bed, tantalizing him with her tongue. *Stop.* Sighing, she pushed aside her fantasy.

"You okay?" He asked.

Scanning the groups coming and going from the airport, she said, "Yeah, why?"

"You moaned."

"Oh, I had a charley horse in my thigh," she lied, rubbing the area. Catching a flash of red hair from the crowd exiting the sliding doors, she sat straight, pointing. "That's my mom."

They opened their car doors. Asher came around to the sidewalk by her, and she stood on the sill of the SUV above everyone's head. Yup. It was them.

They were impossible to miss. Her mom's bright locks, Ted's bald head gleaming smooth, and Miley's sun-kissed blonde hair in a high ponytail.

Damn, she'd missed them. She waved until they caught sight of her. Tears welled behind her lids. Her mother's familiar stride made Lilith homesick and, at the same time, feel like she was home.

Jumping down, she clutched Asher's bicep in excitement. He smiled at her. "Go. I'll stay with the truck."

"Thanks." Without thinking, she kissed his cheek before running toward her family.

Her mother was the closest, and Lilith wrapped her in a fierce hug. "I'm so glad you're here."

"I've missed you," her mom replied, squeezing her tight.

They let go, and Lilith hugged Ted, then Miley. She was bubbling with excitement. It had been too long since seeing them in person. As they walked, she asked about their flight and what they wanted to do during their stay.

Miley wanted to visit Cedar Point, an Ohio amusement park known for its heart-stopping rollercoasters. Lilith was less than thrilled with the idea. She was a total chicken when it came to the dipping and diving rides.

However, she'd take her sister if she truly wanted to go. Besides, Chloe would probably love it and would hopefully partner with Miley.

Mom and Ted's plans were better. They wanted to relax at the lake.

Mom looped an arm through Lilith's and leaned close, nodding toward the SUV. "Honey, if that's your neighbor, I get why you couldn't resist kissing him."

Lilith narrowed her eyes but smiled. "Don't you start. You know we've put that behind us. We're friends."

"Why?" She pointed with her chin. "Have you looked at him?"

"Believe me, I have. He loves to hang out at the lake only in swim trunks." Her mom laughed, and Lilith joined in, finishing with, "But I need him as a friend more than I need his body to get laid. Maybe."

Miley sidled next to them, asking, "What are you two whispering and giggling about?"

"Our lovely chauffeur and Lilith's gorgeous neighbor, Asher," their mother replied.

"The hottie next to the SUV?" Miley asked.

Lilith nodded.

"He's yummy enough to lick." Miley rested her arm across her forehead, pretending to swoon. "Is he single?"

"Yes," Lilith bit out, trying to keep the edge from her voice, even as it cut along her greedy desires. "He's also almost thirty and has a daughter the same age as mine."

"Plus, he kissed our Lilith." Mom quipped, with a skip in her step.

"Oh, are you two together?" Miley asked.

"Um, no. I'm in no position to date. You know, given I'm still married."

"Pssh. That's only on paper," Mom said. "And since Marshall treated it like a piece of toilet paper for years, who cares?"

"Chloe might care. The separation has to be confusing for her. I won't make it more so by dating her best friend's dad."

Miley wiggled her brows. "Well, you don't have to date him..."

"Just screw him within an inch of his life," their mom finished.

"Oh. My. God. Would you two stop?" Lilith patted her flaming cheeks. "We are friends. The kiss was a one-time mistake." *That had felt like the opposite.*

They'd nearly reached the SUV, and Asher was at the rear, popping open the trunk. "No talk of kissing. Or sex. *Please*," she begged.

Her mom made a zipping motion with her fingers across her lips. Miley giggled, nodding.

Lilith hoped they meant it.

For three weeks, she'd been talking herself out of the exact enticing idea they'd presented.

She didn't need encouragement. She needed help resisting it.

CHAPTER SIXTEEN

Asher flipped the burgers, then wiped his brow. Park grills in direct sunlight sucked.

"Ready for me to take over?" Lilith asked.

She was stretched out next to her mom and sister on an old blanket under a massive maple tree. Her lazy smile was hotter than the day's sun.

He shook his head. "It's your birthday. You can't cook your meal."

"Are you going to peel my grapes and feed them to me too?" She joked, standing and smoothing the wrinkles in a tunic that hid her knock-out body.

"Want me to?" he asked.

Next to Lilith, Hope woke from a nap, stretching like a cat. At her left, Miley closed her laptop and stood. "How about you two go cool off? I'll finish cooking the burgers. I need a break from law school applications."

"I don't mind," Asher replied. "I'll swim after we eat."

"No way. I'm going cross-eyed with information overload. You'll be doing me a favor." She took the spatula from him.

"If you insist." He turned to Lilith. "Are you coming?"

"Definitely." She pulled off her cover-up, tossing it on the blanket.

He ate up her curves. Fuck. He wanted to lick them. Wrenching his gaze to her eyes, he saw a flare of heat in hers, and it dragged him back to the memory of her kiss. Needing a distraction, he looked at Lake Huron and spotted their girls floating on neon tubes. Nearby, Tate and Ted tossed a frisbee back and forth.

He pointed toward them. "Want to race?"

She took off running, shouting, "Yesss!"

Once ankle-deep in the lake, he passed her. After a couple of large strides, he dove in, gasping at the cold when he broke the surface. Once he reached Raven, he made a grab for her tube. She screeched and kicked water in his direction. Blinded by the mad splashing, he ducked under, swimming toward Chloe.

He came up to find her a good twenty feet away. Damn. That girl could move. "How did you get so far?" he asked.

She smiled, raising her skinny arms. "I was on the swim team at my old school."

"You need to be on it at your new one."

His buoyant mood dipped. The end of summer marked the end of Chloe and Lilith as his neighbors. Speaking of Lilith...

Huh. He swam in a slow circle. Where was Lilith? She'd been right behind him. Scanning the shore, he found her waist-deep in the water. He allowed himself a moment to admire her modest, yet sexy, bikini.

Before he could drown in immodest thoughts, he shouted, "What happened to you?"

"This is way colder than our lake." She did a little dance, sucking in a breath, pressing her breasts higher in her top. *Sweet sins.*

"Going in slower makes it so much worse..." He swam closer.

"Don't you dare! Don't do it!" Her shriek was filled with laughter as she stumbled away from him.

He chuckled. "Trust me, it's for the best."

Diving into the shallow water, he shot between her legs. He grabbed her ankles and stood before she lost her balance. She sat atop his shoulder with him gripping her knees.

She dug her hands into his hair. "What are you doing?"

"Not letting you escape." He headed deeper into the lake.

"Wait," Tate shouted from the shore. "Don't dump her!"

Asher stopped, "Why?"

"Because he's my brother, and he's going to protect me," Lilith replied, tugging lightly on Asher's hair.

Miley was next to Tate. "We want to play Chicken Fight."

"So much for helping me," Lilith grumbled.

Asher craned his neck, looking at her. "Don't worry. They'll be the ones going down."

"Yes, they will," she agreed. It seemed competition made her indifferent to the cold water.

Miley and Tate waded to them. He kneeled, and Miley climbed onto his shoulders. Lilith wrapped her legs tighter around Asher, tucking her feet into his back. He got a better grip on her knees.

"Aren't you supposed to be cooking hamburgers?" he asked Miley.

"No. Mom took over. She didn't like the way I was pressing on the patties. Said it made them less juicy."

"She has a point," he replied.

Miley flicked water at him, and Lilith asked, "What are the rules? Me and Miley try to throw each other off, and the guys just hold us. Or"—she tapped the top of Asher's head before pointing at Tate— "they also take part in bringing down the other person?"

Chloe and Raven swam closer, full of grins and giggles. One of them called out, "Guys and girls!"

"Fine with me." Asher shrugged, lifting Lilith.

The movement had her tightening her thighs against his ears. His mind flashed with a very different game he'd like to play with her. One that would also make her shriek and pull his hair.

"Me too," Lilith said.

Miley and Tate agreed, and the girls began shouting an excited countdown. When they screamed one, the four of them lunged at each other.

Asher charged at Tate. Raven and Chloe whooped in victory, but it was too premature. Tate got his footing and stepped away. Miley hunched toward him, and he whispered something to her.

Shit. What were those two scheming? By their evil smirks, it wouldn't be good. "What are they up to?" he asked Lilith.

"No clue. Let's get'em before they put us on the defense."

"Good idea." He rushed at them.

Miley reached toward him like she was going to dunk him. Instead, her arms went past him, and a second later, Lilith screeched and bucked violently. He grunted, tipping back. He shot his arms out, and by sheer luck, he caught Tate's slick shoulders. After regaining his balance, Asher pushed. Lilith did the same to Miley. They went under like an anchor thrown overboard.

"Oh my god!" Lilith shouted. "We are awesome! That last move was perfect. Like we'd planned it ahead of time."

"We make a good team," he said, meaning every word.

Lilith would make the perfect partner. *Whoa. Where had that come from?*

Miley and Tate popped up, splashing and demanding a rematch.

He felt Lilith shake her head. "Will you let me down?" She wiggled on him, and he held in a groan.

He'd spent the last five minutes between her thighs, and now she was rubbing against him. Was she trying to make him hard?

He went down on his knees, asking Miley, "What did you do to Lilith? The way she whipped back, I thought you threw a massasauga at her."

"Worse. She tickled me," Lilith muttered. "Cheaters."

Miley scoffed good-naturedly. "Whatever, you still won. Get back on his shoulders. I want a rematch."

Lilith shook her head. "No. I nearly yanked Asher's head off when you tickled me. He's probably tired of having his head between my legs."

Asher choked as images of his very non-family-friendly version of a naked game played through his mind again.

Miley giggled. "Oh, I bet he doesn't mind being there."

Not. At. All.

Lilith's eyes widened, then her face flamed red. "Please. Shut up," she said, sinking under the water to the sound of her sibling's laughter.

He'd have laughed, too, if the image wasn't stuck on repeat in his mind, creating an issue in his swim trunks. He pinched his inner thigh. Hard. Pain shot through him, cutting off delicious desires.

"Food's ready," Hope hollered from shore.

"Come on." Tate pushed Asher's shoulder. "Let's get first pick."

He considered waiting for Lilith but figured he could use a few minutes apart from her. "Shouldn't the birthday woman get first picks?" he asked as they headed toward the shore.

"No."

"Why?"

Tate grinned. "Because I'm a sore loser."

"Did you hear that?" Asher asked, turning to Lilith.

Her gaze flew to his face. It had been on his ass.

"Umm..." Color crawled up her cheeks.

Christ, he wanted to be a good man, but it wasn't easy when they wanted the same thing, and only a bad situation kept them apart.

"Mom?" Chloe said, running and circling around to Lilith.

"Why did you say my name like a question is about to follow?"

"Because there is," Chloe smiled, flashing her slightly crooked incisor. "You never answered me when I asked to have my birthday at Cedar Point."

"Don't you think that's a bit much for an eleventh birthday? You had a huge party last year when you hit your double digits," Lilith reasoned.

"But this year we have grandma and both my grandpas." Chloe took Miley's hand. "And my aunt, who loves rollercoasters."

"I doubt Grandpa Harrison would go," Lilith replied, but Chloe didn't seem to hear. She was too busy talking about coasters with Miley.

"Does your dad not like amusement parks?" Asher asked, stepping next to Lilith.

"He can take or leave them. It's spending the day with Ted and my mom he can't handle. That's why he isn't here today."

Asher frowned. "Not even for his granddaughter or daughter?"

"It's okay. He has a birthday tradition with Chloe they both love. They spend the day together, shopping for her gift, going to the movies, then the restaurant of her choice."

"What about you?" Asher asked.

"Dad took me out to dinner last night and even skipped his usual lecture. And surprised me with a signed book from one of my favorite authors." She laughed, shaking her head. "He actually went to a romance author book signing to get it. I wish I could have been there—my dad in scuffed work boots, jeans, some sports T-shirt, frowning at all the racy book covers."

Just when Asher was certain her dad was a selfish asshole, he redeemed himself. "Oh, I bet he ended up having a great time. I'm sure women attending were interested in a guy buying a romance book."

"Probably. It does say something about a man who reads them."

"Oh, and what does it say about them?"

She leaned close but didn't look at him. "That he knows the clitoris exists and might even know where to find it."

Asher stumbled a step. Had shy, reserved Lilith actually mentioned the clit? After he digested the unexpected treat, he tipped his head closer to her and said, "I read romances."

Her gaze shot to him, to his mouth, then eyes. Her already pink cheeks turned red, but her voice was steady. "I didn't see any on your bookshelf."

"I borrow them from Hope. Whenever she reads one she likes a lot, she gives it to me."

"Mr. Asher?" Chloe called from somewhere ahead of them, making them jolt.

He didn't turn from Lilith, even as he answered Chloe. "I told you, Asher is fine."

"Okay," She said. "Do you like Cedar Point?"

It took him a second to drag his mind from what he and Lilith had been talking about to the question. He blinked, swallowed, then said, "No, I'm not a fan of those Satan-coasters.

Lilith's eyes widened. "Mister Thrill-Seeker doesn't love the 'coaster capital of the world?'"

He opened his mouth to defend himself. Before he could answer, Raven spoke. "I *love* them! But we hardly ever go because Dad's a wuss."

"Hey—"

Chloe let go of Miley's hand and took Raven's. They jumped around, shouting about how much fun they'd have together. That it'd be such a great summer memory. And many other such sentiments directed at their parents.

Asher fell into step with Lilith and Miley, saying, "Why do I suspect a trip to Ohio is in our future?"

Lilith's shoulder slumped. "I fear you're correct."

His brows rose. Did they have another thing in common? "You don't like Cedar Point either?" he asked.

"I loathe rollercoasters." She bumped his shoulder. "But if you're there, it won't be so bad."

Her words slid into his heart. Lilith was dangerous. When he was around her, he always wanted more. More of her time. More of her body. More of her heart.

Instead, all he had was a little of her time, until the end of summer.

He wasn't sure it was enough.

CHAPTER SEVENTEEN

"Rollercoasters, here we come," Asher said, nudging Lilith aside with his hip and grabbing the two small handles of the family-size cooler, hefting it from her trunk.

"Yay," she cheered in a monotone, eyeing the old blue and white wooden coaster at the edge of the parking lot near the entrance of Cedar Point.

It appeared nearly docile next to the new ones further in the park. Those damn near touched the white, cotton-ball clouds. Goosebumps rose on her arms even though it was a warm morning, promising to be a hot day.

Asher skated his palm just above her raised skin. "What made you give in? Why did you agree to come here?" he asked.

"Besides Chloe's guilt trip? You," she admitted.

"Me? Why?"

"Dad, did you pack sunblock?" Raven shouted from next to his Jeep.

He nodded. "If everyone's out, lock the doors and come get it from me."

"Was Chloe well behaved during the drive?" Lilith asked.

"Of course. Hope let Raven have her phone, so she and Chloe played group games online all the way here." He unpacked the sunblock from his backpack, tossing it to Raven when she got closer.

"Oh, that reminds me," Lilith pointed at Miley. "She wants to be in the same car with Hope to talk about UMich. Miley is applying to their law school and wants to talk to your sister since she attended."

"Okay. Tate could ride home with me."

Raven returned the sunblock to Asher, then pushed her sunglasses up her nose. "Dad, can me and Chloe go off together when we get inside?"

Lilith was about to say she was fine with it when Asher answered. "No, you have to be with a grown-up."

"I'm not a baby," Raven huffed.

"This is a big place. Anything could happen."

"Chloe has a phone."

"If someone snatches you two, you'd never know it was coming. And they'd toss the phone in the garbage."

Wow. His mind went dark fast. And his terrifying story had Lilith firmly behind his decision.

"Daaad," Raven cried out. "We'd kick, scream. Make a huge scene."

"No." Asher stared down at his daughter, tight-lipped with arms crossed.

Miley stepped into their tense group. "Tate and I can go with them." She smiled at the girls. "Don't worry, we'll stay out of your way. We just want to ride the coasters too."

Raven smiled at Miley. "Thanks." She eyed her dad, jutting her chin. "Are they adult enough for you?"

"Keep giving me sass, and I'll make you spend the whole day with me."

Her eyes widened. "Love you, Dad. You're the best." She grabbed Miley's hand, then Chloe's, and hurried toward the park's entrance. "We'll, um, meet you inside."

"Do you have your tickets?" Asher called after them.

Raven and Chloe nodded but didn't turn around.

"I don't blame them," Lilith laughed, disengaging the wheel locks on her cooler. She gripped the large handle and began pulling it behind her, following behind the group. "We both hate rollercoasters, so we're not the best people to spend a day with at a park overflowing with them."

Asher turned in a full circle. "Where are your parents?"

Lilith rolled her eyes. "I warned them not to bring such big coffees. They made a mad dash for the restrooms as soon as I had the car in park. We'll meet them at the carousel near the entrance."

"Let me get that." Asher took the cooler from her. "I feel like I should defend myself before my man-card is revoked. The twisty coasters are fun, but those big hills..." He turned, grinning at her. "No thanks."

"I'm not judging. Even the kiddy coasters make me break out in a cold sweat. I'm surprised, that's all. Your garage is stuffed with toys, from the Jeep you take out on the sand dunes to a dirt bike that looks like it is used often. And I bet the snowmobile, winter skis, and skates get just as much use. You've also told me about a mountain climbing trip you took last year, ziplining in Nicaragua, and a million other daredevil things, yet rollercoasters scare you."

"I'm not afraid. It's more that I hate the intense way my stomach drops on the hills. I can't yell or even breathe. I'm powerless."

They'd reached the short entrance line, and she poked his side. "So, it's a control thing?"

"Maybe."

"That answers one of my questions," she mumbled.

Her favorite recurring fantasy, where she had him tied to a four-poster bed and *she* had all the power, suddenly seemed even more unlikely.

"What's the question?" he asked.

Her face flushed warm. "Nothing. Never mind."

He stepped closer. With his hand not holding the cooler, he ran his fingertips over her cheeks. "This blush doesn't look like nothing."

"Next," called the teenager at the gate.

Lilith startled from the trance of Asher's seductive eyes. Dropping his gaze, she gave her ticket to the teen and went inside the park.

Everyone was waiting for them at the carousel. Good. She needed a moment from Asher. The way he was watching her had her wanting so much more than she could have.

"What are you going to ride first?" Chloe asked when Lilith reached the group.

"I'm not sure," she said. "Any suggestions?"

Her daughter smirked. "Planet Snoopy."

"Ha, ha, such a funny girl," Lilith laughed. It was the toddler area. "Why don't we find something we'll want to ride on together before splitting up."

"The Iron Dragon," Raven suggested. "It's a small rollercoaster."

"Bumper-cars," her mom said.

"Ferris wheel," Asher proposed.

Chloe pointed over her shoulder. "The carousel."

Hope was looking at her map. "How's this sound? Since the cars, wheel, and carousel are near each other, we do those together. After, we split and meet at the train later. We'll go on it together before having our picnic lunch."

Everyone agreed. The morning passed in a blur of sunshine, laughter, and memories being made. Lilith didn't want the surprisingly fun day to end. She tried to cherish every single second, even though it felt like she'd blinked and they were all stepping off the train. Another blink, and they were finishing lunch and making plans to meet up again in the early evening.

Lilith and Asher broke from the group, and he asked, "What would you like to do now?"

You. Seriously, she needed to get a grip! Although it would help if everything this man said didn't sound like an innuendo, making her mind dive straight into the gutter.

He quirked a brow. "That is the second time today you've turned beet red. I'd love to know what is going on inside your head."

"Nothing exciting. I'm burning up, that's all." She fanned herself as the lie slid from her tongue. "Want to go on a water ride?"

"The canyon one would be fun to go on with everyone else. Plus, the slides are on the other side of the park. Want to stop at the beach?" Asher suggested. "We could go for a short swim, rest in the sand."

She poked his side. "Do you really want to swim or are you avoiding the drops on those water rides?"

He laughed. "I can handle them." Peeking at her with the cutest shy smile, he said, "And, fine. The slow click to the top of those hills does make my heart pound more than I'd admit to anyone but you."

"I won't tell a soul. Come on," she took his hand, pulling him down the walkway. "Let's go to the beach. I'll bury your secret there."

CHAPTER EIGHTEEN

The waves of Lake Erie crashing against the shore of the nearly empty beach should have soothed her. However, her pulse wouldn't be lulled by the sound. There were a thousand butterflies in her chest, and they could not be calmed. Not when she'd be stripping down to her bathing suit.

She'd left her conservative ones at home, opting for a sexy two-piece she'd bought on impulse two days ago. At the time, she'd told herself it was ridiculous to get something she'd probably never wear, which was another lie. Deep down, she knew it was for today when they'd be together.

Lilith *wanted* Asher to see her. To take notice of the way the top displayed her breasts. To notice how the bottoms curved over her hips, barely covering her butt.

After helping Asher lay a large beach towel on the sand, she shimmied out of her shorts and tank top. She could barely look at him as she settled next to him. *Am I as desperate for attention as Marshall claims?*

"Jesus, Lilith," Asher whispered so quietly the waves almost swallowed it.

She took in his hungry, wandering gaze. It disintegrated all thoughts of Marshall.

Asher rolled onto his stomach, closing his eyes and groaning.

"You okay?" She leaned closer, intending to rub his back, but stopped.

He'd removed his T-shirt before sitting on the towel and was only in the swim trunks he'd worn to the park. She wasn't sure if touching his naked skin was a good idea. The towel didn't seem so big once they were on it. She was close enough to bask in his heat and scent; both were incredible.

"I'm fine." He kept his eyes closed. "It's just you look really good in that bathing suit."

A thrill zinged through her. "Do I look terrible in my other ones?"

He peeked one lid open. "You'd look hot in my grandma's moo-moos, but this,"—he shifted to his side, facing her—"is different."

She glanced at his mouth. "How?"

"You're my friend, one of my best—but, seeing you slide out of your clothes... seeing you in that suit ..."

Pleased, but hiding it, she waved a hand. "You live in a beach community. You see stuff way more revealing than this all the time."

He tucked a strand of her hair behind her ear, resting his hand on the side of her neck. "But they aren't on you."

Lust washed over her, submerging her in desire. Forgetting about tomorrow, only able to see her need for him, she closed the space between them. He didn't hesitate, pressing his lips to hers and deepening the kiss. She skated a hand to his waist, bringing him closer. A hiss escaped from him. Then his tongue played along her lips. She opened, inviting him to take all of her.

Her phone shrilled from the bag, startling her into reality. She touched her lips, glanced at the water, then at Asher. "It might be Chloe."

He nodded at her with fully dilated pupils. "You should check."

The ringing cut off but immediately started again. Twisting around, she pulled it from the backpack's side pocket. She checked the screen, and her stomach dropped. She rejected the call. Ten seconds later, it began ringing again.

"Is it Chloe?" Asher asked.

She faced him and showed him the screen. "It's Marshall. I better answer it. He'll keep calling until I do."

He nodded, sitting and facing the water.

She answered, and Marshall asked, "Is Chloe around? I want to wish her a happy birthday before I go to another meeting."

"No, she's riding rollercoasters, but I'll have her call you when we meet up."

"Why isn't she with you?"

Asher stood, distracting her. "Where are you going?" she asked him.

"Giving you privacy."

"That isn't necessary."

"Who the fuck is that?" Marshall growled through the phone, loud enough that Asher heard.

He raised a brow, his lip twitching. "Join me when you're finished with the call."

"Okay." Everything in her wanted to bury her phone in the sand and follow her kind, sexy friend into the water. Instead, she took a deep breath and answered her vindictive, egotistical husband. "That was Asher."

"Is that the neighbor guy who's always sniffing around you? We've got enough issues to work through without that guy trying to get into your panties."

"Oh, first, I'm throwing myself at him, now it's him?" Lilith dug her toes into the warm sand. "And Marshall, our marriage is broken. We can't fix it."

"It's what our daughter needs."

"I used to think that, but seeing us miserable isn't doing her any favors. Nor do I want my daughter to think it is acceptable to stay with an unfaithful husband."

"And what you're doing is better?"

She smacked the sand. "Excuse me. What am I doing?"

"Spending every spare second with your *friend*. Parading your fuck-buddy in front of our daughter."

"Freaking hypocrite," she whispered. If she didn't, she'd scream. "I'm doing nothing inappropriate."

She ran her fingertips over her lips where Asher's kiss lingered. Guilt didn't touch her.

"Throughout our marriage, you've been unfaithful," she said.

"You have no proof."

"It's the truth."

"The truth doesn't matter. Chloe doesn't know, nor do you have anything to prove otherwise." His voice lowered. "And I'm good buddies with a divorce lawyer who always wins. It's time to drop your *friend* and come home."

"No. You don't love me. Why do you want to stay married to me?"

"Our daughter needs a stable home. Both parents under one roof."

"Chloe doesn't need our farce of a marriage. It doesn't work."

"Bullshit. It has for the last ten years." The line went quiet, then Marshall said, "Listen, if you continue with this crap, you'll be left with nothing."

"I don't want your money."

"Do you want to lose your daughter?"

Lilith gasped, her blood freezing. "I'd never keep her from you. Would you really do that to me?"

"I've been patient. Kind. I've given you space. Let you use my money to redecorate your little lake house. But the waiting period with the courts is almost over, and we need to end this game. You *will* withdraw the request for a divorce. I'm giving you two weeks."

"Or what?"

She couldn't return to him. It'd hollow her out, leave her an empty shell of a woman. However, Lilith's soul would wither and die if she lost Chloe.

"You don't want the life you'll be left with when my lawyer is done with you. Do what's right for Chloe. For me. For you." He hung up.

Blinking back tears, she stared blindly at her phone. A text flashed at her; Chloe needed sunblock and money for a snack. Lilith messaged where to find them, then tucked her phone into the backpack. Falling onto the towel, she gazed unseeing at the sky. The warmth and buoyancy from earlier had drained away.

Her skin was warm, but her heart was as cold and unforgiving as the lake in front of her. Had only five minutes passed since she'd kissed Asher as if she were a free woman? She rolled onto her side, away from him and the water. Closing her eyes, she tried to swallow her tears and gather her shattered peace.

She was building one that allowed her to really live. Returning to her old life would kill something within her. But did she have a choice?

CHAPTER NINETEEN

Asher floated on his back, focusing on the clouds, trying to calm his lust and annoyance. He shouldn't have kissed her, but did it have to be Marshall that ended it?

The guy was a rusty nail in Asher's thumb, even when the ass wasn't around in person. Shifting to tread water, he looked to their spot on the beach. She was curled on her side, facing away from him. Was she off the phone? Had the dickhead upset her?

Annoyance shifted to worry. Marshall wasn't fit to breathe the same air as her, let alone ruin her good mood. Swimming toward the shore, the urge to hold Lilith, to cheer her up, washed through him. Slowing, he groaned. There would be no cuddling.

Friends didn't touch.

And Lilith needed a friend more than a lover. When his shadow covered her, she opened her eyes. They were red-rimmed. Nearly every muscle in him tensed as his heart squeezed.

"What's wrong?"

"Marshall, of course." Her voice cracked a little. "He's a master at wrecking me."

Asher sat next to her, hot anger thrumming through him. "What'd the fucker say now?"

She uncurled herself, sitting up. "He sort of threatened me. He demanded I withdraw the divorce papers and return to him with Chloe. In two weeks."

Asher wanted to rage at the sun, sand, everything. Marshall couldn't have Lilith. He'd tossed her aside like a toddler with a toy that no longer amused him. That is, until someone else had shown an interest in what he deemed his property. Asher suspected his friendship with Lilith made Marshall's tantrum worse.

Good thing he couldn't see what was taking place when he'd called. Guilt warred with anger. He wasn't supposed to complicate Lilith's situation.

His chest constricted, even as his blood thirsted for Marshall's pain. "What do you think he'll do?"

"Leave me penniless. Gain full custody of Chloe." She pressed her palm over her heart as if the thought pained her.

"It takes a real asshole to threaten to get what he wants, but really, what could he use against you? You're a great mother, with a spotless reputation... unlike him." He cupped her cheek and saw her eyes were drowning in worry. "If you need a witness to testify about him being with other women, there are plenty who saw him. He didn't hide his activities while visiting your lake house."

"That's nice of you to offer," she said. "But I couldn't ask you to be a character witness—"

Adrenaline shot through him. "Lilith, I can't be, um... I've got some stuff in my past that might hurt, more than help your case..."

The whole shitty story of what he'd done to the scumbag all those years ago sat on the tip of his tongue. But her wide eyes and the way she leaned away from him had him swallowing his words.

"A little trouble when I was a teenager." He looked toward Lake Erie, unable to hold Lilith's gaze. "The records are sealed, but the courts could and would probably look at them."

She sagged, resting against him. "I'm sure the Friend of the Court won't care about a little reckless fun when you were a kid. Anyway, it doesn't matter. I couldn't use you as a character witness. Marshall made sure of it."

The worry whirling in him stalled. "How?"

She grabbed a handful of sand, letting it slide between her fingers. "He's going to tell the courts I paraded my 'boy-toy' in front of my daughter while still married."

Confusion rippled through him. "Who's your 'boy-toy?'"

The tips of her ears reddened. "You."

"But you aren't even playing with me." He rubbed his lips together, tasting her phantom kiss. "Much."

She laughed, and it held him like a summer breeze.

"I told him that. He didn't believe me. Also, what if his lawyer asked if we ever kissed? I can't lie." The worry was back in her eyes, and this time he was the cause of it.

She plunged a hand into her hair and twisted the strands around her fist. "I was an idiot not to gather evidence of his cheating before I left. He didn't try very hard to hide it. It would have been easy."

Asher gently removed her hand from her tortured hair, trying to ignore how much he wanted to run *his* fingers through the soft locks. "Last summer, I saw him at The Hill getting hot and heavy with a friend of mine. As his neighbor, I, um, was aware he wasn't looking for a girlfriend. I warned her."

"Your point?" Lilith asked. She didn't sound hurt or even bitter, just tired.

"Juliet told me she wasn't looking for a boyfriend, only a little fun. But unless she changed a lot, she wouldn't have knowingly slept with a married man. If I ask her to speak against his character, I bet she would."

Lilith looked toward Lake Erie. "That is something. A grain of hope." She exhaled, and to his ears, it sounded relieved. "However, I pray it doesn't come to that. I don't want to drag others into my mess."

"It seems more like Marshall's mess, and he's waiting for you to clean it up."

She tilted her head from left to right as if saying, 'What's new' or 'It's the same thing.' What she said out loud was, "Enough talk of him. We won't find a solution today, so I'm going to let it go for now."

"Fair enough," Asher said. "Do you want to swim?"

Lilith told him about Chloe's text. "I thought they'd be here by now. They must've gone on another ride."

"Let's chill until they get here. Then they won't have to search for us." Propping the backpack behind his head, he laid back, patting the spot next to him.

Sometime later, he woke to Lilith sleeping on his chest, his hand resting on her waist. Three sets of eyes stared at them, each wearing different expressions. Hope squinted, her mouth in a tight line. Raven scratched her cheek, her uncertain gaze bouncing from him to Lilith. Chloe studied them with open curiosity. He ignored their glances, reaching for his T-shirt. Lilith woke and sat, rubbing her eyes.

Raven busted out, "Mom's coming by tomorrow. Can we go out on the boat? Take her tubing? She's never been."

Okay... "Um, sure, honey."

"And have her stay for dinner?"

"If she wants."

Eden and Raven were closer since she'd moved to Michigan, and it was great. But what was up with this odd behavior? "What's this about?"

"No reason." Her gaze skittered to Lilith, then away. *Uh-oh.*

"You're weird, Mom," Chloe said. "We're surrounded by rollercoasters and a million other rides, and you choose to sleep on a beach."

"I'm not the only one." Lilith had been applying sunblock and pointed the tube at Asher before tossing it to her daughter. "And what happened to you? I thought you'd be here right after texting for money?"

"Hope bought our snacks, so we went on a few more rides." Chloe grinned at her mom. "Unlike you boring old people."

"Guess that's why we make such good *friends.*" He stressed the last word, wanting his daughter and sister to hear it. Even if his body wasn't listening.

Standing, Lilith brushed the sand off her feet before putting on her shorts and tank top. She strapped on her sandals. "Since we have half the group here, lets message the rest and see if they want to meet at the water rides. Those are better for large groups."

They agreed, and Lilith sent a group text while he shook the large towel and folded it into his backpack. Usually, he loved water rides, but leaving behind his alone time with Lilith stole most of his enthusiasm.

CHAPTER TWENTY

Glancing in her rearview mirror, Lilith saw her mom was already asleep, and Hope was on the precipice. Every time she blinked, her eyes stayed closed longer. Lucky lady.

Halfway through the drive, Lilith had stopped to get an extra-large, almost-not-disgusting coffee from the gas station. And Miley had switched places with their mom, taking the front passenger seat. During the first part of the drive, she'd talked to Hope about UMich and now seemed too pumped about the possibility of attending to doze—for which Lilith was thankful.

Miley's current stories of college life in Florida had Lilith awake, laughing, and cringing. Also, a little sad that she'd never gotten the chance to experience it.

She patted her sister's knee. "I hope you get accepted to UMich. You could live with me."

"You'd want me to stay with you?" She sounded surprised.

"Definitely." Lilith had no hesitation. "I regret never living with you, getting the chance to really know my little sister."

"Plus, we're older, so we'll skip the teenage drama of stealing each other's clothes and boyfriends," Miley joked.

Lilith laughed, taking a sip of her coffee. "Doesn't that stuff only happen on TV shows?"

"Hell if I know. I didn't have any siblings at home to steal from, or them from me," Miley giggled.

"Yeah, and Tate never stole my skirts or boyfriends," Lilith winked, her voice shaking with humor.

Miley reached over the center console and tugged gently on a lock of Lilith's hair. "And for the record, I'll stay away from your man."

"Asher isn't my man."

"Then how'd you know that's who I was talking about?"

She rolled her eyes. "What other guy do I talk to?"

"Jackson, Max, that cute guy at the grocery store." Lilith snorted at that last one. "Not that it would matter," Miley continued.

"What do you mean?'"

"Oh, come on, Lil. I could pole dance in front of him naked, and Asher wouldn't notice because he'd be too busy staring at you."

Mom's quiet laughter drifted from the back seat. "So true."

Lilith scanned her rearview mirror. Hope was quietly snoring, but Mom was now wide awake and looking very amused.

Squinting at her, Lilith said with mock seriousness. "Go back to sleep."

"Not a chance. This is way too interesting."

"What? My sister's delusions?" Lilith quipped, her mouth going a little dry.

"I'm not the delusional one," Miley scoffed. "You two were rather cozy on the beach."

"Oh, please. There wasn't much room on the towel. Plus, we were taking a nap, not making out in the sand."

Lilith was thankful she was driving. Then they couldn't see her lying eyes.

"You were sprawled on him, and his hand was curled around your waist. Oh, and during the fireworks, you were tucked into his side the whole time and wearing his hoodie." Miley gave Lilith a heavy dose of side-eye. "Which you kept sniffing."

Lilith's cheeks warmed. She kept her gaze resolutely on the road. "I was cold. As for the hoodie, what can I say? He smells good."

In fact, so good she couldn't stop imagining herself wrapped around his naked body, his scent all over her skin.

She held the cuff under her sister's nose. She breathed it in. "Damn. He does smell good."

"I rest my case."

"Um. Not at all." Miley twisted sideways in her seat, facing Lilith. "I know you said you've both decided it was better to be friends, but why? You two seem great together, and he's an awesome guy."

"Or as I've said," their mother muttered, "they could be friends-with-benefits."

"Would you stop?" Lilith squeaked. "You're my mom. Aren't you supposed to be lecturing me about safe sex and waiting for love?"

"Daughter, last week was your thirtieth birthday. I'd hope by now you know all about safe sex. As for love, yes, I want you to find a person who treasures you and is worthy of your heart. But it doesn't have to be now. For a decade, you were married to an incredibly selfish man; it's time you grabbed a bit of fun and pleasure for yourself with a good guy."

"Yeah," Miley chimed in, "take Asher. He's that man."

The two women high-fived, and Lilith shook her head. They were incorrigible. She'd heard similar remarks during most of their visit.

Not wanting to get into Marshall's troubling phone call and bring down everyone's upbeat mood, she took a different direction. "That's a terrible idea. Sex, even the no-strings kind, could ruin a friendship. What if he finds it boring with me? Or he's terrible at it? It'd make things awkward. He's my neighbor."

"Neither is likely. And if by some infinitesimal chance that happens, you'll only have him as a neighbor for another month or so," their mother reasoned.

That was it? Her insides filled with melancholy sadness. Not seeing Asher nearly every day was on the horizon.

"Our daughters will probably remain friends, and we'll still be visiting the lake house often to clean up between renters since I can't afford to hire a cleaning service."

"Fine. Fine. You'll still see each other, but it will be easier to avoid him," Miley reasoned. "Also, really, is there any kind of sex guys find boring?"

Lilith couldn't have been all that much fun if Marshall had continuously strayed, but she kept her insecurities to herself.

"And I doubt Asher would be an awful lay," Mom said.

"I know I'm going to regret asking, but what makes you so certain?" Lilith asked.

"Because he's thoughtful and loves adventure. Those are great traits to have in a lover."

Lilith waved a hand. "Would you two quit? He and I will remain friends. Without any benefits."

"Yes, please stop," groaned Hope from the backseat. "Sex and my brother is a conversation I'd rather not have awoken to."

Lilith slouched into her seat. She wanted to sink through the car onto the highway, where a semi-truck could run her over.

"Don't worry. I don't plan on trying to seduce him," she said.

"That's good because I don't think he'd resist." Hope's yawn filled the car, but what Lilith heard was the underlying disapproval.

It hurt, but she understood. Who'd want someone they loved with a disaster like her?

She floundered for a topic change and wanted to hug her mom when she began to regale them with stories about her first boyfriend and disaster dates. Before long, she had them laughing and sharing funny dating stories.

It almost made Lilith forget about Hope's stinging rejection. Almost, but not completely. And that was good. The reminder was needed. Lilith needed more and more reasons not to give in and invite Asher to her bed.

CHAPTER TWENTY-ONE

"Hello?" called a man from inside Lilith's house.

Asher tilted his head. It couldn't be Ted. He'd returned to Flordia with his family this morning. Setting aside his wrench, Asher grabbed his discarded shirt and wiped his face with it. Tossing it on the nearby deck chair, he stepped around the A/C unit and strode across Lilith's lower balcony, opening the sliding door of her walkout basement.

"Hello?" he called out.

A man in pressed khakis, a peach polo shirt, and perfectly styled, short black hair appeared at the top of the stairs. The infamous estranged husband up close.

He looked as arrogant and douchie as Asher remembered—-good-looking in a sleek, slimy way.

"You're the neighbor," Marshall stated flatly.

"Yeah. Asher." He climbed the stairs but couldn't bring himself to offer his hand to the other man. "You're early. Lilith and Chloe are at my house. My phone's downstairs. I'll get it and call 'em."

"I've got mine," Marshall said, pulling out his cell. After a few rings, Lilith answered. "I told you I'd be here at four. Why aren't you here?"

Asher couldn't hear her reply, and he didn't think Marshall was listening. Might have even hung up before she'd finished replying.

His steely gaze traveled from Asher's bare feet to his old boardshorts and lack of shirt, stopping at his face. "Any reason you're hanging out at *my* Lilith's, alone?"

The possessive way he spoke bugged the shit out of Asher, and he couldn't resist poking. He scratched the thick stubble on his cheek, asking, "'My?' Didn't she serve you with divorce papers?"

Marshall bared his teeth, glaring. "We have a history together. A daughter. She'll always be mine." He stepped closer. "Never yours."

Asher ignored the last part. "When Lilith *was* yours, you didn't seem to care. Why start now, when she's giving you an out?"

"What are you talking about? You have no idea how I feel about my wife or how I treat her," Marshall growled.

Wow. He didn't even remember their near fight.

He tapped his chin with his finger. "Funny, in the summers of the past, I saw women here all the time, but never your *wife*."

The other man's eyes glazed arctic. "Mind your own damn business."

"I will, unless you keep threatening Lilith."

A vein pulsed on Marshall's forehead. "Are *you* fucking threatening me?"

"Nope, just stating a fact."

"Are you going to run,"—Marshall swung his index and middle finger back and forth in a running motion— "to Lilith's lawyer to tattle on me? Mine will tear you apart. He'll paint you as her lovesick neighbor willing to say anything to get in her panties."

"We're friends." Asher curled his hands into fists, locking them at his sides to keep from punching the other man. Although, the satisfaction of hitting the asshole might be worth the fallout of another arrest.

"Friend," the prick scoffed.

"This might be a foreign concept to you," Asher said, "but men and women can be friends."

"Only if the woman's ugly."

Asher jerked back in disgust. "You're a dick."

Marshall shrugged. "Maybe, and that's why I can recognize another one. You're just another dog sniffing after pussy."

Asher stepped into Marshall's personal space. "Don't *ever* compare me to you. I'd never treat Lilith like she's disposable."

"All women are. Though I doubt you'll get the chance to taste her. She likes her men,"—he sniffed, eyeing Asher's worn shorts— "a little more sophisticated."

The front screen door swung open, and Lilith stopped short. Her gaze bounced from him to Marshall, unease tightening the corner of her eyes. Chloe was right behind her, with a similar expression.

"Is everything okay?" Lilith asked.

Marshall pasted on a smarmy smile. "Great. I'm talking to your friendly neighbor, trying to figure out why he was snooping around our house."

"Snooping? I invited him. Plus, it's nice you finally got to meet him in person," she said with false sweetness.

"Why? Because he's your special *friend*, willing to be at your beck and call?"

"No, because he probably feels like he knows you from all your visits here the last few summers."

"What do you mean, Mom?" Chloe asked, her brows pulling together. "We didn't come here last year. Or the year before."

"Oh, yeah, that's right. *We* didn't..."

"Chloe, get your bag," Marshall snapped. "It's time to go."

She nodded, moving around the adults. Her footsteps retreated down the stairs, growing fainter. Lucky girl. She got to escape from the smothering tension.

Marshall pointed at Lilith. "We agreed not to do this shit in front of our daughter."

"Yes, we did, but that doesn't mean you can make underhanded comments, and I have to swallow them to keep the peace. Those days are over," she shot back. "You were insulting Asher, and he wasn't the one in the wrong. You were."

"You've changed, and not for the better." He shook his head, his gaze flickering from Lilith to Asher, as if making sure they were both listening. "We'll work on losing it when you come home. You're down to a week."

Lilith didn't answer, but everything in her seemed to deflate. Was she giving up? A cold gloom coated Asher.

Chloe appeared at the top of the stairs with her suitcase. "I'm ready, Dad."

She kissed her mom. "See you on Sunday. Miss you." She turned and hugged Asher. "You, too."

He returned it, and a little of his darkness faded. Even more evaporated when he glanced at Marshall and saw the hug had annoyed him.

When the door shut, he pressed a hand against the frame. "I'm sorry if I made things worse."

"You didn't. Things have been shitty for a long time." She looked at her flip-flops. When her gaze met his, she was smiling. "Plus, having an excuse to push back felt great. I spent ten years biting my words, being blind around him. Looking him in the eye and telling him I see his bullshit was fantastic. Freeing."

Asher chuckled. "You were impressive. Crowley Construction could use you as our bill collector. You'd scare them shitless. No one would pay late."

She waved aside the compliment, but her gaze sparkled, and her smile widened.

"How's the A/C?" Lilith winced as if the question hurt to ask.

But it made him laugh.

"What's so funny?" she asked.

Digging into the deep pockets of his cargo shorts, he pulled out his unexpected find in the A/C unit. "I think you might have a smutty Easter bunny that likes to hide interesting eggs throughout your house."

Lilith blinked a few times. Then doubled over with laughter, holding onto her sides. Between gasps, she said, "Well, I won't need Google to figure out that sex toy."

"Nope." Asher hit the suction base of the rubber dildo against the nearest wall, and it stuck, making Lilith laugh harder.

The woman was so damn beautiful.

"Is this,"—she flicked the head of the dick—"the reason my house won't cool down?"

He grinned. "I want to say your A/C was hot-and-bothered, but no. It was wedged into a corner, not in the way. After removing it, I cleaned out the dirt and leaves that made it inside the unit. I also changed the air filters."

"Thank you," she said, her lips twitching with mirth.

He shifted so his back was to the screen, hoping for a breeze. "Let me know if it doesn't help."

She nodded, but she probably wouldn't tell him. Stubborn woman.

The sweltering heat had him talking without thinking. "You should stay with me tonight."

Her eyes widened. "Wow, um..."

Oh shit. That came out wrong.

"I meant in my guest room." He scratched behind his ear. "If the air conditioning still isn't working, and you're miserable here in the heat."

She covered her mouth, but her laughter broke through her fingers, halting his babbling. "Sorry, I know. I was messing with you," she said between giggles. "The look on your face was priceless."

"I wonder if it was better than yours when I pulled this,"—he removed the dildo from the wall— "from my pocket."

"Probably not." Her cheeks hurt from laughing.

Going into the kitchen, he tossed it in the trash under the sink. "Anyway, that wasn't nice," he teased. "I wanted to sound like a caring friend, and you had me worried I sounded like your friendly creep."

Following him, she patted his back. "I'm sorry, I couldn't resist. Anyway, I'm fine. If it doesn't cool off, I'll keep the window open at night and sleep in Chloe's room. Since hers is downstairs, I should be fine."

"Do your windows have tabs that stop from opening too much?" he asked.

Her brows pushed together. "What's that? And don't I want them open?"

Well, if they did, she wasn't using them. Worry replaced his levity. "It's a safety feature. You can have an inch or so with the tabs out. It means no one can easily enter through a window."

"It also means I only get an inch or so of air. No thanks."

"I don't like the idea of you alone at night with all the windows unlocked."

Her spine stiffened. "I'm not a child. I can take care of myself."

Shit. He'd overstepped, so he took a step back. "You're right. I'm sorry. I had a Dad moment."

She laughed, and it sounded genuine. "It's fine."

Returning to the foyer, he opened the screen door. "But if cleaning the A/C didn't help and your house stays this hot, my invitation stands."

She nodded. "Okay."

At the edge of the porch, he turned, but whatever he was going to say disappeared.

Inside, Lilith was slumped against the foyer wall. She looked defeated.

Was she still upset with him, or was it Marshall's threat?

"You won't go back to him, will you?" Asher asked.

She jolted, meeting his gaze. The hopelessness in her eyes made his pulse spike. He feared her answer.

"I don't want to." Her voice cracked on the last word.

He reopened the door and brought her into his arms. She hugged him tight, whispering, "I'm running out of options."

They stood like that until she loosened her hold and stepped away. "You'd better get home. Didn't you say it was movie night with Raven?"

"Come with me. Watch it with us."

Lilith smiled, but her eyes remained troubled. "No. I think I need to be alone. Try to figure some things out."

Indecision pulled him in opposite directions. He wanted to insist, but his early protectiveness had pissed her off, and the last thing he wanted was to upset her more.

"Go," she said, pushing him gently. "Enjoy movie night."

"Are you sure you don't want to join us?"

"I am."

He left, but discontent trailed him home.

CHAPTER TWENTY-TWO

Lilith yawned and settled deeper into the deck chair's cushion. The lake was calm. The morning sun warmed her skin, and the scent of coconut creamer and coffee wafted from her mug. She picked up the book her dad had recommended to her. He had a keen eye for knowing which stories she'd loved, but today she read the same paragraph over and over.

Setting it down, she rubbed her eyes. Sleep had been fitful, full of nightmares and anxiety. Time was running out. Why hadn't she gotten proof of Marshall's cheating before she'd left? If she could return to the past, she'd kick herself. Then hire a P.I.

...Or a teenager.

Her phone sat under her current read. She grabbed it and called Asher.

"Good morning," Asher said. "I hope you're calling to tell me you had a wonderful night's sleep in a cold house with all your windows locked and closed."

"It still wasn't cooling much, so I shut off the A/C, but I still managed to survive the night, McGruff," she teased.

"McGruff," he laughed. "How do you even know who that is? That dog is from the eighties."

"He's still around. He came to my elementary school. Left an impression."

"Yeah, my dad dressed up as him for Halloween one year when I was a kid." Something banged, followed by a man's tenor and a woman's indecipherable voice in the background. "Did you know the actor who played that dog was arrested and sentenced to something like sixteen years in prison?"

"What was his crime?" She paused. "Also, why do you know this?"

He snorted. "A bunch of stuff—drugs, weapons. I think he even had a grenade launcher. As for me, I am a fountain of useless information."

The word information reminded Lilith why she'd called. "Is Raven around?"

"No. I'm working today, so I dropped her off at her my parents. Why? Do you need her?"

"Yeah, could you ask her to call me? I just have a quick social media question."

"I thought you hated those sites."

"They might have their uses," she said vaguely, glad he didn't ask why she wasn't calling her own daughter for the information.

She trusted Asher but didn't want to get her hopes up by telling others. After looking into it, she'd tell him if it was a success or bust.

Someone called his name, and he told them to give him a minute. "I'll call her now," he said to Lilith.

"They said their goodbyes and hung up. Less than five minutes later, her cell rang. "Hi, Raven. Do you remember when you and Chloe were on the computer the other day and found a girl you both know?"

"Anna? She was at Chloe's old school but now goes to mine."

"Yes, her. Could you tell me how you found so much information about her?"

"I searched her @."

"Her what?"

"The name she uses on her socials."

"Social media?"

"Yeah."

"Hold on." Lilith ran inside, grabbing a notebook and pen. "Continue, please. What do you do after you have her name?"

Raven launched into a plethora of tips and tricks. By the time she finished, Lilith had a page of notes.

Her pulse thrummed. "Thanks. This is really helpful."

After hanging up, she went inside her house, and grabbed her laptop from her downstairs office. Then she headed to the screen porch at the walkout basement. Once inside, she flipped the switch on the ceiling fan and dived into social media.

Finding Marshall's accounts was easy. They weren't set to private. No shocker, given most posts were of bland work stuff. He had the link to his company in his bio, and she scrolled through photos of the most recent Christmas party. In nearly everyone with Marshall, there was a sexy brunette next to him. Since everyone was tagged, finding the woman's personal account was simple.

There, Lilith hit priceless gold. Taking a screenshot, she called Marshall.

"Good morning, wife," he said. "Are you calling because you're ready to come home?"

Arrogant ass.

"Please send Chloe over to a friend's or your brother's. We need to talk in private. I'm leaving now and should be at your place in an hour."

"Our place. And it's about damn time."

He might not feel the same when she arrived.

A little before noon, she was typing the code to the gate at her old home. Her hands were clammy, and she was glad for the extra swipe of deodorant, but her mind was calm. She'd looked at the upcoming confrontation from every angle, and there was a good chance she'd walk from her old, suffocating life as a free woman.

Marshall opened the front door and stepped aside. "Why are you knocking? This is your house."

He was cocky and so self-assured that some of her confidence and certainty disappeared.

She grasped at false bravado. "Yes, it is, and I'll take my half in the divorce."

He halted outside the living room, all congeniality sliding from his face. "I hope you didn't drive all the way here to harass me with this shit. We. Are. Not. Divorcing."

She continued walking. "I disagree."

Taking a seat on the nearest couch, she perched on the edge of the leather cushion. The room was as stiff, stuffy, and uncomfortable as she remembered. She'd argued for comfy furniture that begged people to stay and chat. Walls that were light and airy, with intricate art that enticed the eye. Not gray walls and modern art that looked similar to the prints at her doctor's office—except Marshall would only have originals on his stark, cold walls.

"Did you spend last night with that asshole neighbor of yours? Did he fill your head with lies and make-believe? Do you think he's your knight, out to rescue you?" Marshall stalked into the room, towering over her. "Don't count on it. I reached out to my lawyer friend this morning. He called right before you arrived—"

She stood, forcing him to step back. "This isn't about Asher, but you, me, and your threats."

He crossed his arms over his chest. "They aren't threats. Merely incentives to come home."

"We may live in a no-fault state, but the courts won't favor a parent who's a chronic cheater," Lilith said. "I might not be able to afford your lawyer, but I know how to read. I've learned a lot about Michigan divorces. If adultery is involved, the one who was cheated on is usually awarded alimony, more of the marriage assets, and custody of the children."

His nostrils flared, and she half expected him to breathe fire. "You have no proof," he said through clenched teeth.

She took her phone from the pocket of her linen shorts and showed him the screenshot she'd taken from Instagram. It was of Marshall kissing the brunette in the living room they were standing in now. In the background was last year's Christmas tree with its distinct blue crystal lights. Below the photo was the date—last New Year's Eve.

"Nice, Marshall. So, when Chloe and I flew to Florida during Christmas break because I was so distraught over our marriage, you threw a freaking party."

He was still as a statue. "Where did you get that?"

"You should be careful what your 'friends' are posting on social media. I also have someone who's willing to go on record saying she went home with you after a night of dancing and drinks at The Hill—"

"The Hill?" he repeated, sounding dazed.

She nodded. "It was over two years ago, but she remembers you."

That part could be total bullshit. She might have forgotten about Marshall. Lilith had never spoken to the woman Asher had mentioned on the beach at Cedar Point. However, going by Marshall's expression, he was plenty worried.

He slumped into the nearest chair and ran a trembling hand through his hair. "Fuck. Fine. You win. I'll sign the papers."

The accumulated weight of a decade in a loveless marriage lifted from her. She could have floated to the ceiling.

He kept his gaze locked on his polished shoes. "Please don't take Chloe from me."

Lilith returned to the couch across from him as a shard of unexpected sympathy seeped into her. "I won't. She loves you, and while you treat me like crap, you are good to her. She can stay with you every other weekend. Same with holidays."

After a loaded silence, he nodded.

Lilith tipped her head and closed her eyes, relief coursing through her. "Okay. Good. I'm going to leave now. But, Marshall—"

She waited for him to look at her.

His gaze met hers. "Yeah?" Wariness threaded through his voice.

"I'm holding on to this picture and the one I printed—don't worry, it's hidden. We wouldn't want Chloe to see it. She'd recognize the tree and the brand-new lights she and I had picked out last year." She put her phone in her purse. "I want the papers signed and notarized this Monday. I'll throw the evidence out when the divorce is final."

Marshall's spine went straight. "Are you threatening me?"

"No," she said, making it sound like a lie. In truth, she'd never purposely drag Chloe into the middle of their mess, but she didn't want him to know this fact.

"Wow, you really want out."

"Can you blame me?"

There was another long pause. "No, I guess not."

She left her old home, which no longer felt like a home, striding toward her new life.

CHAPTER TWENTY-THREE

L ilith adjusted her wireless earbuds, glancing at Asher's house. When was he going to be home? She'd called her mom and Miley after leaving Marshall, but she wanted to share her fantastic news with her best friend.

Something quiet and deprived whispered that might not be the only reason she wanted to see him. Ignoring it, she concentrated on her thankless task—weeding her front yard. Gathering the pulled ones, she dropped them in the yard waste bag.

Did they grow on spite and humidity? Each day was warmer than the last, and it hadn't rained in a week, yet they were everywhere, trying to choke her roses, daylilies, and poppies.

She turned up her music and sang, yanking out the unwanted intruders to the beat of a great song.

Someone grabbed her shoulder, and the lyrics clogged with fear in her throat. Swiveling around, she faced a surprised-looking Asher.

He straightened, holding up his hands and mouthing, "Sorry."

She plopped on her butt, hand over her racing heart. After a moment, she removed an earbud. "My fault."

"I'd wondered why you didn't answer me," he replied.

Pulling the case from her front pocket, she placed the earbuds inside. "They're noise-canceling and I had the music loud."

"Do you think that's safe?"

His frown of worry sent a ripple of annoyance through her, and she gave him a frown in return. "Christ, Asher, I'm in my front yard not running down the worse part of 8 Mile at midnight."

He held up his hand as if in surrender. "Sorry. Good point." Sitting next to her, asking, "How's your Saturday going? You seemed excited when you called this morning."

The reminder of her success melted away her lingering annoyance at him. She looked at him, really looked at him. He had on a faded baseball hat. There was sawdust mixed in with the light hairs on his arms. It was also sprinkled on his shirt, which stuck to him due to a light coating of sweat.

Two words described him. Masculine and sexy.

"It's after six on a Saturday. Why were you working today?" she asked.

He groaned, lying flat in the grass. "Because one of my jobs is killing me. The client ordered custom-made cabinets and deck. Both are intricate and time-consuming. And they paid extra to have it finished by the end of the summer." He rubbed his flat stomach through this threadbare shirt. "So that means weekends for me."

"Do you have to work tomorrow too?"

He shook his head.

"Good." She patted his firm chest. "Now, it's time for you to relax. Enjoy this muggy, cloying summer day."

"When you put it like that, I want to zone out in front of my TV in the A/C. Oh—" He shifted to his side. "When you called this morning, did you say yours wasn't working?"

She shrugged. "I'm not sure."

"How can you not be sure in this heat?"

"It might have just been me. I tossed and turned most of the night, and ended up shutting it off for the lake breeze and sound. Then I took off this morning, only getting back about an hour ago. I've been out here since."

"Did your busy day have something to do with your phone call with my daughter?"

"Yes." Lilith twisted to face him, sitting crossed-legged. Her heart skipped a few beats. "I convinced Marshall to sign the divorce papers."

Asher's eyes widened, and he sat up. "How?"

As she told him the story, she scooted down, resting on her hip, mirroring him. "All these months and his downfall was an hour of internet snooping," she finished.

"Does it feel like you've won the lottery?" he asked.

She plucked a blade of grass from the ground and wound it around her finger. "Yes, but also like a loss."

He took her hand. "Why?"

Entwining her fingers with his, she said, "I don't know. Perhaps because my marriage was a long chapter of my life, and I failed miserably at it. The younger me had all these plans when I said, I do... and here I am back at the start, none the wiser." She shook her head. "I've made so many mistakes."

"Believe me, everyone has mistakes and regrets." He scratched his face and looked away, going quiet, but it wasn't like usually calm. This one was loaded with heavy discontent.

"Are you okay?" she asked.

He nodded, then squeezed her hand. "You don't give yourself enough credit. You're a strong woman."

She wasn't sure if that was true but said, "I hope you're right."

"I am."

This time the quiet that fell between was pleasant, and soothing. She listened to the gentle song from the cicadas and enjoyed the comfort of Asher's hand in hers.

"So, what's next?"

Was he asking about them? She bit the inside of her cheek, leaning closer as her gaze fell to his mouth. In a week or less, her dying marriage would no longer separate her from Asher. She could have him.

If he wanted her.

She looked into his eyes. They were cloudy with desire. A flush of warmth spread between her legs.

Swallowing, her throat clicked with sudden dryness. "What do you mean?" she asked.

"I'd meant, when the papers are signed, are you automatically divorced? But after watching you watch me, that's not what I'm asking now." He shifted closer. "What does it mean for us?"

A hollowness flooded her stomach, and she dropped his gaze, taking in their surroundings. They were alone. She couldn't even hear a motorboat on the lake. But her current recklessness was foolish—for her heart and her equally precarious situation with Marshall.

She let go of Asher's hand. "I'm technically still married until Friday. Then the mandatory waiting period is over, and everything will be finalized."

"Did you pull away because you're worried Marshall will try to get some last-ditch dirt on you?" Asher crooked a knee and rested an elbow on it. "Or did my question upset you?"

"I'm afraid he'll try something." She stared at her nails, focusing on the dirt under her thumb. "But I also don't know how to answer your question. It's a bit like stepping onto a rollercoaster."

"That bad?" He poked her above the hip.

"Not the tickle spot!" She yelp-laughed, wrapping her arms around her waist. "And, fine, that was a terrible analogy. How about skiing instead?"

"I like this one better already," he teased, rolling his index finger in a keep-going gesture.

"Some of those runs scare me silly, but every limb in my body tingles to rush down them. Experience them... even if I'm not ready."

Crunching gravel snagged her attention, and she looked toward the sound. A red SUV drove up the road.

Asher waved. "That's my dad with Raven," he told Lilith, standing and then helping her up. "Listen, I'm attracted to you, but I can handle if you don't want more. It won't ruin our friendship. Okay?"

"Okay," she replied.

He squeezed her hand briefly. "I better get home. I promised Raven I'd make tacos, then go kayaking with her."

"What happened to vegging in front of the TV?"

"I said I wanted to do that. That doesn't mean I'd actually get to do that," he laughed. Then his smile faded and his eyes turned serious. "You believe me, what I said about us being friends or lovers, don't you?"

"I do." And she meant it.

Asher was one of the most honorable men she knew. Her worry was her. She might be the one to destroy them with her messy emotions and desires.

CHAPTER TWENTY-FOUR

Lilith sighed, lifting her hair as a strong gust of wind blowing from the lake reached her inside the screened-in porch. After nearly a week of her A/C blowing out slightly cooler air, it had rattled and died in the afternoon.

Chloe had been with her grandpa, and upon learning of the A/C's death, she decided to spend the night at his house. Even at eleven o'clock at night, the temperature was sweltering, so maybe Lilith should have done the same.

No way. It was her first true day of freedom, and she didn't want to spend it with her father, filling her head with doubt. As promised, Marshall had signed the divorce papers on Monday, and five days later, he was her ex-husband.

Unrolling her yoga mat, Lilith set a sheet and pillow on it. Her sleeping nest was complete. Returning to her favorite wicker rocking chair, she settled in with an exquisite white wine. The soothing breeze and water lapping against the shore was a recipe for a perfect night of contemplation.

Her foot bounced, and she tapped her nails on the armrest. Memories and anxious worries pinged and leaped within her.

She stood—forget contemplation. After being smothered under the weight of Marshall refusing to divorce her, and now she could finally breathe. She wanted to shout and howl at the moon. Release her pent-up anxiety and anticipation surging through her veins.

Pushing through the screen door, she grabbed a towel hanging over the nearby banister and didn't stop until stepping onto the cool sand. Digging her toes in, she glanced around. There was a full moon, but most of the lights in the neighboring houses were off.

The refreshing cold was exactly what she needed. She stripped, ran down the dock, and dove into the lake. Breaking the surface, she whooped.

A rustling of bushes to her left had her heart in her throat. She sank lower into the water and squeaked, "Who's there?"

Asher's voice floated from his yard. "It's me. What are you doing?"

"Swimming," Lilith replied.

The dock creaked with his heavy footsteps. Then his silhouette materialized from the dark. He was shirtless, in a pair of swim trunks.

"Why are you out here all alone?" He sounded irritated.

"Because it's hot, and I wanted to swim."

"It isn't safe."

She quirked a brow. He was drowning her good mood, but she tried for playfulness. "Not safe? Is there a Loch Ness monster in this lake I'm unaware of?"

"What if—" He held up a hand. "Sorry, I'm being ridiculous."

"Yeah, you are," she huffed.

"Sorry. I'm stopping now." The dock creaked as he shifted. "I'd come out here planning to swim too. Mind if I join you?"

"You can't swim in the middle of the night." She sucked in a dramatic breath. "It isn't safe."

"Smartass," he said good-naturedly, stepping to the end of the dock.

Lilith sank lower into the water. "If you want to swim with me, you have to strip."

"Why?"

"Because I'm skinny-dipping. The rule is, if one does it, so does everyone," she joked.

He went completely still. "What if someone sees you? They might—"

She held up a hand, disappointed. She'd expected him to play with her or maybe be intrigued, not this serious-as-a-heart-attack tone. "Please. You promised to stop."

"I'm worried about your safety, that's all. I care about you."

She understood he was a protective person, but the last thing she needed tonight was a man lecturing her on how to take care of herself. However, she didn't want to argue with Asher, so she changed the subject. "So what prompted your late-night swim?"

"I fell asleep during movie night with Raven. Now I'm restless. I was going to go for a quick swim."

"Then join me." Emboldened by her new freedom, she added, "But don't forget to strip."

He shrugged, hooking his thumbs in the waist of his shorts, and slid them down. She treaded water, her gaze glued on the abdominal V appearing before her hungry eyes.

"Should we play music? Do you have any dollar bills?" he teased.

Her eyes widened, noticing the hair she was looking at now wasn't just the trail from his belly button to the waist of his shorts. She *was* ogling him like he was a stripper.

She whipped around, giving him her back. "Sorry, but in my defense, you have the body of an erotic dancer."

His chuckle carried over the silent lake. "Thanks."

A second later, something heavy clunked onto the metal dock. Startled, she turned, "What was—"

She caught a flash of Asher as he jumped into the lake. He was all lean, corded muscle. He was hard everywhere. *Everywhere.* And *wow*.

He broke above the surface, pushing his hair from his forehead. "What did you say right before I dove in?"

"I heard a knock or thump that would weigh more than your swim trunks. I worried we had another guest trying to join our little swimming party."

"Ah," he nodded. "It was probably my wallet."

"Why would you bring it for a swim?"

"I couldn't find my keys and didn't want to leave the house unlocked with Raven inside. I keep a spare in my wallet."

She couldn't help laughing. "You lost them again?" He misplaced them at least twice a week.

He swam a little closer, sending electricity racing through her limbs and belly. She could reach out and touch his naked body. "Why are you out so late?"

"I'm too wired to sleep. Plus, this afternoon my A/C flatlined." She skimmed her hand over the water. "A swim seemed perfect."

"Shit. That sucks. I'll take another look at it tomorrow. And my offer for you to stay in my guest room still stands."

"Actually, I made a little nest in my screened-in porch." She pointed in its general direction. "I plan to sleep there tonight."

He tensed. "Isn't there only a tiny flip lock on its door?"

"Stop." She pushed him. Her palm met solid muscle and a dusting of soft hair, momentarily distracting her. "I'll be fine. I can take care of myself."

"Ugh. Okay. I'm done." He shook his head, sprinkling her with droplets of water, then grinned. "But if you wake to find me sleeping outside, blocking the door, don't be mad."

She giggled, unable to figure out if she was touched or annoyed. "Are you this bad with Raven?"

"Worse." He swam a big circle around Lilith, then stopped and stood in front of her. Water ran down his broad shoulders and the top of his chest. "Is it only the heat that has you wired?"

"You don't remember me telling you what today is?" She was a little hurt he'd forgotten.

His face scrunched, then cleared. He bumped his forehead. "Sorry, coming out for a swim and finding you naked distracted me. How did it all go?"

"Surprisingly smooth."

"How's Chloe?"

"She was quiet when I dropped her off at my dad's before meeting with Marshall to sign the divorce papers. Then she asked to stay the night with her grandpa. I called her before heading out here. She seemed fine. Subdued, but good."

"And you, are you okay?"

"I thought I'd be sad or at least melancholy for all the mistakes he and I made, but..." She twirled, the water holding her. "It's like I've been treading in quicksand, and suddenly I'm in fresh water."

Flinging out her hands, she hugged Asher around the neck. He stiffened, and reality hit her. They were naked, her breasts pressed against his equally bare chest, her lower half floating inches from his.

She didn't let go of him, didn't move.

His hands slid to her waist. His hold was light enough that she could easily get away if she wanted.

That wasn't what she wanted.

"Say something," she whispered, staring at his mouth.

They were inches apart. His desire stoked hers.

"There's so much to say. I don't know where to start," he whispered.

"What's screaming the loudest?"

He brushed his lips against hers. "That I want you."

"Then have me." She wrapped her legs around his hips, making him hiss.

"I want more of you than I have the right to ask for."

Did he mean he wanted more than sex? She'd always assumed he didn't do commitment.

It was a struggle to think around her lust, but she had to be upfront with him. "I'm not ready for a relationship. Even thinking about giving my heart to a man is impossible."

His hands loosened on her waist. "I understand."

"But Asher, I trust you with my body." She tightened her legs around him, and his groan dripped with hunger.

He cupped her bottom with his large hands but didn't bring her closer. "What exactly do you want from me?"

"We enjoy each other's bodies. That's it. No romance, no dating. Only orgasms. When I move to my condo, we stop."

Now he brought her against him, his erection pressing into her, sending fireworks of need shooting through her. "There are so many reasons we shouldn't."

"Maybe, but they won't stop me. Will they stop you?" Her forwardness and honesty shocked her. Yet, expressing her needs to Asher came easily.

"No," he whispered against her mouth before kissing her, drenching her in desire.

She dug her hands into the short hairs on the back of his head, hungry for him. His lips pressed and moved, devouring all her fantasies of him. The reality was so much better. But she had to have more. The weightless water wouldn't allow for the friction her body craved.

"Let's get out of the lake."

He nodded. "You go first," he said against her mouth.

"Why?"

His gaze caressed her. "Because I want to watch you."

Insecurities wiggled in around her lust. She tried to smother them and was marginally successful. Her scramble up the ladder wasn't seductive or sexy, but she did it. As she wrapped a towel around her body, she heard the water part around Asher as he climbed out. Suddenly shy, she couldn't turn to watch him.

A moment later, his arms came around her from behind. His erection pressed into her lower back. "Are we good?" he asked.

"Yes. I haven't been this sure about anything in a long time." She took his hand, leading him to her porch. Right outside the door, she kissed him.

With Lilith walking backward, they went inside. When her feet hit the mat, they stopped. She expected him to lower her to the ground and take her with a quick urgency. Instead, he continued to kiss her, teasing and tormenting in the best way possible.

When she began to worry she might melt from need, he lowered her to the makeshift bed, bracketing her between his arms, keeping most of his weight off her. She wanted all of him and tugged at his shoulders. He didn't budge and ran kisses along her collarbone to her shoulder, her skin rose in anticipation. He tugged at her towel with a wandering hand, and it fell open. The night breeze stroked her naked skin.

"You are perfect," he whispered, and the sincerity in his voice almost had her believing him.

He ran a finger down her throat, between her breasts, to the underside of each, before cupping them. He leaned in, tasting her with a deep groan. His lips were erotic magic. He kissed, licked, and bit in a way that had her nearly climaxing.

Gripping the back of his head, she reveled in his delicious weight and the way his arousal pressed in all the right places between her legs. She arched into him, rubbing against his length. He growled her name, thrusting while his sinful mouth met her lips.

"I need more," she pleaded.

"Whatever you want, love."

The endearment melted into her heart, even knowing their night wasn't about love. This was lust and pleasure.

Her entire world narrowed to the feel of him against her. He shifted to his side, and she glided a palm over his flat stomach to his erection. Wrapping a firm hand around him, she stroked him from base to tip. His head fell against her shoulder, and his firm hand gripped her waist.

His hunger amped hers, and she was ravenous, wanting to devour him. If she were a different woman, she'd shove him onto his back, climb on and ride him until an orgasm or two ripped through her.

She wasn't, and so she waited, urging him with her touch. He was an observant man, and it didn't take long for him to slide between her legs.

Finally.

He'd take her now. This part usually felt like a race, with her trying to grab onto her bliss before it was too late. At least she was so turned on there was a good chance she'd climax before he was even all the way inside her. It'd be a first. However, she'd never been this aroused.

Again, he surprised her, moving down her body instead of up. A whimper of frustration escaped her, and he chuckled.

"Don't worry. I don't think you'll mind the detour."

After teasing her nipples briefly, he continued lower. When he circled her belly button with his tongue, nerves fluttered in her stomach. Would he go lower?

Sure, friends went on and on about how great oral sex was, but the few times she'd experienced it with Marshall, it was just okay. Nothing mind-blowing, more frustrating than fun.

Should she stop him or fake it? She didn't want to ruin the moment.

He stilled. "Do you want me to stop?"

Damn it. I'm already messing things up.

She rested on her elbows, meeting his eyes with difficulty. "I'm fine. Why do you ask?"

"You tensed."

"I'm sorry—"

"Lilith, please don't apologize if I'm doing something you don't want." His sincerity and tenderness had tears prickling behind her lashes.

"I do. It's just... I usually can't, um, get off from oral. I don't want to upset you."

Even in the near dark, she saw his brow furrow. "Your pleasure turns me on. If you like it great. If not, I don't mind stopping or skipping. Your choice." He rested his chin on her belly. "Woman, your body is a paradise. Believe me, I'll find plenty to keep us both entertained. Okay?"

His words and the honesty behind them loosened her inhibitions. "Okay," she laughed, running her hands through his thick hair, nudging him south.

"Are you sure?" he asked.

She laid back. "Yes."

He kissed her stomach, bringing his hands under her, then took her with his mouth, moaning as if tasting a fine wine. He sucked and twirled his tongue in a way that had bliss exploding through her. She gasped, unable to remember it feeling this good. His licking and teasing were phenomenal—sensual magic.

Needing more, she tugged his hair, pushing him into her without shame. Her ecstasy burned away reserve. Not that he seemed to mind, giving her exactly what her body craved. Her hips bucked, desperate for release. Slipping his fingers inside her, he gave it to her.

She shattered, unable to even call out his name. Words and thoughts disappeared. All that remained was his touch and her euphoric bliss.

His caresses and licks became softer, helping ease her from sensitive ecstasy. He made his way up her body, taking his time with kisses and gentle nips.

When every part of him pressed against her, he breathed against her ear, "Did I change your mind?" Lust echoed in his every word.

"Yes," she nearly slurred, drunk on pleasure.

He chuckled, twisting off. His back was to her, and his muscular behind momentarily distracted her. It was perfect. The statue of David had nothing on this man.

She tip-toed her fingers along his spine. "Where are you going? I'm not done with you."

Huh. I guess explosive orgasms make me bossy.

He grinned over his shoulder. It dripped with wicked intent. "Good. I'm nowhere near done. I'm getting a condom from my wallet."

Oh. Yeah. Protection.

She smiled. "Good thing you lost your keys tonight."

He shifted onto his back, and she watched in erotic fascination as he rolled on the condom. "I'll never complain about it again."

She laughed, loving that they hadn't lost the ease between them.

He settled on top of her, kissing her gently. "Are you still okay with this?"

"I couldn't be more okay."

His mouth returned to hers, making love to it as he slid inside her. "You're fucking nirvana," he growled against her lips.

He thrust deep and hard. She loved the way he filled her and moaned in pleasure. His breathing caressed her ears, and his sweat mingled with hers as they moved. She never wanted the night to end.

"Wrap your legs around me," he demanded.

She obeyed and was immediately rewarded. The deeper penetration had her second orgasm building.

"Oh… oh. My…" Carnal bliss stole her ability to form coherent sentences. She gripped his biceps, her short nails digging into him. "Don't stop."

"Never," he promised, his breathing choppy as hers. Dipping, he kissed her.

His arms went under her, cradling her head. She held him tight, treasuring his closeness as his scent mixed with hers. His pace never faltered, and it had her spiraling into an orgasm so intense she shouted his name into the crook of his neck.

She clenched and pulsed around him. He covered her mouth with his, groaning and moving faster. The rough tempo was perfect, prolonging her climax.

He stiffened, and his thrusts became less measured as he came, his kisses turning deliciously brutal. She continued to rock under him, greedily enjoying the after-shocks of their pleasure.

As they lay entangled, she ran the pads of her fingers up and down his spine, listening to his breathing even out, noticing it had begun to rain. She waited for inhibitions or regrets to overtake her satiated calm. They never arrived. She was home in his arms.

It was a dangerous illusion. This was about physical satisfaction. She had to be careful not to mistake it for more.

Later, he murmured against her damp skin, "I want to stay here until morning, but I can't have Raven waking up tomorrow and finding me gone."

She loosened her legs still locked around his waist. His reasoning was valid, yet it hurt to let him go.

He disposed of the condom and put on his shorts. Sitting next to her, he ran a hand through her hair. "Will you come with me? To my house? I won't be able to sleep knowing you're out here alone."

Was he asking as a friend or lover?

And what answer did she want?

She should stay here. Create a little distance from her overwhelming urge to cuddle into him, to make a home in his arms.

She covered her breasts with the sheets. "I should stay here. Raven will wonder how I ended up at your house when I wasn't there when she went to bed."

"Nah. She's used to my midnight wanderings. I'll tell her you were out here, and we talked. That I convinced you to sleep in the spare bedroom."

He ran a finger along the top of the sheet, drawing it down and exposing a nipple. He skated his thumb over it. She gasped as heat pooled between her legs, and her need for distance evaporated.

"I'll just leave out the part about our very fun and incredibly satisfying interlude." His gaze met hers, and she smiled at the wicked glimmer in his eyes.

"Good idea." She tilted closer, craving his lips.

He took the hint and kissed her.

CHAPTER TWENTY-FIVE

"Dad, why's your door locked?" Raven shouted, knocking.

Asher went from satiated sleep to *oh shit* in two seconds flat. He rolled to face an equally alarmed Lilith.

Damn it. In hindsight, insisting she stay a little longer after they made love again, this time in his bed, might not have been the best idea.

He ran a hand through his hair. What the hell was wrong with him? He wasn't a cuddler after sex. Also, that was what they were supposed to be having—sex, not making love.

Lilith pointed to his ensuite bathroom, where they'd had an incredibly erotic shower after stumbling over from her house. Getting out of bed and grabbing her clothes, she tiptoed toward it. The sway of her hips and plump ass had all of his attention.

Next time she'd be on top, so he could grip—

The doorknob rattled. "Are you in there, Dad?"

Fuck. Focus, man.

"Yeah," he answered, grabbing a pair of shorts. "Must have locked it without realizing."

Opening the door, he slipped out and closed it behind him. Trying to erase the sleep and the vision of Lilith's naked backside from his mind, he pointed toward the stairs. "Are you ready for breakfast?"

"More like lunch," Raven huffed.

Asher blinked, rubbing his eyes. "What time is it?"

"After eleven. I thought you died. You never sleep in."

That was true, but he'd been up with Lilith until the sun was peeking over the horizon. The woman had worn him out in the best way possible.

"Were you worried about my demise or your pancakes?" he asked.

Raven smiled at him, wide and bright. "Both."

He laughed, hugging her from behind and tickling her ribs. "Thanks, daughter."

She screeched and tore loose from him, running past the guestroom. Asher gave an inward groan. The door was wide open, and the bed was made. Hopefully in her distraction to get free, she hadn't noticed.

Yeah, right. She saw *everything*.

"We'll have breakfast for lunch." He pointed with his thumb toward his bedroom. "I'm going to grab a T-shirt. I'll meet you there."

"Can I have chocolate chips in my pancakes?" Raven wheedled.

He usually refused, wanting her to start the day with something healthy. However, setting her to search for a bag of them might give him extra time.

"Okay, I'll make a few." He held up his index finger before she took off. "But I expect you to eat some fruit and eggs."

"Deal," she groused.

"You gather the ingredients. I'll be down in a sec."

He backtracked to his bedroom, and Lilith peeked from around the bathroom door. "Want to keep her in the kitchen, and I'll slip out the front?" She smiled shyly. "I feel like a teenager sneaking out."

He laughed, "Except we're hiding from a ten-year-old instead of our parents."

"Because we are the parents. What an odd turn of events," she giggled.

"I have a better idea." He gripped the top of the door, his gaze taking in her tempting, naked body. "Go to the guest room and take a shower. After, meet us for pancakes."

She scrunched her nose, appearing alarmed. "Do I stink?"

Coming closer, he ran his nose along her collarbone. "No, you smell like temptation."

Sighing, she tilted her head, giving him more access. Kissing from her jawline, he found her lips. When she slid her tongue into his mouth, he groaned, already half hard.

"Dad!" Raven shouted from the stairs.

He and Lilith jumped apart. Adjusting himself, he cursed under his breath and twisted around, yelling, "What?"

"I can't find the chocolate chips."

"Try the freezer. I might have put them there because of the heat."

Raven's feet pounded toward the kitchen, and he exhaled in relief. Lilith did the same.

"She's the reason I'd mentioned taking a shower," he said. "The guestroom door was open, and she might've noticed the made bed. If she does, you'll say you made it before getting in the shower."

"Make sense, but,"—Lilith pointed to her discarded towel from last night—"I can't wear that to breakfast."

She had a point. Speaking of points, he brushed a thumb over her nipple, and she sucked in a breathy moan.

"Don't start," she admonished with a flicker of heat in her gaze.

"I can't help it. You're irresistible."

She rubbed a brow, looking away. "Whatever."

Everything in him wanted to take her back to his bed and show her. However, with the risk of Raven returning, he settled for gently kissing Lilith. "Woman, you exude sensuality, and you've tempted me since I first laid eyes on you." He rested a hand on her hip. "And now that I've had a taste, I'm addicted."

"So, it isn't just me? It's a little overwhelming how much I want you," she whispered.

Her words soothed and made him ache for her. "Definitely not."

She laid her head against his chest. "Where do we go from here? Is there anywhere to go? I'm moving in a month."

He didn't want to think about the future. "Let's take it one day at a time. For now, we're friends who indulge in each other when the mood strikes."

"Okay," she agreed. "Now, about my clothes…"

Last night, he'd meant to have her bring something to wear for the next day, but she'd started kissing him, and all his thoughts had focused on sinking inside her again. He'd had only one condom in his wallet, and getting her in his bed and under him was his top priority. Clothes had been the last thing on his mind.

Moving to his dresser, he got a T-shirt for himself and a pair of cotton boxers along with an old concert T-shirt for Lilith. "They'll be big, but should work."

"Thanks." She left for the guest bathroom.

Making his way to the kitchen, he asked Raven if she'd found the chocolate chips. She pointed to the bag on the counter with her chin while gathering two plates from the cupboard.

"Take out an extra one," he said.

Pausing with the dishes in her hand, she asked. "Why?"

"Lilith's here." He told the nice, innocent story they'd made up.

Raven nodded slowly, frowning. "The bed was made, and she wasn't in the guestroom."

Asher chuckled. Of course his daughter noticed. With her attention to detail, the girl would make a great engineer.

"She could've made her bed in the morning. Unlike a certain girl I know."

"Unlike a certain girl I know," Raven mimicked as the pipes to the guest bathroom rattled above them. She looked at the ceiling. "It sure took her a long time to get in the shower after making the bed."

Forget engineer. She had a bright future as a detective. "Maybe she wanted to snoop through the cabinets first," Asher said.

"Do you have any of those magazines in there for her? The ones you and Aunt Hope really liked as teenagers." Raven smirked. "Playboys and girls."

Asher's cheeks heated, and he tossed a chocolate chip at his daughter. "Ugh, you googled what they are, didn't you?"

She grabbed the chip, shoving it in her mouth, and looked away, but that answer was in her eyes. *Not to self—check the parental control again on the internet.*

Changing the subject, he asked, "What do you want to do today?"

"Is Chloe at her dad's this weekend?" Raven asked while mixing her small batch of chocolate pancakes.

"No. She's at her grandpa's, but I don't know when she's coming home."

Or if it would be a good idea for him and Lilith to spend the day together.

He'd discovered last night that she was shy but had a wild side struggling to get out. He wanted to be the one to free it, to break down each and every inhibition until she had none. But that didn't mean he wanted her heart too. Right?

Shit, one night with her, and he was addicted. Time apart might help him put things into perspective. This was sex with no emotions. That was her stipulation and something he usually preferred. Nothing needed to change.

"Dad? Are you listening?"

"Uh, no. Sorry."

"Gee, thanks."

He pointed to the coffeepot. "I haven't had my caffeine, and you know I'm useless before my first cup. What did you say?"

"Want me to make the coffee?" Lilith asked, hovering at the kitchen's entrance, biting her bottom lip and looking damn adorable in his too-large clothes.

She tugged at the concert shirt. "I hope you don't mind. I was so tired last night I forgot to pack a change of clothes but didn't want to put on yesterday's pajamas. I found these in the guestroom."

Asher smiled, swallowing his mirth as she finished her long-winded story. Her eyes narrowed, but her lips quirked.

Holding her bowl of pancake batter, Raven studied Lilith. Asher's heart raced, afraid of what she'd say.

After a forever pause, Raven said, "Keep it. I hate when Dad listens to that band. You can take it home and burn it."

"Hey," Asher play-shouted, pretending to whack his daughter with his spatula. "They're the best."

"Sorry, I have to agree with Raven. They suck," Lilith said, high-fiving Raven and laughing.

The two of them were so at ease and happy with each other that it pulled at Asher's heart, filling him with a longing he refused to acknowledge.

CHAPTER TWENTY-SIX

"What do you think?" Tate asked.

Lilith took in the stark white walls, bamboo floors, and the large windows overlooking a forest park of her soon-to-be condo. The place would be hers, with no ties to Marshall. She should be excited—thrilled. Digging deep, she found none. There was only dull disappointment at leaving her lake house. Leaving Asher.

"It's nice."

"The place was built right. It's sturdy," Asher said from behind her.

He'd insisted on coming, had said he didn't trust anyone but him to do the home inspection. Though he didn't sound very happy about finding the place built well.

"The unit won't be ready until the first week of September," Tate told Lilith. "I know the other one we looked at doesn't have the view of the park but is move-in ready. You could be in by the end of the week and get some extra cash with end-of-the-summer renters from your lake house."

End of the week. That was two weeks less with Asher—the same amount of time they'd been sleeping together. She needed a little more time with him. Or maybe this urge to keep him close was a sign to back off. She shouldn't be so attached so soon.

"I like this one." *I'm so weak.*

"Me too," said Asher. "The rooms are a little bigger, and the largest windows are on the west side. It will keep your place cooler in the summer."

"That's what I was thinking," Lilith lied.

"Suit yourself." Tate put an arm around Lilith. "It'll be great having you as my neighbor."

"You're on the other side of the complex," she said.

"It's closer than your old place with Marshall or the lake house." Tate rubbed his hands together. "Now, who's ready to eat? Chloe texted me about five minutes ago, saying dinner was delivered."

"Go ahead. I'm not super hungry, and I'd like to do another walkthrough." Afraid her intent was written in her eyes, she refused to look at Tate but hoped Asher got the hint.

He did.

"I, um, want to check out the furnace and A/C," he said. "Make sure the contractors didn't use the brand that has a ton of recalls."

Tate shrugged. "Fine, but don't blame me if the food's all gone when you get to my place."

"Could you at least save us a few kebabs and hummus?"

"I make no promises."

"Nice brother," she said.

He held up his hands. "It's the girls, not me. They're bottomless pits."

Asher chuckled. "This is true."

She heard the door click shut, and three seconds later, Asher was pressing her against the hallway wall. "Finally," he murmured, his lips finding hers.

She broke away from his kiss with a hungry gasp. "I thought I'd never get you alone."

He skimmed a hand up her thigh, lifting her summer dress to just below her butt. "Now that you have me all to yourself, what do you want?"

"You." *Always you.*

What was she going to do when she moved here, when this ended? Pushing the thought away, she pulled him to her mouth.

His kisses were light and teasing. As were the fingers skimming along the edge of her panties. He stilled between her legs and asked, "How do you want me?"

"Badly," she panted as he pressed into her. She hummed at the contact, arching against him.

"Same, but, how? Teasing and touching, but no sex—"

"Please, don't tease. I need you too much." She unbuckled his belt.

"That's a start." He removed a condom from his wallet. "Over here or on the kitchen counter?"

She removed her panties in a stroke of boldness, putting them in his pocket. "Here. Against the wall."

Pushing his jeans to his knees, he put on the condom, then lifted her. She wrapped her legs around his hips, moaning as he filled her.

His muscles pressed and flexed, straining his T-shirt. It was beyond sexy.

"Take off your dress," he grunted, rocking into her.

She pulled it off, then her bra. He rewarded her with his commanding mouth. The pull on her nipples reached between her legs, pushing her closer to orgasm.

Gasping his name, she clutched him. He pressed her against the wall, the connection and friction deepening. It took her over the edge, and she fell into bliss.

His rough strokes and choppy breaths told her he was close. "What can I do for you? For your pleasure," she whispered in his ear, licking it.

"Stay," he panted.

In this position? Or with him?

He repeated his request, shuddering and moving faster, his climax overtaking him. Breast to chest, their hearts raced to the same rhythm, and their heavy breathing echoed through the empty condo.

Afraid to delve into what he'd meant, she joked, "I know you said stay, but my back's getting a little sore against the wall."

He chuckled into her temple. "And I'm sure the contractors would love the view of you, but they'd be less than thrilled with the sight of my naked ass."

She slid her legs to the ground, then palmed his butt. "I'm not so sure. You have a very fine one."

Pulling up his jeans, he nuzzled her neck. "I'll be right back."

She had her dress situated and was smoothing away the new wrinkles when he returned from the bathroom.

"Come here," he said, opening his arms.

She went into them, loving and hating how they felt like home. A strong, independent woman wouldn't be so needy.

Picking her up, he moved to the kitchen, setting her on the counter. "Do you have to move here? Can't you stay at your lake house?" he asked.

She hugged him, loving that he didn't want her to leave. But oddly enough, it reinforced her determination to do it. She *wouldn't* change her path for a man—she'd sworn to never do that again.

"I can't," she said. "The lake house is booked solid through the winter. I need that money. Marshall's child support covers Chloe's needs, but the rental income will cover this place and my classes. I'm going to get certified in bookkeeping," she said proudly.

He kissed her neck. "I could pay for your classes."

"No." She pushed on his shoulders, needing space from him and his safe arms.

He stepped back but kept his arms around her waist. "Why? I want to take care of you."

"It isn't your place to take care of me." *I need to learn how to take care of myself.* "You aren't even my boyfriend."

He squeezed her hips. "I could be."

"It's too soon. I've been divorced for only a few weeks. How would that look to Chloe?"

Nor could Lilith look at herself in the mirror, knowing she jumped from one man to the next, never standing on her own two feet. She could hear her dad's disapproval mixing with her shame.

"Then let me do it as a friend."

She tilted her head. "Why are you so insistent?"

"Because I like you and Chloe near me. I like knowing you two are safe and can come to me if you needed anything."

That was precisely why she had to leave. His constant willingness to take on all her problems was a confusing mixture of smothering and comfort.

She didn't want to hurt his feelings, so said, "I can't. Tate is looking forward to us moving here, and it'd be wrong to cancel on all my renters."

"Lil—"

"Please, Asher. It's going to be hard to move here. I'm excited, but also scared of all these changes." Especially when her heart begged to stay in his arms. "I need you to celebrate with me, not make it more difficult."

He nodded, resting his forehead against hers. "Okay."

"Thank you." She kissed him, thankful for his surrender even as she dreaded each tick of the clock that pushed them apart.

CHAPTER TWENTY-SEVEN

Asher couldn't believe it was the last week of August. The end of summer was rushing toward him, and he hated it. This year was worse because Lilith and Chloe would be gone. Her condo was ready, and most of their stuff was there. Sure, they'd be at the lake once or twice a month to clean the house between renters. Still, things would change. How much, he had no idea.

"Ready to go, Dad?" Raven asked, closing the front door behind her.

He flattened his feet, stopping the porch swing. "I thought—hoped—you'd all changed your minds." He smirked. "Damn it."

Lilith made her way up his sidewalk, looking sexy and cute in a bright summer dress. "School shopping isn't that bad," she said.

It was the worst damn activity ever, yet another reason to hate the end of summer. At least this year he had Lilith to help ease the torture.

"We should drive separately," she said.

Shit. Maybe he would be suffering alone. "Why?"

"My dad just called. He bought Chloe a tablet for school and loaded it with her reading list and a few of her favorite authors. She's beyond excited to get her hands on it. I promised her and my dad I'd stop at his place and grab it today."

"I don't mind going there with you. And," he grinned, "school shopping is torture. I can't risk letting you out of my sight. You might bail on me."

"Wow. You really hate it." Lilith laughed.

"It's Dante's ninth circle of hell. With you, it'll be the third." He smiled. "Plus, it's a waste to take two cars when we are going to all the same places."

She rubbed the toe of her sandal against the bottom step of his porch. "Except for my dad's."

He stood. "I really don't mind going there with you. You've mentioned he's a big reader. How can we not get along?"

"You say that now…"

He paused. She could be trying to draw a line between them. Keeping some of her family separate from him.

"Would you rather I didn't meet him?"

She came toward him. "Why wouldn't I? You're one of my closest friends."

Friend. Asher was beginning to dislike that word.

"It's more… he's prickly. I don't want to subject you to him if he's in a mood," she finished.

"I'll be fine," he said.

"Okay." She turned, walking toward his Jeep. "But don't say I didn't warn you.

Sliding into the backseat, Chloe said, "I can't believe school starts in a week. I hate Labor Day. It's the most depressing, lame holiday."

"Tell that to the workers who fought and died for better working conditions," Lilith replied.

"Well," Chloe huffed. "All it means to me is that *my* work starts the next day."

"Yeah, I'm not ready to go back to school," Raven said, clicking her seatbelt. Then she asked Chloe, "Are you nervous about starting a new school?"

"Yeah," Chloe replied. "I wish I could stay here and go to school with you."

That sounded good to Asher. Starting the Jeep, he asked the girls if they had their school supply lists.

They held them up, and Raven asked, "And I tried on my jeans. None of them fit. I need more."

"It's still shorts weather," Asher nearly whined.

Lilith laughed. "Going to the mall isn't that bad."

"Oh, if you think your dad is difficult, just wait. This girl," he said, pointing at Raven, "is picky. Forget picky. Impossible is a better word. She will try on a hundred and fifty things only to find one or two she likes."

Raven shrugged. "I have to be comfortable, and most things are itchy or fit bad."

Lilith nodded. "I get that. I have the same problem."

Groaning, Asher pulled onto the street. "Please tell me you aren't clothes shopping today too."

"Maybe." She winked. "My new favorite summer activity has caused me to lose weight."

They had been *very* active. If they'd hoped to burn through their lust, it hadn't dimmed. He wanted her more, not less.

"Being healthy is important." Especially when it involved her naked body against his. "But would you mind if we stopped at your dad's first? Leave me there and you three can take my Jeep and go shopping. Pick me up in a week when you're done."

Lilith smiled. "How about you come with us, but I'll take them shopping? You can go to a coffee shop or visit a bookstore."

He tapped a short dance on the steering wheel. "Woman, I owe you. Big. Time."

"Oh, and how do you plan on paying me back?"

"Ice cream at your favorite parlor?" he suggested.

Raven and Chloe cheered their approval and had a heated debate on which flavor was the best.

Lilith's gaze licked over him, sweeter than any ice cream. "That's a start. What else?"

He braked for a red light and leaned over the center console. "Next time we *exercise* together, you're in charge."

Her eyes flashed molten heat, and she sucked on her bottom lip. Releasing it, she whispered, "Okay."

The want in her voice tugged at his lust. Fuck, he wanted to kiss her. Pull her onto his lap. Claim her as his.

A horn beeped, jerking him from his desire. Shit. The light had turned green.

"When did you start running with Dad?" Raven asked.

"What?" Lilith shook her head as if trying to clear her mind of the same X-rated images dancing and grinding in his mind.

"Dad said you guys are exercising together. I haven't seen you in his workout room, so you must be running together."

Pink infused Lilith's cheeks. "Yes, that's it. We started a few weeks ago."

Asher couldn't help laughing. He'd asked her once to go running with him. She'd told him the only way she would run was if someone was chasing her.

Lilith poked his thigh, smiling. Changing the subject, she asked the girls what store they wanted to visit first.

The rest of the drive and afternoon passed quickly. It helped that Lilith's offer to take the girls clothes shopping had been sincere. While they tried on outfits, he browsed a local bookstore; drinking coffee, and buying a few books. He'd even earned a stolen kiss from Lilith when the girls were in the restroom for getting her the new release of her favorite author.

However, she became quieter the closer they got to her dad's place. When he parked in the driveway, the girls took off, Chloe calling out for her grandpa. Lilith stayed behind, lingering with her hand on the door, not pushing it open as if she needed more time. As if she needed to fortify herself for the visit. From what she'd told him about her dad, he understood her hesitation.

He rubbed her shoulder. "Ready?"

"No." She looked from the house to Asher. "I love him. I really do. He's just so old-fashioned. I hate the constant push and pull with him. I want to please him yet be strong—something he doesn't seem to believe I am capable of. Or maybe it isn't me, personally, more that I am a woman. Who knows."

His father wasn't that kind of man, but he'd met enough to know the type. You were golden if you fit into their expectations, their tiny box. If you didn't, things could be stressful.

A tall older man with close-cropped, thinning blond hair opened the front door, stepped out, and embraced Chloe. When the girls disappeared into the house, he looked toward the car. Even from their distance in the driveway, Asher saw he had his daughter's same piercing blue eyes.

He motioned for them to come inside.

Lilith sighed. "We better go."

Asher followed close behind, wishing he could take her hand and offer his comfort. Once inside, it took a minute for his eyes to adjust inside the house. The thin, horizontal blinds on the windows were half shut, and the leather couch was brown, giving the room a gloomy feel. Although the floor-to-ceiling bookcases on the farthest wall were spectacular.

"Grandpa, can I show Raven the antique dollhouse?" Chloe asked.

Lilith's dad nodded. "Sure." The two girls ran past him, down a narrow hallway. He turned to face Asher, the warmth he'd had with the girls disappearing. "Who are you?"

"Asher Crowley." He offered his hand. The other man hesitated before taking it.

Lilith exhaled loudly. "This is my father, Harrison Siren. And, Dad, I told you I was coming by with a friend."

"You didn't say the *friend* would be a man." He pointed them toward the couch.

Taking the recliner, he asked Asher, "Is the girl with Chloe your daughter?"

"Yes. Raven."

"Are you married?"

Okay..."No."

"Of course not. Why bother raising kids in a family environment? Anything goes nowadays," Harrison muttered. He faced Lilith. "Don't you think it's too soon?"

"Stop, please. He's my friend."

Harrison harrumphed. "You should be trying to fix things with Marshall, not go out and make new *friends.*"

"I didn't break things between me and him," she ground out through clenched teeth.

"Try harder. It's better for Chloe."

Lilith wasn't kidding about her dad not holding back with his opinions. Asher's admiration of Lilith grew. To be raised by such an overbearing man, she had to fight and struggle for every slice of independence.

"Some things can't be fixed," she persisted. "Also, you and mom divorced, and I turned out fine. So did Tate."

Harrison huffed. "That was your mother's choice. She has no discipline. Runs from one thing to the next, searching for what makes her happy. If we'd set a better example, you probably wouldn't be divorced at thirty."

"If I'd married a better man, I wouldn't be divorced."

"Possibly," Harrison conceded. "But how's jumping from him to another man a good idea? I understand that as a woman you're afraid to be alone, so you push yourself and Chloe into an insta-family—"

Christ, the man was relentless. Asher was tempted to tell Harrison to butt out of their business, but Lilith spoke first. "We haven't told the girls."

"Why?"

"I'm moving to Royal Oak at the end of the summer..."

Harrison's lips pressed into a thin line of disapproval. "So, this is just a fling?"

His gaze landed hard on Asher, and he had to restrain himself from looking away, fidgeting. Or arguing that he'd happily have more with his daughter, but she wasn't ready.

Lilith sat ramrod straight, crossing her arms over her chest. "If I'm in a relationship, it's wrong. If I'm not in one, it's wrong. You're never satisfied."

"It's not about satisfying me. It's about making the right choices."

Asher leaned forward. "It might not be my place—"

"It isn't," Harrison said.

"It isn't yours either. She's a grown woman able to make her own choices. And personally, I think she's making the right ones."

"Of course you'd think that, you're—"

"I've met Marshall. He doesn't deserve your daughter. Maybe I don't either, but he definitely doesn't."

Harrison stared at Asher for three eternally long beats, then said. "Maybe you're right."

"Can we please talk about something else?" Lilith pleaded. She tapped her nails on her knees. "How about those Tigers?"

Asher snorted. "Baseball starts in April."

"Well, at least this one seems to know something about sports," Harrison muttered, then pointed to the kitchen. "What do you two want to drink?"

"Nothing," Lilith said. "We can't stay long. Asher's sister invited us to dinner."

"You can stay for a little bit," Harrison said, heading to the kitchen. "It's been nearly a month since you and Chloe have visited."

Lilith leaned close to Asher and whispered. "Can he blame me? I get the run-down of my faults every time I stop by. I bet when he returns, he'll suggest Chloe and I move in with him. He'd love to micromanage my life."

Asher wasn't her dad's biggest fan, but he empathized with him wanting to protect his daughter and grandkid. Even if his method was heavy-handed and a little misguided.

"What do you want to do?" she whispered. "Stay or run?"

"Your dad, your call. We have time, but if you want to use Hope as an excuse, I'll go along with it."

She scooted closer, kissing him hard and fast. "Thank you."

He stole another before asking, "For what?"

"For having my back."

"Always."

A throat cleared, and they turned to see Harrison holding three drinks. His mouth opened, probably to offer more *advice*, but Lilith asked. "Do you want us to stay longer?"

"Of course," he replied.

"Then drop whatever you are about to say."

Harrison's gaze bounced between them, those damn penetrating eyes making it difficult not to squirm. Then he shrugged. "Fine." He handed each of them a can and settled into his recliner.

The rest of their time at his house wasn't as painful as the start. However, Asher was relieved when Lilith stood an hour later, announcing they had to leave. Shaking the older man's hand goodbye, unease seeped into him. Lilith had stood up to her father, but she didn't always. He recalled the night at the firepit when she'd mentioned her father had convinced her to marry Marshall. Could he talk her into returning to her husband?

CHAPTER TWENTY-EIGHT

Lilith walked toward Hope's boat, crowded with women, and put on a happy face. She loved spending time with her friend, but this was her last weekend before moving into her condo, so she'd rather spend it in bed with him. Which was possible because Chloe was with Marshall, and Raven was spending the night with her grandparents. However, Lilith hadn't come to the previous pontoon party because she and Asher had a free evening alone. She couldn't blow off Hope again.

Though maybe it didn't have to be her final weekend with Asher. He might be willing to continue with their arrangement.

Could she convince him? Should she convince him? Her addiction to him was strong, but being two hours away would offer her emotional and physical distance. They'd grow apart gradually instead of her giving him up cold-turkey.

"There she is," Hope called to Lilith. "Are you ready to toast to the end of the summer?"

She wasn't but nodded. Stepping onto the boat, she accepted the plastic wine glass filled with white. Scanning the group, her heart flipped when her gaze snagged on Paloma's black hair. *Fantastic.* An evening stuck on a boat with the last person Asher "dated."

She sucked in a breath before releasing it through her nose, willing away her stress and focusing on the gorgeous evening. Even though Labor Day was next week, the temps were in the high eighties, and it looked like they were in for a spectacular sunset. She took the seat next to Emma, asking if her husband was meeting with Asher. She told Lilith he was, and they were at Jackson's dirt biking on his property.

They slid into an easy conversation, and when Hope dropped the anchor in a favorite cove, Lilith was surprised to find she was relaxed, even enjoying herself. She rested her head against the railing, studying the wispy clouds as the sun warmed her and different conversations flowed around the boat.

"Hey, Hope," a woman called out. "How come your brother doesn't stop by The Hill anymore?"

Lilith's stomach pitched like they were on rough water. She didn't want to listen. The idea of jumping overboard and swimming home held great appeal.

"I have no idea, but I swear if you start talking about sex and Asher, I'm going to throw you in the water," Hope groaned, her gaze flickering to Lilith as laughter rippled through the women.

Lilith's already roiling belly sunk further. Did Hope know? She was close to her brother and might have figured it out. Would she be more pissed that it was kept from her or that the woman he was sleeping with was Lilith?

Emma pointed at Paloma. "Besides, shouldn't we be asking you?"

She shook her head. "Nope. I broke the cardinal rule, told him I liked him for more than sex. He did his usual and ran."

"You think he's running to Eden?" questioned another woman.

Lilith glanced at a blonde who'd just spoken. Hope had been talking to her when Lilith had first arrived. Going by her glassy eyes and sloppy grin, she'd had a few drinks before getting on the boat.

"No way," Hope said. "She left him with a newborn, to live it up on the west coast. She doesn't get to come back into his life ten years later." Her gaze landed on Lilith. "Asher doesn't need a woman who waltzes in and out of his life. Raven too."

Seeming oblivious to the brief but intense stare aimed at Lilith, Emma asked, "Didn't she go to California for medical school, not to party?"

"Doesn't matter. She left. Now, please, new subject," Hope pleaded.

"I don't know," the blonde insisted. "She's gorgeous, a surgeon, and Raven's mom. Those reasons might be enough."

Curiosity and self-consciousness leaked into Lilith's veins. Compared to Eden, she felt incredibly inadequate. Combine her beauty and success with the conversation Lilith had with Asher earlier in the summer about the importance of family, and every ounce of contentment floated away.

Emma leaned into Lilith and whispered. "Who do you think she's lusting after? Asher or Eden?"

As if hearing the question, the tipsy woman continued. "I mean, have you seen her? She makes me want to be bi."

Lilith laughed, even though it burned.

"Oh, do tell," Paloma spurred on the blonde.

Hope waved her hands in front of her face. "Please don't. Discussing Eden fantasies is right there with the torture of talking about my brother's sex life."

"For Jessica, it might be one and the same. She'll take 'em both," Emma quipped.

The blonde nodded, making everyone laugh.

"Who wants a refill?" Hope asked, obviously trying to change the subject.

Nearly every cup was raised. Drinks were topped off, and they toasted to a perfect summer while wishing the same for autumn. The chilled wine soothed her nervous edges, and Lilith tried not to chug it. She reconsidered when Paloma's gaze locked on hers.

Whatever she was about to say couldn't be good.

"Besides, if you want to know who Asher's sleeping with, ask *her*." Paloma pointed her glass at Lilith. "Those two are always together, and he seems rather possessive of her."

Crap.

Lilith stared at her wine. "He's my neighbor. My friend." She looked up and locked gazes with Hope. She was studying Lilith with an intensity that made it difficult not to fidget.

Then her focus shifted, and she glanced around the group. "Seriously, please, enough about my brother." She faced Emma. "Why don't you tell us about your sex life since it won't involve Asher."

The other woman arched a perfect brow. "Are you sure? Wyatt does like to try new things."

Hope's mouth fell open, and every head swiveled in Emma's direction. Lilith snorted, knowing it was total bullshit.

Emma struggled to hold in her laughter. She lasted all of five seconds.

Once she could breathe, she said, "I'm kidding. I'm sorry. I couldn't resist."

Hope's lips twitched. "You're such a bitch."

"This is true," Emma agreed, holding up her cup as if toasting to the declaration.

Thankfully, that ended talk of Asher. His name wasn't mentioned again, and by the time the sun had set and Hope had docked her boat in front of her house, most of Lilith's peace had returned.

"Come inside, ladies. I have more drinks and food." Hope pointed to the drunk blonde and grinned. "And I have coffee for you."

Lilith glanced toward the lovely craftsman home with its navy board-and-batten siding, then in the direction that would take her home—and into Asher's arms. "I'm going to head out," she told the group.

She hugged Emma, and when she did the same to Hope, she said, "I'll walk you to your car."

Lilith's brows twitched as she took in the group. "I'll be fine. Stay with your friends."

"They'll be okay. They've all been her a million times."

A peculiar, weighted silence fell between them as they walked the bricked paved path around the house toward the driveway. When they reached her car, Hope asked, "Are you going over to Asher's? Are you two dating?"

"Aren't you the one who told me he didn't date?" Lilith deflected.

Hope put her hands on her hips. "Fine, you want to play semantics. Are you two sleeping together?"

"Is that really any of your business?"

"So, you are," she sighed as if disappointed.

"Again, it isn't your business." Lilith tapped her nails on the roof of her car. "And your obvious disapproval hurts. I'm good enough to be your friend, but nothing more to your brother, huh?"

"You're barely out of a bad marriage. I don't want you destroying Asher's heart as he heals yours from the damage caused by your ex."

"I would never hurt Asher. He's not some nameless rebound. He's my friend." Heat flushed through Lilith, beginning to boil in her veins. "And he's well aware of my baggage and that I don't want anything serious—which works for him. You know as well as I do, he doesn't do relationships."

"I've seen the way he looks at you. Hear the way he talks about you. You're different."

Lilith's heart thumped, heavy and quick. *No.* Asher was her best friend, but she couldn't give more than her body.

"You're wrong," she insisted. "He's known all summer I'm leaving."

"Yes, and it's next week. Are you going to break off whatever's going on between you? Let him go before you hurt him."

Lilith's stomach flipped and her throat tightened. Hope wanted Lilith gone, far away from her brother.

"That is between me and Asher." She opened her car door. "I have to go." *Before I cry like a damn fool.*

"I'm sorry. I don't want to hurt you, but I'm worried about my brother. He's been through so much shit—"

"And I'm more of it." Lilith choked on her words and hurt.

"No!" Hope came closer, holding out her arms like she wanted to pull Lilith into them.

She slid into the driver's seat, closed the door, and started the engine.

"Please, let me explain myself better," Hope said through the window.

Lilith blinked at the burning in her eyes. She would *not* cry. "You've made yourself very clear. Good night." She put the car in reverse, backing out slowly, giving Hope time to step away.

Pulling onto her street a few minutes later, she tried to shrug off her heavy sadness. The emotion was useless. She was leaving next week. Her friendship with Hope probably would have faded just like things would with Asher, so it was fine their friendship had ended tonight.

Parking in her driveway, she shut off the engine and glanced at his house. There was a sleek SUV parked in front she didn't recognize. Maybe one of the guys had come over after the dirt bike outing. Disappointment and relief mixed within her. Staying away from Asher might be for the best, but that didn't mean she didn't want to be in his arms.

She opened her car door just as his porch light flicked on, and a second later, a woman stepped out. She had wavy black hair past her shoulders, mile-long legs, and an impressive chest. Eden.

Right behind her was Asher, wrapped only in a towel.

What the ever-loving hell?

CHAPTER TWENTY-NINE

Asher crossed his arms over his bare chest as Eden walked to her car. The brief visit had been strange and uncomfortable. Right after he'd shut off the shower, layers of mud still circling the drain from his dirt biking, the doorbell rang. He'd wrapped a towel around his waist and sprinted to answer it, figuring it was Lilith.

Swinging open the door, he froze. Eden stood on his porch wide-eyed, her gaze taking in his near nakedness.

She blinked rapidly a few times, eyeing him from head to toe. "Is this how you always answer the door?"

He gripped the towel around his waist tighter, stepping inside and out of view from any passing cars or people. Eden took it as an invitation to come inside.

"I thought you might be Raven," he lied.

"She knocks at her own house?"

"Like her dad, she always loses her key." Now that was the truth.

Eden nodded, smiling. "Ahh, remember the first night we met, Hope had to climb through the bathroom window of the place you were renting because you'd lost your key?"

Asher chucked. "Yeah, I still can't figure out how she contorted herself to fit."

"Or managed to not crash to the tile floor." Eden stepped closer, poking his chest with a short red fingernail. "Anyway, I don't mind you answering the door like this. Seriously, you look even better than back in those days."

"Um. Thanks." He backed into the living room and away from her, his humor fading. "Anyway, sorry you wasted your time. Raven isn't here."

"Will she be home soon?" Eden asked, remaining in the foyer.

"No, she's staying the night at my parents," he blurted, halfway to his bedroom, planning to put on a pair of shorts.

"Then why did you think I might be her at the door?"

He considered lying again but decided, why bother? What did it matter if Eden knew he was expecting a woman? "I didn't really think it was Raven."

"Then who?"

Asher waited for her to connect the dots. She was an intelligent woman, and it took a matter of seconds.

"Oh!" Surprise and something he couldn't name flashed across her features before she smoothed them out. "I see, um, I better get out of here before whoever you were expecting shows up."

She opened the door, then stepped onto the porch. He followed, clutching his towel, wishing he'd grabbed his shorts before answering the damn door. "I'll let Raven know you stopped by," he said.

"Thanks. Will you two be free tomorrow?" she asked.

Raven would love for the three of them to spend an afternoon together, but he'd been busy at work, and Lilith was spending a lot of time at her condo getting it ready. They'd barely seen each other, so he didn't plan on picking up Raven until late in the afternoon if Lilith was free.

"I'm not sure," he said. "Could you call tomorrow? I'll let you know."

She nodded before turning to her car. He sighed, glad that was over. Nothing said awkward like chatting with an ex in only a wet towel.

When Eden reached her Mustang, she waved. Then her attention shifted to Lilith's driveway, and she frowned. He followed her line of sight.

Shit.

Lilith was sitting in her car. The interior light was on, and even from across the yard, he saw her confusion and shock. Her gaze met his, and the hurt in her eyes gutted him.

He had a brief internal debate. Run inside for a pair of shorts and a shirt or, haul ass to her house to explain. Not willing to take the chance of her getting inside and refusing to open the door, he took off across his lawn.

It was the right move because when he started toward her, she nearly sprinted from her car, calling, "You owe me nothing. We'll talk tomorrow."

"Lilith, wait!"

Ignoring him, she walked faster. He caught up as she was unlocking the door. He covered her hand. "Please, stop."

She shook him free. "It's been a long evening. I can't have this conversation right now. We don't even need to have it. We aren't a couple. I'm leaving next week. You're free to do as, or who, you please."

He turned her, and when she tried to twist away, he cupped her face. "Look at me."

She did, and the tears that gathered at her lashes tore at his heart.

"It's fine, Asher. Really."

"Listen, that's Eden."

"I figured as much," Lilith whispered, sounding crushed.

"I'm not sleeping with her. I haven't been with anyone since you."

"Don't lie." A steely flint sparked in her eyes. "My days of choking them down are over."

"I'm not Marshall," he said, pissed but trying not to sound it. The unspoken accusation angered him, but he couldn't blame her. He wouldn't like to come home and find her in only a towel talking to her ex—hell, any man.

"No," she spat. "But you two seem to view relationships the same."

"That isn't fair," he said with a touch of heat.

Her shoulders slumped as if defeated. It extinguished his anger.

"You're right," she whispered. "But we aren't together. So, why the lies?"

"I swear, I'm not." He rested his forehead against hers, and thankfully, she didn't move away. "And we do have something. I have no idea what, but I don't want anyone but you. I'm in deep enough that picturing you with another man makes me damn near psychotic."

"Yet it's fine for Eden to be leaving your house late at night with you practically naked?" Lilith stated flatly.

He told her what had happened. After, she didn't reply. He listened to the crickets chirp, giving her time.

When he couldn't take the silence any longer, he asked, "Do you believe me?"

She nodded.

"Thank Christ," he breathed, brushing his lips back and forth on hers.

She brought him closer and deepened the kiss.

He ran his lips along her collarbone. She smelled of summer sunsets, promises, and flowering desire. He forced himself to move away from her.

Her brows furrowed. "Why'd you stop?"

"If you want to continue this, we should go inside." He clutched the front of his towel, trying to keep his hard-on covered. "Unless you want to give Mrs. Wilson a show. She'll be by anytime now, walking her dog."

Lilith's gaze traveled to his towel-clad waist, and she gasped. Yanking open the door, she pulled him inside. Soon as the lock clicked, he pressed her against the wall as she tugged off his towel. Her legs wrapped around his waist, hiking her sundress to her hips. Everything in him wanted to take her there and now, but they had the whole night. He would savor her.

She ground against him, and he nearly caved. Gripping her hips, he stilled her. "Hold tight." He walked toward her bedroom. "Remember when I promised the next time we were alone, you'd be in complete control?"

Her teasing trail from shoulder to Adam's apple with her lips, tongue, and teeth stopped at his words. Her fully dilated eyes met his, and she nodded.

Damn. His woman wanted this and desperately.

His woman. Was she?

"That's tonight," he finished, pushing aside his question.

They'd reached her bedroom. He loosened his hold, and she slid from around him.

"I don't know how to be in charge," she admitted, looking both lost and found.

He kissed her, opening her mouth and feasting on her desires. But when she melted against him, waiting for his next move, he stopped and whispered, "Take what you want."

"On the bed," she demanded in a shaky voice.

Without a pause, he fell onto the mattress, scooting to the headboard. She took off her dress and stood before him in pink panties and a matching bra. It was on the tip of his tongue to tell her to remove them too, but he managed to keep quiet. This was her show, and he'd pay any price for admission.

She prowled up him, her hands gliding up his legs. Stopping at his waist, her molten gaze crashed into his. Nervousness and excitement seemed to swirl around her.

Leaning down, she ran her lips lightly along his dick, making him shudder with need. He fisted the sheets, resisting the urge to bury his hands in her hair and guide her. After a few playful licks, she took him into her mouth, her tongue running over every pleasure pulse.

Her name fell from his lips, and it sounded like he was praying. Fitting, as her touch was heaven. He couldn't stop his hips from pumping, but she didn't seem to mind, taking him deeper, gripping him tighter. His body began to tighten and coil.

The urge to bring her around, to taste her desire, was overpowering. With enormous effort, he denied the impulse, keeping his word to give her control. But damn, he was losing his.

"Lilith," he warned. "If you keep doing that..."

She sat up, leisurely stroking him. "Do you want me to stop?"

The hooded lust in her eyes and swollen lips nearly did him in. He had to hold her hand to stop her perfect movements. "I want you to come at least once before I do."

Her gaze skittered from his, and she bit her lower lip, piquing his curiosity. "Damn, what's in that look? What do you have in mind? Role playing? St. Andrew's cross?"

She tilted her head. "What cross?"

He laughed, "Never mind. Tell me what you're thinking."

"I want to go without a condom." She shifted, lying next to him. "I was tested after Marshall and I split, and I've been on the pill for years."

His mind and body went to war. He hadn't gone without one since Eden. It had been another unbreakable rule since the pregnancy. Yet, now he considered it. Not only because the thought of sinking into her without a barrier made him even harder, but he craved the closeness with her.

It slammed into him then. He was falling for her.

He sucked in a breath. "I—"

I should stick to my rules and back off before everything between them crashes and burns.

He was supposed to enjoy her body and friendship but never her heart. She didn't want to give that to him, and she'd be even more reluctant if she knew of his past.

She rested a hand on his cheek. "I'm sorry. I shouldn't have asked." She twisted toward the nightstand. "I have condoms."

His wants and, okay, a piece of his heart, claimed his brain. He gripped her hips, bringing her on top of him. "I don't want anything between us either. I haven't been with anyone but you since I got tested in the spring. I have a clean bill of health."

She smiled, the edges of it nervous. "So, yes?"

Kissing her, he said against her lips, "Yes."

"I want to stay like this. I've never been on top," she admitted.

Shock ricocheted through him. "Never?"

"I'm not good at taking control."

"Are you kidding me? You're doing a fucking fantastic job." He grinned. "I'm willing to be your submissive any time, babe."

She laughed, playfully swatting his chest. Shifting onto her knees, she took him into her, inch by glorious inch. Her tight heat pulsed around him.

At that moment, she owned him.

Watching her rock, the way her nipples tightened and peaked, begging for his mouth, mixing with the glassy bliss in her eyes, had him impossibly hard. He was damn near going into sensory overload.

"You're gorgeous," he grated, running his palms up her, cupping her breasts.

"You make me feel beautiful," she hummed.

Rising a little, she paused, then slammed down. Her mouth formed a cute, surprised, "oh!"

"You like that?" he asked.

"Yes." She did it a few more times, sending shock waves of ecstasy coiling around his slow-building orgasm.

Her brows furrowed and her pace slowed. Lilith discovering what she liked was a mix of sweet and sexy.

"What's wrong?" he asked.

She licked her bottom lip. "Nothing."

He grazed a finger where her tongue had just been. "Tell me, love."

She blushed, the color reaching her chest. "This feels good, but not enough to take me over." Switching to rocking against him, she continued, "This might work, but I want... *more*."

The hungry way she said 'more' fed his craving for her. As she moved, he pressed his thumb where they were connected, caressing her in a circular motion.

She gasped, exhaling his name.

"Press harder," she instructed.

He did as told, and she gave another breathy cry that became sharp gasps.

He was familiar with the sound. It was his favorite. It meant she was riding that wave of euphoria, about to come.

She shifted closer, offering him her mouth. He greedily accepted, being too rough, but her moans said she loved it.

Her pants became chants of his name, whispered against his lips. Her body clenched around him as she rode into her orgasm.

When her sounds and movements became less frantic, he rolled on top of her. Her nails dug into his ass, pushing him impossibly deeper with each thrust, closer to his bliss.

A growl ripped from his throat as he came. Pleasure poured from him, so intense it bordered on pain. He never wanted it to end.

Eventually, the strength of his climax ebbed, and his hips slowed as lazy waves of euphoria returned him softly to earth.

A few sweaty strands stuck to Lilith's forehead, and he wiped them away, kissing her hairline. "Damn, woman, you're incredible."

She laughed into his neck. "I'm boring. What thirty-year-old woman has never been on top during sex?"

"It's about passion, not positions." He tipped on his side, taking her with him, cupping her ass. "Although, I'm surprised that you didn't at least pause that time we had the quickie in the bathroom. There was no hesitation when I bent you over the sink. Or that other time against the wall. Or—"

"It's not about positions," she countered. "But my inability to ask for what I want."

"Why is it difficult?"

He felt her shrug. "All I know is it's easier to ask you."

His body filled with warmth, and it had nothing to do with lust. He hugged her tighter as a lone owl called out to the night.

"You think I'm passionate? Not cold?" she asked quietly. The desperate reassurance in her voice made him want to rip Marshall to shreds.

Shifting, he faced her. "Lilith, look at me." When her gaze met his, he said, "You are hot as the fucking sun. If anyone told you differently, it's their shortcomings—not yours."

"Thank you." She blinked, and a single tear escaped from the corner of her eye.

He wiped it with his thumb, a range of emotions shredding him. He wanted to kiss away her every pain and insecurity. Then drive to her ex-husband's house and beat the shit out of him.

Smiling, she shoved his shoulder, and he went willingly onto his back. "You might regret this insatiable monster you've created in me," she teased, climbing on him.

He arched into her, and her quiet moan had him rapidly going from half-hard to granite. "Oh, I doubt that."

CHAPTER THIRTY

Lilith floated into wakefulness. With Asher pressed against her back, one leg between hers, it felt like she was still dreaming.

This was a new level of contentment. Other than their first time, they hadn't spent the whole night together. Plus, neither could call that morning relaxing. She giggled, recalling him springing naked from the bed as she ran for his bathroom.

He kissed the top of her spine and tickled her belly. "Do I want to know why you're laughing?"

"I was thinking about the only other time we woke up in bed together. When Raven knocked on your, thankfully, locked door."

His deep chuckle filled the room. "Shit. She would have been scarred for life. An eye-full of her naked dad and her best friend's mom." He brought her closer, his erection pressing into her lower back, his palm skimming lower. "This is much better."

She wiggled her butt. "I agree. Waking to your sleepy kisses and busy hands is way nicer. Although, where do you get your stamina? You wore me out last night. I'm too languid to move."

"Don't worry, love, I'll take care of you."

She couldn't decide what she liked more, his endearment or how his hands teased and tempted her. When he thrust between her legs, not sinking in but sliding along her swollen need, she decided his touch won this round.

"Are you sore?" he asked, nipping her ear.

"A little," she admitted.

He froze, his hand shifting to her stomach. "Rest. I'll make coffee."

There wasn't a trace of irritation in his voice, and she adored him for it. He didn't guilt her for his desires and didn't realize what a gift it was for her. It slowly eased and untied a tight knot in her. She'd lived with it for so long that she hadn't noticed how it had bound her in a million different ways.

When he made to leave, she held tight to his arm resting on her waist. "I want you. Not coffee." She rocked against his arousal, making it clear what she desired.

He sucked in a breath, murmuring in a voice thick with lust, "We shouldn't if you're sore."

"I'm fine." When he didn't continue, she twisted to look at him. "I swear."

She loved the way his compassion fueled her passion. In fact, there was so much to love about him. She had to be careful not to mistake it for actual love.

He kissed her, but when she started to roll onto her back, he stilled her with a hand on her hip. "Arch," he ordered, positioning her butt against him.

Opening her legs from behind with his knee, he pushed gently inside her. She sighed in relief, giddy anticipation building. His hand glided down her belly to continue his play from earlier. Combined with his perfect thrusts, she reached nirvana in a matter of minutes, her climax somehow both lazy and intense.

As her body floated in euphoric bliss, Asher nudged her onto her stomach, keeping his rhythm gentle, even as his breaths became ragged. He told her how good she felt, how he wanted to stay buried in her. Until he began to shudder then his words were lost as his body stiffened, and his orgasm consumed him.

He collapsed, tipping onto his side, probably trying not to crush her. She wouldn't have cared. Not when the last thing she'd hear was the thumping of his racing heartbeat.

"Lilith." Her name sounded serious on his lips.

Her heart dipped, and she rolled toward him. "What's wrong?"

He brushed a thumb over her cheek. "You're moving to your condo next weekend. And I think we both assumed this would end then."

She tensed. He was ending it like they should, but she wasn't ready. Moisture gathered along her eyes, and her chest ached. She wanted to turn away, so he couldn't see her disappointment, but before she could, he said, "But I'm not ready. Are you?"

Relief crashed into her so fast her head spun. Her pragmatic side whispered that wasn't good. She was in too deep too soon. Muzzling her worries, trying to convince herself this was still a casual thing, she tightened her arms around him. "No."

He exhaled loudly. "Thank Christ. We're going to try the long-distance thing?"

She nodded into his chest, a little anxiety creeping into her relief. "But I still think it's best we don't tell the girls."

"Why?" He sounded hurt. "Is it only about sex for you?"

"No, but I want to see how this goes first. Chloe's life has been in upheaval since I left Marshall. Learning I'm already with another man and it's her best friend's dad would add more. Especially if we grow apart in a month or two. We need to see if long-distance will even work."

"I wouldn't let us not working affect their friendship, and I don't think you would either," he reasoned.

"True, but it might be awkward for the girls." She met his gaze. "Also, to be honest, I'm not ready to look too closely at what you and I are to each other. I've only officially been divorced for a month. Nearly everything in me screams it's too soon for a relationship, so not giving us a label, telling our kids, makes it easier."

He ran a large palm along her hair, smoothing it. "Fine, if that's what you need, I'll go along with it for now."

"Thank you."

After a moment, he asked. "Are you ready for coffee?"

She smiled into her pillow. "Definitely."

"Me too, but I have a problem."

"What's that?"

"I have no clothes." He rolled onto his side, propping his head in his palm. "Remember, I arrived in a towel."

She giggled. "What is with us and no clothes during our sleepovers?"

"That's right. It was the same with you."

"Crap." Her grin fell. "You left your house unlocked all night."

"I'm sure it's fine, and if not, at least no one was home. So, would you mind running to my place and getting me clothes?" He wiggled his hips. "Or would you rather I have coffee in the nude?"

"You can cream my coffee any time, Asher." She slapped a hand over her mouth, then giggled through her fingers.

He fell onto his back, his loud laughter filling the room. "In that case, make sure you keep the curtains closed."

"And disappoint Mrs. Wilson?" She tickled his torso, loving the way his muscles flexed. "You should hear her talk about your butt when you walk away."

"I'd rather not. You ladies make me feel like such a piece of meat," he teased, tweaking her nipple.

"No. Never. You're not a piece of meat to me." She scooted to the side of the bed, twisting around to kiss him. Against his lips, she said, "What did Marshall call you? Ah, yes, my boy-toy."

He nipped her lip. "Play with me anytime."

Someone knocked on her front door, and Lilith startled. "Who would be here this early on a Saturday?"

"What time is it?" Asher asked.

"It can't be past nine." She slipped her arms into her blue silk robe. "I'll find out who it is, then run to your house to get you clothes."

"I'm going to take a quick shower. That way I can stay here until I have to pick up Raven this afternoon."

"Okay. I'll be back before you're finished," Lilith said, leaving the bedroom.

"Perfect," Asher called after her. "Then you can join me."

Smiling, she opened the door and froze. Hope stood on her porch.

"Did we have plans this morning?" Lilith asked. "And if we did, I'm surprised you kept them."

Hope winced. "I'm really sorry for yesterday. I was out of line." She held up a tray with to-go mugs. "I brought a peace offering."

Lilith moved aside, opening the door wider. "Three cups?"

"Well, I figured Asher would be here. Or you at his house." She glanced around. "Is he here?"

Lilith ignored the questions and the ache in her chest. "You've made it clear from the start you don't want me with your brother. What changed?"

Hope rested a free hand on Lilith's arm. "I'll admit, I'm worried. That hasn't changed. Asher doesn't trust easily or often, so when he's hurt it cuts him deep. However, I've never seen him this happy. You make him happy. All I can do is hope you won't let your past get in the way of your future."

Lilith couldn't reassure her friend. Committing herself to another man, even one as great as Asher, was terrifying. But maybe she could offer him the present and not think too much about the future.

Hope walked into the kitchen, setting the coffee tray on the table. Turning, she widened her eyes briefly. "So... yesterday on the boat must have been awkward. You and Paloma."

"It wasn't too bad. I might not be her favorite person, but she seems too confident to be mean or petty because things didn't work out with Asher." Lilith shook her head. "It couldn't have been any worse than you having to deal with some of them openly lusting after your brother."

Hope rolled her eyes. "I've been listening to that shit since middle school. I'm used to it."

"I hear you," Lilith said, shaking her head. "My friends are the same with Tate."

"I can't blame them," Hope winked. "Your brother is cute. His dark red hair and green eyes remind me of a sexy actor from my favorite TV show."

Lilith groaned. "Not you too." Setting her mug on the table, she said, "I have to run to Asher's house real quick."

Hope's gaze darted to Lilith's bedroom, where they could both hear the shower. "Why?"

"He, um, doesn't have any clothes."

Hope's brows rose. "He came over naked. That was a bit presumptuous of him."

Not wanting to get into Eden and the misunderstanding, Lilith laughed, saying, "It's a long story."

Hope took a sip from one of the coffees. "Are we good?"

Lilith nodded. She'd been carrying a heaviness from their fight, and now a lightness tingled through her.

Reaching across the table, Hope squeezed Lilith's hand. "I'm so relieved."

The shower shut off, and a minute later, Asher called from the bedroom. "Lilith, are you back?"

"She hasn't left yet," Hope answered.

Silence beat between them, then Asher said, "Good morning, sister."

"I bet mine hasn't been as good as yours," she replied.

Asher called, "That's a bet I'm not willing to take."

"I'll be right back," Lilith said, tightening her robe around her pajamas and escaping through the door.

CHAPTER THIRTY-ONE

Lilith gazed out the kitchen window, taking in her tilled and dormant garden. It seemed like yesterday she and Chloe were canning and freezing vegetables with Asher and Raven. How was it already the end of October? Time was playing tricks on her—going too fast when she was visiting her lake house and dragging at her condo.

"Is your chili almost done?" Tate strolled into the kitchen. Stopping next to her, he bent and looked into the stove. "My mac-and-cheese is almost done."

Lilith stirred her chili, testing a small bite. "Yup, mine is ready."

Gazing out the same window Lilith had just been staring out, Tate said, "The colors are peaking. I can't believe you didn't have renters this weekend."

"I could've. A few had even offered double the price, but this is Raven's Halloween birthday party. We couldn't miss it."

Monday had been her actual birthday, but she'd told Lilith she always waited to celebrate it on her favorite holiday. For a social butterfly like Raven, a big costumed party with friends and family was perfect.

Nor would Lilith skip the chance to be with Asher. Long distance wasn't lessening her desire to be with him. Their late-night talks and constant texting brought him closer to her heart even as the miles and time apart made her aching for him.

Tate pulled on oven mitts and bumped Lilith lightly with his hip, nudging her out of the way. Then he opened the stove door. Cheesy goodness filled the kitchen, and she inhaled deeply. "Yum. We don't need to take that to Asher's. I could happily eat it all."

"Can't. I already told him I was bringing it." Tate flashed her a fanged smile before pulling out the casserole dish.

She couldn't help laughing. "When did you put in the teeth? Costumes are for kids, not the adults."

"I will never be too old for Halloween. It is the best holiday ever. Candy, ghosts, and all those slutty costumes."

She shook her head. "You are the worst."

He set the dish on the granite counter, then fished inside a bag he'd slung on a kitchen chair when they'd first arrived. From it, he pulled out a pair of black devil horns. "These are for you. I figured they're fitting."

"Um, why?"

"In Jewish folklore, Lilith was Adam's first wife. She chose to become a demon instead of submitting to him."

She quirked a brow. "Why do you know this?"

He shrugged. "Got me. I'm full of information that doesn't help in everyday life."

"Yeah, 'full of shit' sounds right," Lilith muttered.

"Hey!" Tate said, placing the horns rather roughly on her head.

She laughed. "Any chance you know what your name means?"

"Yup. It's Norse. It means cheerful."

"Nice. I'm possibly named after a demon, and you're a positive emotion. Guess we know who's our parents favorite." Leaving the kitchen, she yelled from the stairs, "Are you two almost ready?"

"Yeah," Chloe called back. A few seconds later, she and Raven bounded into the living room, all smiles and costumes. "Let's go!"

"I'll get the chili. Chloe, you set candy on the porch." Lilith pointed to the bowl sitting on the ledge that led downstairs.

Locking her door, she eyed Asher's lawn, the part facing the road, not lake-side. There were at least three dozen people, some milling around the tables with food, others by the metal firepit.

"Let's get some caramel apples before they're all gone," Raven said.

Chloe nodded, and they shot off toward the food. Lilith took a deep breath, glancing over her shoulder toward her cozy, comfy house.

"Is your inner introvert coming out to play?"

She bit her lip. "Yes. She's telling me to hide."

Tate shifted his crock-pot to one hand, then rubbed between Lilith's shoulder blades, nudging her forward. "Most of the people here you already know. Many of them you even like."

"Yeah, but there will be lots of others I've only met in passing." She shuddered. "What if I have to make small talk?"

"Oh, no, the torture and cruelty," Tate teased, waving to someone.

It was Jackson, and he was gesturing to a few empty chairs next to him by the fire. On his other side was Asher. He was ruggedly handsome in a pair of faded jeans and a thick gray hoodie. His head was thrown back, and he was laughing with Eden. She was stunning in skinny jeans, knee-high boots, and a tight cowl-neck sweater. Her cherry-red lips were smiling adoringly at Asher.

Why did she have to be a doctor—no, a *surgeon*—and look like freaking Salma Hayek?

Lilith's insecurities piled on top of each other. It was beyond her how Asher even noticed her with Eden around. Yet, he did. His gaze drifted from her to Lilith, his grin widening as he waved them over.

She held up her chili, indicating she needed to set it down. He nodded, turning back to Jackson and Eden.

"Whoa, who's that woman?" Tate asked.

"Raven's mom. Eden." Lilith's voice was smooth as her insides rioted.

"Seriously?! Damn, I'd never want to leave her garden."

Lilith slapped her brother in the chest, trying not to be amused but failing. "You are the worst."

"True. But that doesn't change the fact that Asher's baby-mamma is hot."

She couldn't argue. The woman was all curves and sex. Next to her, Lilith looked like an adolescent girl.

"First, Hope. Now you're drooling over Asher's ex. Is that why you're friends with him? For the eye-candy?"

Tate grinned. "It helps. And Hope *is* gorgeous. But Jackson would kick my ass if I hit on her. And I wouldn't anyway. I'm dating a woman from work."

"You are? Since when?"

Tate placed his mac-in-cheese on the table. "Not long. Just a few weeks. He name's Katrina."

"I can't wait to meet her." After setting her chili next to Tate's dish, she asked, "So, you also think Jackson likes Hope as more than a friend?"

"Oh, definitely. He has it bad for her. I'm not sure why he doesn't make a move." Tate handed her a hard cider before getting himself a beer. "Maybe he's afraid it'll fuck with his and Asher's friendship."

"Perhaps, but if you're really attracted to someone, would that be enough?"

"No, probably not."

She scanned the crowd, looking for Hope or the girls. The last place she wanted to sit was around the fire, coming up with idle chatter with Eden. It might be petty, but she couldn't help it. The woman made Lilith feel incredibly inadequate.

"Does it bother you?" Tate asked.

She paused with her drink halfway to her mouth. "Why would it bother me that Jackson and Hope aren't dating?"

Tate rolled his eyes. She could almost see the teenage version of him when he used to do that constantly. "No. Dork," he said. "Eden hanging out with Asher."

"She's here for her daughter. Not him."

"I wouldn't be so sure. She's sitting pretty close to him, and the adoring look in her eyes says she might be here for more than her daughter."

Lilith took a large swig of her drink, trying to swallow the distaste of Tate's observation. Hope had made similar comments.

"Why should I care?"

She did. A lot. Too much.

"Because you two are sleeping together," Tate said like he was commenting on the weather.

Mid sip, Lilith choked on her drink. He laughed, rubbing her shoulders.

"Do you think I really bought that whole 'we need to take another look through the condo together,' last month? You two totally christened the place, didn't you?"

Her face flamed hot. "Are we that obvious?"

"Yup. And you're worse, now. You make those eyes at him."

Lilith snorted. "What eyes?"

"The same you made whenever you saw that musician guy who lived down the street from us when we were teenagers."

She rested the back of her hand on her forehead like she was swooning. "I remember him. He was sex in faded jeans and a leather jacket."

"Ugh. If you say so. As for Asher, he's a little better at hiding his horny eyes, but whenever us guys meet at The Hill, he doesn't flirt or dance with any of the single women. Even when they hit on him. When we rib him about it, he refuses to look at me," Tate finished, laughing.

"Do you think our girls know?" Her stomach fluttered and flipped.

"No," Tate said without hesitation.

"You sound very sure."

He shrugged. "I'm one hundred percent sure."

"Why?"

Tate chuckled. "Because Chloe always says how cool it'd be if you two got together. Raven would be her sister. Plus, if she suspected, you know she'd say something. Subtle and Chloe don't go together."

So true. "She's like her uncle in that regard."

He nodded in agreement.

"Anyway, that's what I was afraid of—her dreaming of me marrying Asher." She shook her head. "I've only been divorced a few months. I'm not ready to play house again. I'm not sure if I will ever be ready."

"Asher isn't Marshall," Tate said. "And I'm talking about dating, not marriage."

"That doesn't mean what we have will last. I don't want to drag the girls into it until we know for sure."

"Know for sure?" Tate repeated, his brows rising toward his forehead. "This has been going on since the summer, right?"

Lilith nodded.

"It's fall. You've been sleeping with him for, what, months? And he's been a close friend since nearly the day you moved in, yet you're not sure if you want to date him?" He rested a hand on her shoulder. "I mean this in the nicest way possible. You have your head up your ass. Let me say this nice and slow, so you understand; You two are already together."

She laughed, even as the flipping and fluttering in her stomach reached her heart. Was he right?

"I'm not ready. And I'm never getting married again." She'd served her time in that prison.

He gave a dismissive wave. "Again, I never mentioned a wedding. But it probably isn't just sex."

Lilith sipped on her cider, taking in everything he'd said. Maybe he was right. But was she ready to admit there was more?

She eyed Tate. "When did you get so smart, little brother?

He tapped his bottle against hers. "I've always been wise beyond my years."

"Lilith! Tate!" Asher called. "Come here. Try these apple donuts my mom made."

They went to him. Being near him eased her racing-rabbit heart. She couldn't decide if the strength of her feelings for him made her weak. If they did, she was clueless as what to do about it.

CHAPTER THIRTY-TWO

The setting sun shone on Lilith's red hair, and it flamed bright as the autumn leaves around her. Damn, he'd missed her. Two weeks—hell, two hours—without her in his arms was too long. But every time she returned for a visit, the longing and missing her was worth it.

She bit into her donut and moaned, the sound licking against his constant desire for her. Everything about her was so damn sexy. She swiped some sugar from her bottom lip with her tongue. *Christ.* He should look away but couldn't, and going by her wicked grin, she knew just what she was doing to him.

"Dad," Raven called, running toward him, with Chloe behind her. "Are you ready to go trick-or-treating?"

He nodded, turning to Lilith. "Are you coming too?"

Raven called to her mother on the other side of the firepit, "Want to go with me?"

"Sure," Eden replied. "But since I have to move away from this heat, I need to grab my coat from the car. I'll be right back."

"Mom, ready?" Chloe asked.

"Um..." Lilith's gaze bounced to Eden's retreating form. "Do you mind if I stay here, sweetie? I ate too much junk food and my stomach is bothering me."

"Okay." Chloe stood on her tip-toes and leaned closer to her mom. "If you have to poop, don't use that bathroom next to the guest bedroom. It clogs really easy."

"Thanks for the tip," Lilith said, choking on a laugh as Asher swallowed his own.

Raven took Chloe's hand. "Let's get our bags." She looked at Asher. "We'll meet you by the road."

He nodded, and when they were out of earshot, and no one else seemed to be paying them any attention, he asked Lilith, "Are you sure you don't want to go? It might be nice for you to get to know Eden."

She shook her head. "No thanks. Not tonight."

He cupped her elbow gently. "You aren't feeling pushed aside, are you?"

"No." A small smile flickered at the corner of her mouth. "Maybe territorial. I mean, your hot ex wants to hang out with you—"

"With Raven, not me."

"I've heard rumors she wants both."

"No way. Eden is here for her fellowship and possibly her daughter, not me."

"But even if she was after you," Lilith said, "she wouldn't be doing anything wrong. You aren't mine."

Disappointment skittered through his veins. He wanted to be hers. After all these months, was it still only orgasms and friendship to her? Even with her moving to Royal Oak, he'd thought they were becoming closer, but maybe he was wrong.

"We're together as much as possible, in and out of the bedroom. We enjoy each other's company, and neither of us is interested in dating other people. Wouldn't you say we have more than merely casual sex?" he asked.

Lilith blinked as if waking from a dream.

Or a nightmare.

From the start, she'd told him he could have her body, not her heart. Now his dropped to the pit of his stomach. Would she end it?

Lilith swallowed. "Yes, what we have is more than sex. We are together, but our daughters don't know. Which is why I don't want to go. I'd have to pretend to be your friend while hanging out with your ex, who eyes you like you hold all her answers. It's more than I'm up for this Halloween. Sorry."

He squeezed her elbow, sliding his hand down her arm, holding it briefly before letting go. "You're wrong about Eden, but I get it. I wouldn't want to trick-or-treat with Marshall."

"Dad, let's go. My bag isn't going to fill itself!" Raven called from her spot next to Eden. It struck him like lightning at how much they looked alike.

A blur of purple flashed past him, hugging Lilith. She laughed and returned Chloe's embrace, asking, "Are you already on a sugar rush?"

She giggled. "Uncle Tate brought me candy. So did Hope."

"Great. Perhaps I'll send you home with one of them," she said, not sounding truly bothered.

"Fine. That means you won't pick through the candy with me tonight, taking all your favorites."

"Oh, right. Never mind." Lilith kissed Chloe's forehead. She took off running toward Raven.

"Do you have a kiss for me too?" Asher asked.

"Oh, I always have them for you. And I hope to give you lots later tonight." She tilted her head toward the girls rocking on their heels, talking and gesturing wildly to Eden. "But right now they're waiting for you."

He smiled. Eden was laughing at whatever they were saying and replied with equal enthusiasm. He hated leaving Lilith behind, yet he had to admit that having Raven's mom in her life was great. She'd always been a happy-go-lucky girl but had become even more carefree and content since her mother's return.

He turned to Lilith to reassure her—and him—they were fine.

She was gone.

CHAPTER THIRTY-THREE

Asher listened as Eden's usually clipped, serious cadence was light and relaxed as she chatted with the girls. And they seemed equally smitten with her. For someone who had run from motherhood, she had an effortless way with kids. She listened when they spoke and talked to them, not at them, as many adults tended to do.

"Oh! That house gives out full-size candy bars." Raven and Chloe took off, bags held aloft as they cut across the lawn, leaving him and Eden to trail after them.

"Are you glad you came since they only remember us when it's time to cross over to a new neighborhood?" Asher asked.

"I don't mind. Their exuberance is fun to see. And the little pocket of chatting time between streets is great. Plus, you aren't the worst company. Unlike, say, your sister," Eden teased. "The stink-eye she gives me is the scariest thing I've seen all Halloween."

Asher chuckled. "She's protective of me. If you stay around, she'll come around."

"I picked UMich because I wanted to be near Raven. I hope to be around for a while."

He didn't reply, noting she didn't say she was staying when her fellowship was over. Her plan might be to return to New Mexico when it ended.

"Sooo…" she said, dragging out the word. "You and Lilith, huh?"

His mouth fell open. He closed it, laughing. They were the worst kept secret.

"What makes you think she and I are together?"

"Remember at the end of summer, when I stopped by and you opened the door in nothing but a towel?"

He snorted. "Yeah, it's not something I do often enough that I'd forget."

"Well, that's too bad for your neighbors," Eden joked. "Anyway, I saw her expression as I left. It wasn't one of a disinterested friend. And then this evening, you two might not hold hands or kiss, but there's an intimacy in the way you watch her. She's the same with you."

Huh, a perceptive Eden was unexpected. The woman he'd known when they were barely adults had been self-absorbed, noticing only what affected her.

"Yes, we're together," he replied. "But keeping it quiet for a few reasons."

"She doesn't seem your type."

"I have a type?"

"Sure. The first time I met you, you were dancing with a girl who had a black mane down to her ass. Then there's me." She ran a hand through her hair, that was darker than the night sky.

"That was a long time ago," he said flatly.

"True, but when I moved back here, the rumor was you were hooking up with Paloma."

"Why do you know this?" Asher huffed. "Don't people have anything better to do than gossip about my sex life?"

She held up her hands in a what-can-you-do gesture. "It's a small town."

"Besides, my type has more to do with personality than a body or hair color."

"Ahh," Eden nodded. "So, you like them pretty and damaged."

Asher stopped walking. "What are you talking about?"

"I don't know Paloma, but my history is a trainwreak. And I can see it in Lilith's eyes—in her body language. She's been hurt bad and is struggling to overcome it."

Lilith was wrestling with a few demons, but she wasn't damaged. And he was unwilling to share any of her personal life, so he focused on Eden. "What are you've talking about ? You're one of the most responsible and composed woman I've ever met."

Eden scoffed. "Only a damaged person would leave their child."

"Maybe things would have been different if I hadn't been on probation, and unable to follow you to Stanford."

"No. It wouldn't have changed anything," she said bluntly.

Her unspoken words cut. *I didn't want you to come with me. I didn't want to raise a child with you. A derelict.*

"I get it. Being stuck with a guy like me wasn't what you signed up for when you moved here for college."

"You misunderstand me." She looked at him. "I'm not going to lie. I panicked when you first told me about your past, but after the whole story sunk in, I was fine. I mean, come on, I might not have wanted to be a mother, but there is no way in hell I'd have given my baby to a man who scared me or might harm a child–any child, mine or a stranger's. No, I left because *I* was terrified of becoming a parent."

Asher scratched his jaw, trying to bury old resentments. "So was I."

"Sure, because of your age. Mine was that and my upbringing. My mom was a terrible mother. Did and said things no parent should say or do. I feared, still fear, turning into her. I didn't want Raven to have a childhood anything like mine. I thought the best way to make sure that didn't happen was removing myself from her life... but I never could completely."

A heaviness, an ache, squeezed his heart. "Why didn't you ever tell me this?"

His past was not a dream. Some of it was a damn nightmare. But his parents' love and support never wavered. What had it been like for Eden to be denied such a basic need?

"Because the past is better left buried. I'm telling you now for a few reasons."

"Such as?"

"Whatever Lilith is struggling with, whatever's hurting her, might hurt you."

"Now you sound like my sister."

"Maybe she's giving good advice."

Asher quirked a brow. "Want to hear her advice about you?"

Eden winced. "Nope. No, thank you."

"What are your other reasons?"

"I want you to understand it wasn't an easy choice. Leaving Raven has haunted me. I love her and would like to be a bigger part of her life. I hope you will let me."

"Have I ever stopped you?"

"No. And it means the world to me. Thank you."

He'd done it for Raven, not Eden, but he didn't see a reason to clarify that point.

She squeezed his bicep. "Anyway, that was my rambling and oversharing way of saying thank you for never keeping my daughter from me. For your willingness to let me be in her life. I'll put my ghosts and demons away for the rest of the Halloween stroll."

"Mom. Dad!" Raven yelled, running toward them, Chloe a step behind. "Mrs. MacSon said you two deserved candy for taking us out."

Her gaze fell to Eden's hand resting on his arm. *Uh-oh.* The delight flickering in her eyes was impossible to miss.

He took the offered candy bar, and Eden's hand fell from him. "Those are Lilith's favorite. I'll save it for her," he said.

Chloe held up hers. "I was going to give her mine..."

Smiling, he said, "Go ahead, eat it."

"Thanks!" She ripped off the wrapping and shoved half of it in her mouth, then struggled to chew it.

"I'm beginning to regret my offer. Please don't choke on your candy."

She tried to answer, but it was garbled around all the chocolate and nougat.

"It'll be fine. I'll help her. I always have a scalpel in my pocket. I can get the sweets stuck in her throat," Eden teased, rubbing her hands together. "Surgeons love to have a reason to cut people."

Chloe's eyes widened, but she was smiling. After managing to swallow, she said, "I think I'll stick to bite-size pieces when you're around."

Eden snapped her fingers like she was disappointed. Chloe and Raven laughed, taking a quick step back and pretending to shake as if scared. Asher shook his head at their antics. They were cute together.

"Want to switch to a street that'll lead home?" he asked.

The girls agreed, and the conversation between him and Eden flowed easily without touching on anything heavy again. Yet, her warning weighed on him.

Lilith could hurt him. Hell, her reluctance tonight to admit they had more than orgasms and friendship had been painful.

But was it better to be stuck in this limbo with her than to risk losing her?

CHAPTER THIRTY-FOUR

Sitting with Asher's family, Lilith peeked at her watch. His parents were lovely, but listening to his Aunt Tammy go on and on about how great it would be if her nephew reunited with Eden was wearing thin.

Lilith pushed back, her lawn chair scrapped into the dying grass. "I'm going to head h—"

Asher's tall, broad frame materialized from the darkness, looking like her favorite Halloween treat. Not so sweet was Eden next to him. A step behind them were the girls, dragging bags stuffed with candy.

Aunt Tammy noticed them too, and cooed, "Oh, there they are. Aren't they adorable together, Irene? A perfect little family."

"I guess," Asher's mom drawled, sounding like she disagreed.

Eden hugged Raven, then Asher. She waved to someone Lilith couldn't see before walking to her vehicle. A minute later, the tires of her Mustang crunched under the gravel as she drove away. Aunt Tammy sniffed. "Second chance romances are the best."

Irene patted her sister's hand. "Honey, you need to watch something besides the Hallmark channel."

"And you need to watch more of it," Tammy countered.

Chloe ran, her bag dragging along the ground. Close on her heels was Raven. "We got a ton of candy!" she exclaimed, running into Lilith's arms. "Can we go inside to trade?"

"Sure, if Asher doesn't mind you dumping piles of candy in his house," Lilith replied.

"I don't care if each of you let me pick a few things from your loot," he said, coming up behind the girls.

They nodded, taking off. Their laughter carried as they disappeared into the house.

"You know Raven's going to hide the good stuff from you," Asher's father said.

"She probably should." He patted his flat stomach. "I foraged through her bag when she asked me to carry it. I had more than my fill." He pulled a full-sized candy bar from his pocket and handed it to Lilith. "Your favorite, right?"

She nodded, delighted he remembered. "Thank you."

"Those jeans look a little loose. Extra sweets and meals won't hurt you." Irene tugged on Asher's pant leg as she rose from her seat.

He helped her up. "It isn't from the lack of eating. It's my job. My boss is relentless," Asher said, smirking at his dad.

James stood. "Don't whine to me. Your sister makes the schedule, not me."

"We had a great time, but we're exhausted," his mom said, embracing Asher. "We're going to say our goodbyes then head home."

Lilith rose and was pleasantly surprised when Irene and James hugged her. After they went into the house, she and Asher scooted closer to the fire.

He stared into the flames. Minutes ticked by, and he remained silent.

"Something on your mind?" she asked.

His gaze met hers, and it was serious. Tiny prickles of agitation sparked in her veins.

"We should tell the girls about us tonight," he said.

Lilith gripped her knees. The urge to run from the conversation was fierce. "Why are you pushing and poking at what's between us?"

"One. It's the worst kept secret." He leaned closer, the flickering flames casting shadows on his handsome features. "My sister figured it out a long time ago. Tonight, Eden asked if you and I were seeing each other."

Huh. What had been Eden's reaction? Afraid to know the answer, Lilith said, "Tate knows too."

Asher chuckled. "Really?"

"Yup. He said something about me making lusty-eyes whenever I look at you."

Asher full-out belly laughed. When he caught his breath, he leaned into his chair, crossing his legs at the ankles. "Can my nickname for you be Lusty-eyes?"

She giggled, shoving his shoulder playfully. "Absolutely not."

"Damn," he muttered.

"What's your other reason?" Her voice shook on the question, matching her emotions.

"What I mentioned earlier." He traced her knee with his fingers. "We aren't interested in dating other people. I like you. A lot. I want to take you out to dinner. To the movies. On a picnic. Whatever we want, without this quasi-sneaking around."

"We already do those things." Admittedly, it was usually with the girls or their friends. Rarely alone.

"Then why not make it official? Or are you losing interest since moving to your condo?" he asked.

She nearly laughed at the absurdity of the question. "No. Not at all."

Asher closed his eyes, tipping his head back, muttering, "Thank Christ." He looked at her. "I want to hold your hand, hug you, kiss you, and not just stolen ones late at night or when no one's around."

She wanted the same so bad it made her heart hurt. But where was the independence and backbone she was supposed to find now that Marshall's needs and expectations were no longer stifling her? Once free of him, all she'd done was immediately replace him.

She was as weak as her dad insinuated—afraid to be alone, so she ran straight into Asher's arms before the ink was even dry on her divorce papers. Worries and insecurities pounded into her, beating her down. What had she done on her own? Nothing.

Asher was always there to help her around her homes, to talk with, to give her pleasure she didn't even know existed. He was a definite upgrade but a crutch nonetheless.

"Should we pull back?" Asher let his hand fall from hers.

"What do you mean?"

"We go back to being only friends."

She craved their intimate moments, inside and outside of the bedroom. Giving them up was impossible.

Tate was right. Whatever was between her and Asher wasn't just sex and stolen fun.

Running a palm roughly over his cheek, he said, "We should probably take a break from each other. At least temporarily."

Wait. What?

She stiffened. "You'd punish me because I hesitate about going along with what you want?" Loss and regret stung at her eyes, but she refused to let a single tear fall.

Asher gripped her elbow gently. "No. Never. I swear, I'm not trying to hurt or corner you, but I'll need space and time to return to being just your friend."

No matter what he said, she did feel cornered. "Why can't we continue as we are? Things are great. Nearly perfect. Why risk ruining it?"

He sighed. "Because I can't keep doing this. I can't keep pretending all I want from you is sex and friendship. Also, if nearly everyone close to us can tell we're more than friends, how long do you think it will take for Raven and Chloe to figure it out? And when they do, what do we tell them? That we don't date, just fuck?"

"Isn't that what you do, what you like?" Lilith snapped, needing to attack. "According to Paloma and the other women you've been with, you don't do relationships. What's changed?"

"It's you. You're the difference." His eyes were sad, his voice gentle. "We've been doing this since August, don't you want more?"

Yes, but that doesn't mean I'm ready. However, as Tate had said, it was already happening. She was merely ignoring reality.

Asher rose. "I'm going to check on the girls."

She had to decide—face her feelings or turn from them.

Grabbing his wrist, she choked out, "I feel the same, but I'm scared. I don't want to lose myself while dating you." Her fears rushed forward, smothering the rest of her words and thoughts.

"I am too," he admitted, returning to his seat. "I haven't done the whole relationship thing in a while, and the more entangled we become, the harder it will be to return to friends. I don't want to lose that, but staying in this in-between doesn't fit anymore."

She entwined her fingers with his, acknowledging the truth. "You're right."

Her heart hammered, doubts chasing her insecurities. She buried them under her hope of having both Asher and her independence.

He stood, offering her his hand. "Ready to go inside?"

Lilith wasn't sure, but nodded.

CHAPTER THIRTY-FIVE

Walking into Asher's spacious living room, Lilith focused on the simple cream walls and stunning framed travel photos that hung over a gray sectional. In the cozy fireplace, a few logs crackled. She watched them pop for a few seconds before turning to Chloe and Raven.

They were sitting crisscrossed in the center of the plush burgundy rug. The girls had changed out of their costumes and were chatting away with a good size pile of discarded candy wrappers between them.

She and Asher took a seat on the couch next to each other. A fluttering bat flipped in her stomach. Telling the girls would make everything real.

The same worry line as Lilith's pulled between her daughter's eyes. "Mom, what's wrong? You guys look serious."

"Nothing bad, but we want to talk to you both about something important," Lilith replied. She took a deep breath and dove in. "How do you two feel about us dating?" Asher took her hand, sliding his fingers through hers.

Chloe broke into a wide grin, but Raven's jaw tightened. She glared at her dad. "What about Mom?"

He frowned. "Eden? What about her?"

"She's here now. Back in Michigan... and I thought... I thought... you'd want to date *her*." Raven's words stumbled over each other as she expressed what was apparently a secret wish.

"But we could be sisters. Wouldn't that be cool?" Chloe asked.

"Yeah, but my mom's been coming around a lot. The three of us have been going out. It's fun. Really nice." Raven's shoulders slumped. "Don't you like it, Dad?"

Lilith's chest tightened, strangled by her daughter's aching hopes and Raven's disappointment.

"I d-do," Asher replied, looking as if he'd been hit by a two-by-four. "But your mom's my friend. We aren't interested in each other romantically."

"When I've asked before, about her." She pointed at Lilith. "You said the same thing."

Lilith stared at her hands, torn. What could she say? It hurt, yet coming from a divorced home, she understood Raven's wish.

"It's different—" Asher began.

"How?" Raven asked. "You're friends with mom too. Spent time with her. Get along with her. And you already liked mom enough to date her before. Why not again?"

He shook his head. "No. That wouldn't happen."

"Why not?"

"We aren't the same people we were ten years ago. We'll always be your family and love you, but not each other."

Raven grabbed a discarded wrapper and began shredding it. Except for the muffled rip of paper, the room was silent.

Lilith slid from the couch, sitting across from Raven, mirroring her cross-legged position. "You are too important to me, and I don't want to hurt you. I won't date your father if you're against it." She tapped Raven's knee, but she didn't look at her. Lilith continued anyway. "However, from what I've seen, your mom and Asher are a great team, but if friendship is all they have in their hearts, there will never be more, whether or not I'm here. Believe me, I know."

Raven met Lilith's gaze. "How do you know?"

"My parents divorced when I was younger than you. I carried the same wish as you, clung to it for years. But emotions and life are difficult, uncontrollable. I couldn't wish or beg my parents to feel things they didn't have."

I'm learning this all over again with Marshall and Asher.

"In the end, I'm happy they didn't get back together," she finished.

Raven's straight brows pulled together. "Why?"

"My mom is with the man who was meant for her heart."

After a solid minute of silence, Raven said, "Okay. Fine."

"Okay, what?" Asher asked, shifting onto the floor next to her.

"It's cool. You two dating." Raven offered a shy smile in Lilith's direction.

Returning it, relief and worry tugged at her uncertainties. Was Raven speaking the truth or merely putting on a good show?

Asher asked Chloe. "And what about you? Do you mind if I date your mother?"

"My dad makes Mom sad. You make her laugh and smile, so I'm happy."

Tears swelled in Lilith's throat. Her daughter's words were simple and straightforward but true.

As if the matter was over and she had never been upset, Raven shoved two bite-size chocolate bars in her mouth, chewed for a second before storing it in her cheek like a chipmunk, and asked if Chloe could stay the night.

Asher nodded, and Lilith agreed. The girls whooped and began gathering up their candy.

CHAPTER THIRTY-SIX

Asher relaxed into the couch, clicking from one television channel to the next. Nothing held his attention. Not when his brain couldn't stop replaying his rollercoaster ride of a day. He'd been certain Lilith would end things between them, and his damn heart had plummeted into a pit of misery. Only to beat again when she took his hand instead of letting him walk away. Then, a few minutes later, his daughter ripped it out.

He'd assumed the girls would be thrilled. He should've seen Raven's wish, her longing to have both parents with her. She'd even mentioned it when Eden had first returned to Michigan. Scratching the stubble on his cheeks, he groaned. Some days he truly failed as a parent.

His phone vibrated, and he muttered. "Please, be that needed distraction."

It was Tate asking if Asher wanted company. He messaged back that the front door was unlocked and to come over. Less than ten minutes later, there were heavy footfalls on his porch, and Tate ambled into the living room.

He took a seat on the end of the couch, propping his feet on the ottoman. "Where are the girls?"

"Upstairs in the sitting room. They have on an old black and white Dracula film. They'd wanted 'Tales from the Crypt' after hearing Hope and I talk about our tradition as kids. We used to binge on them every Halloween. But a few of them scared the shit out of me, so I crushed that idea. I'd hate to send Chloe home with a case of the nightmares."

Tate laughed. "I remember that show. There was always a marathon of them during October. They were a mixture of corny and creepy."

Asher scrolled until he found the show. Clicking on an episode, they sat in silence as the crypt keeper gave his oddly funny spiel.

During a lull in the show, Tate asked, "Do you know what's wrong with Lilith?"

Shit, maybe he shouldn't have pushed her. His throat clicked with dryness as he swallowed. "What do you mean?"

"She seemed down when we walked home from the party. I asked what was wrong. She said she didn't want to talk about it."

"We told our girls that we were dating." Asher tapped his fingers against his leg before running them up and down his jeans. "Raven was a little upset. She had this fantasy of Eden and me getting back together."

Tate nodded. "When our parents divorced, Lilith wanted the same thing."

"Not you?" Asher asked.

"No. They split when I was a kid. Practically a baby. I barely remember them together. And I don't need parents who stayed together for me but are miserable. My mom and Ted are great together. I'm happy for them." He paused, taking a drink of his water. "Now Lilith, she bought into the shit my dad lectured throughout our childhood—family above everything. I'm certain it's the reason she stayed with Marshall for so long."

"Hmm," Asher hummed, taking in Tate's words.

"Anyway, what I'm saying is, I'm sure Lilith's sympathetic and wasn't hurt by Raven."

Asher wasn't as sure. "Do you think it'll cause her to break things off? That she wouldn't want to stand in the way of me possibly getting back with Eden?"

"No," Tate replied immediately. "Lilith's martyr complex died when she finally left Marshall. She's no longer under the storybook illusion that a nuclear family is the only way for kids to have a good childhood. However, she still might run.

To tell you the truth, I'm shocked she even hooked up with you. When she left Marshall, she swore off men and meant it."

"Yeah, I got that vibe from her." Asher shook his head. "I thought I had commitment issues, but your sister has me beat."

"Marshall did his best to kill Lilith's spirit. When she finally decided to walk away from him, she was a shadow of the person she was going in. It will take time for her hurt to heal. If you really want to be with her, you're going to need patience. A lot of it."

"That I have."

His worry was it might not be enough. He recalled Hope and Eden's warning about him having to pay for Lilith's ex-husband's mistakes. He was going to find out if he could afford it because Lilith would cost him his heart.

CHAPTER THIRTY-SEVEN

Lilith had always admired Asher's dining room table. He'd crafted from different pieces of reclaimed wood, and the result was stunning and unique. She especially loved that it was big enough to fit multiple families, as it did on this Thanksgiving day. Chloe and Raven chattered two seats down on her left. Her dad sat on her right, talking with Tate and his new girlfriend, Katrina. Asher's parents and sister were across from her, laughing at a story Jackson and his mom were telling. Even having Eden at the lovely table couldn't ruin Lilith's mood. Not with her belly stuffed from Thanksgiving dinner and her heart full of contentment.

Asher returned from the kitchen holding the turkey's wishbone he'd let dry out in the oven's heat. "Do you two have your wishes ready?" he asked, handing it to Raven. She shifted in her seat, holding it up to Chloe. Right before they pulled, he stopped them. "Wait. Both of you should hold the bone from the bottom."

His pointed look landed on Raven. She gave a guilty smile and adjusted her fingers. Chloe narrowed her eyes. Lilith swallowed her laughter. The girls nodded and yanked in opposite directions. The bone snapped, and Chloe let out a triumphant whoop, holding the bigger piece.

Raven tossed hers on the table, a slight pout tugging at her mouth. "Why'd you have me move my hand?"

"If you cheat, your wish won't come true," Asher admonished.

"Says who," Raven muttered.

"Don't worry," Chloe said, patting her best friend's hand. "You'll like my wish."

Lilith could guess what it was. Her daughter wanted two things: a puppy or Asher to ask Lilith to marry him. While she no longer got heart palpitations at the mere thought of being in a relationship, the dog was a better bet. Things were great, almost perfect, but she wasn't willing to return to matrimony's cage.

"Was it to get out of clearing the table and washing all these dishes?" Raven asked Chloe, eyeing the mess of plates and food.

Asher laughed, "If that's the case, your wish has come true."

The girls cheered, stopping when he held up a finger. "But you are in charge of the dessert dishes."

"Deal," they quickly agreed. Then Raven asked, "Can we try out the video game Grandma got me?"

"Only if your grandma promises to stop buying you Thanksgiving gifts," Asher joked.

"I make no promises." Irene winked. "And you two can still play the game."

Raven grinned at Asher. "You have to listen to her. She's your mom. If you don't, she can ground you."

Asher laughed. "Fine. Go ahead. Just make sure you're back to help later."

The girls nodded and headed downstairs. Lilith wiped her hands on a napkin. Under the table, she ran her palm along Asher's thigh. His warm fingers slid through hers, squeezing.

"Did you get enough to eat?" he asked.

"Too much," she groaned, patting her stomach with her free hand. "The turkey was delicious."

"Thanks. It's my parents' recipe."

"You should have let us cook it," Irene chastised, though her tone sounded more pleased than upset.

"I don't know honey." James held his hands, palms up, like he was weighing his options. "Sleeping and going for a long, leisurely walk before coming here to stuff our faces. Or... spending all day in the kitchen."

Asher smirked. "Don't get used to it. Next year, when it's Hope's turn, you might want to help, so we don't end up with a raw or burnt bird."

"Hey!" Hope tossed her half-eaten biscuit at Asher. He caught it and took a bite.

Laughing, Lilith let go of Asher's hand and began gathering the plates. "I need to get away from this table. I'm beyond full, yet the stuffing and cranberries are calling to me."

"I'll get those." He took the pile of dishes from her and strolled toward the kitchen. "You rest."

Standing, Hope grabbed a half-empty green bean casserole and a bowl that held a few lonely kernels of corn. "I should move too before I fall asleep at the table like Grandpa Crowley used to do after every meal."

"Anything I can do to help?" Eden asked.

"No," Hope said with such harshness that Lilith felt its bite.

"Hope..." Asher's tone was full of warning. Silence fell around the table.

Lilith cleared her throat. "People will probably want coffee with dessert." She looked at Eden. "Do you want to make it?"

"I'd love to."

"I'll show you where it is," Asher said. He shot Hope another warning glare, leaving with Eden.

When they were gone, Irene reached for Hope's arm. "Be nice."

"Why?" she scoffed. Tight-lipped, she stacked dirty dishes and took them to the kitchen.

Lilith drew into herself, frowning. Was Hope like this with all Asher's exes? Damn. She'd probably dump Lilith as a friend if she and Asher ended things. It made her heart a little heavy to think of losing them both.

Her dad leaned in and murmured, "You really want to get in the middle of all that? Do you want to be the Mexican's competition?"

"Dad," Lilith choked. "Don't call her that."

"What? I don't mean disrespect. It's what she is." He waved a hand. "Along with being Raven's mom. What if she's back here not for that fellowship, but for her family? Will you step aside for Raven? Maybe do that whole independent thing you were blathering on about when you first left Marshall."

An arrow of pain shot into her. "Blathering. I shared my pain and fears with you and that's what you call it—blathering?" she whispered, tears burning behind her eyes.

She pushed back her chair to stand, but her dad rested a hand on her arm. "I'm sorry, that came out wrong. Like I told you when you first met Asher, I'm think you're rushing into things. He's a nice guy, but he's got his ex in the picture. And you, you haven't even been divorced a year…"

"I'm fine. I'm a big girl. I can take care of myself."

"Are you sure? Jumping from one man to another."

"Dad…" Tate warned.

Lilith looked at her brother, then around the table. Thankfully, no one else but Katrina was paying attention to their conversation. "I'm going to get these dishes to Asher," she said.

Tate stood too. "I'll help."

Lilith quirked a brow. Her brother despised cleaning. He'd rather do all the cooking than wash a single cup. Either he was trying to impress his new girlfriend, or he also needed to put distance between himself and their dad.

"I'll come with you," Katrina said, following Tate.

In the kitchen, Lilith found Hope and Asher at the sink. He was drying, and she was washing. At the opposite counter, Eden was filling the coffee filter. The scene should have been oozing comfort and contentment, but everyone was stiff. They were all ramrod spines and jerky movements in a room as silent as a winter graveyard.

Lilith glanced at Tate. He shrugged.

Eden closed the filter's lid. Her gaze flickered to Asher, admiration playing on her every feature. Lilith wanted to offer the other woman friendship, but it was difficult when she saw how Eden looked at Asher. In those moments, Lilith wanted Eden to disappear.

Her gaze met Lilith's, and apprehension replaced the admiration. She tapped her nails on the bottom of the plates she'd carried in, her stomach churning as she forced herself not to break eye contact. Holding on to her confidence was hard. Eden was everything Lilith was not—self-possessed, beautiful, and successful.

"Hey, Eden. Katrina and I are going to check out the game the girls are playing. Want to come with us?" Tate asked.

Lilith could see the relief wash over Eden, and she grabbed onto Tate's offer. "Yes, sounds fun."

Katrina's lips flattened, her gaze turning cold. *Uh. Oh.* Lilith hoped her brother's kind offer wouldn't cause a fight.

After they left, Hope warned, "You better watch that one around your brother."

"You noticed he brought a girlfriend, right?"

"Um, yeah. How could I not? She's a bit territorial. I swear, whenever I talked to him, she looked like she was planning where to stick the pins on the voodoo doll she's going to make of me."

Lilith laughed. "Good to know I'm not the only one who found her a tad... intense." She waved a hand, returning to their original topic. "Anyway, he only offered to get out of helping with the clean-up."

"Whatever the reason, I'm sure Eden *loves* the attention," Hope drawled.

Asher bumped his sister with his leg. "Cut her some slack. She isn't the girl she was in college. And if you don't want to believe that, do it for Raven. This attitude will hurt your relationship with her."

Hope handed him a clean plate, her expression pinched. "Fine, but I don't want her to get any ideas about us being friends again. That's not happening. Ever."

"I think she got the message loud and clear," Asher said dryly.

"Good." Hope returned to washing the dishes. This time, a little too viciously.

It might be prying, but Lilith asked, "Were you friends when Eden was dating Asher?"

Jackson walked into the kitchen and answered, "Hope knew Eden first. They met in college and were close. It was Hope who introduced them."

"Ah."

"Exactly." He set the turkey pan on the counter. "She feels like Eden betrayed her and Asher."

"I don't give a shit about our stupid college friendship," Hope seethed. "I care she abandoned Asher with their kid."

That might be true, but there was hurt in Hope's voice. Lilith understood it. She'd lost her friends when marrying Marshall. Yes, it had mostly been her fault. She was the one who hadn't called back or canceled plans, but she'd cared about them, and the way they'd let her go so easily still stung.

"She didn't want to be a mom back then. I wanted to keep our baby. We made our choices a long time ago and now we live with them," Asher said. "Hope, you need to let go of your bitterness. Raven's thrilled to have her mom finally take a bigger part in her life. Be happy for your niece."

"I am," Hope snipped. "But I worry how much it will hurt her when her mom takes off again. Her fellowship is only a year. I'm sure once it's over, she'll be gone."

Jackson picked up a washcloth. "She might not leav—"

The door to the basement opened, and the woman they were all talking about emerged. The silence was immediate and telling.

Eden's brow wrinkled, then smoothed out. "Don't worry, I'm grabbing an extra controller from Raven's room and heading back downstairs. Go ahead and continue talking about me, if you wish."

Lilith laughed, admiring the other woman's brazenness. Eden smiled at her before leaving the kitchen.

Her brief appearance effectively ended the topic. And Lilith, Asher, Hope, and Jackson joked, talked, and had an all-around good time while getting everything cleared away.

As Lilith filled the last container with leftovers, Asher came up behind her and rested his chin on her shoulder. "We're almost finished, so why don't you get a cup of coffee and relax with everyone in the living room? I heard my mom mention getting out cards for a game of Euchre."

"I notice you didn't include me," Hope joked.

"Or me," Jackson added.

"Neither of you is my girlfriend," Asher replied.

Hope sauntered next to him. "No, but I am the sister who offered to have your girls over for a slumber party, giving you all night and morning with your woman."

"You make a good point," Asher agreed. "You can go. I'm sure Jackson won't mind picking up your slack."

"Uh, yeah, I do," the other man groaned. "I ate so much. I don't want to even look at food."

"You and Hope go rest," Lilith said. "Asher and I will finish. I need to move, or I'll go into a turkey coma."

"Will everyone please stop mentioning food? Just talking about it makes my belly hurt," Hope groaned.

"Not even dessert?" Asher asked. "I made my pumpkin pie."

Lilith laughed as Hope clutched her middle. "Are you trying to make me explode?"

"You don't have to eat it."

"Let's not get crazy." Hope rested against the counter, and after a couple of ticks of silence, she hedged, "About Jackson and me leaving..."

Asher shoved her playfully toward the living room. "Go ahead. Leave. We're almost done anyway. Lilith and I will get dessert ready."

"Thanks." Hope tugged Jackson's shirt sleeve. "Let's get out of here before they change their minds."

Asher removed the tinfoil from his pumpkin pie, setting it between Lilith's homemade chocolate-chip cookies and the baklava from Tate's favorite Middle Eastern restaurant.

"There are so many sweets. We also have Jackson's apple pie and Hope's cupcakes," Lilith sighed. She'd overindulged at dinner, yet her taste buds were salivating to try everything.

"Don't forget my mom's banana cream pie. And I'm definitely having a glass of that whiskey your dad brought." He sighed. "Oh, and Eden brought flan. I have to try that."

Lilith tucked into his side. It was becoming her favorite spot. He wrapped an arm around her waist. She ran a finger along the counter where most of the desserts. "I'll be stuffed worse than the turkey before dinner. I'm won't be able to climb the stairs to your bedroom."

"We'll have the whole night and house together." His hand drifted to her ass and squeezed. "We can work off our calories and lethargy with a slow, naked workout in any of the rooms."

"That sounds fantastic." She nuzzled into him, yawning. "Let's hope I don't fall asleep first. I swear, there is something in turkey that makes me sleepy."

"If you do, I don't mind. I'm a happy man no matter how this evening ends because I get to spend the entire night with you." He kissed her temple, working his way to her lips. "Plus, there's always the morning for naked fun."

"True." She twisted, facing him and looping her arms around his neck, giddy with having him all night. That had only happened once since her move to the condo. "I slept so good during our last slumber party. I don't know if it was because you wore me out or if it was having you next to me all night."

"Hard to say. You're an energetic and wanton woman. Keeping up with you takes a lot of stamina."

Her cheeks flushed pink. "Is it too much? I get lost in your touch. It makes me so—"

He waggled his eyebrows. "Turned-on, horny, lusty?"

She buried her face into his chest. "Yes."

"I love it, and it will never be too much." He hugged her. "Have you talked with Marshall about Chloe's Christmas vacation?"

The coffee finished percolating, its hiss filling the quiet kitchen. Lilith stepped from his embrace, already missing it. She removed the carafe from the warming plate, setting it on the tray with cream and sugar.

"I did," she said, filling a mug and tasting it. She moaned in appreciation before offering it to him.

Thanking her, he took a sip, then said, "And…"

"Sorry." She smiled. "The tasty caffeine distracted me."

He took the hint, passing her the mug. She smiled before bringing it to her lips.

After swallowing, she continued, "Marshall wants to pick her up on Christmas day and take her to his family, have her stay a night or two. After, he's going to Vegas, so I get her for the rest of her break."

"What do you think of going up north with the girls? My friend, Ryan Green, has a cabin at Boyne Mountain. We could go skiing. Visit Tahquamenon Falls. Those sorts of things."

All the recently eaten food hardened in her stomach, even as her heart danced. A vacation was what serious couples did together.

But it would be fun—she should focus on the pleasure, not the possibility of pain. Although, as she entertained the idea, her dad's words came back about her rushing into things with Asher.

"What about Eden?" she asked. "Does she have any plans with Raven?"

Asher blinked. "Huh, I don't know. I'm not used to having to take her into account. I didn't ask. Anyway, for Raven, I'll invite her to Christmas Eve or the morning of."

Lilith dropped her gaze, focusing on her mug.

He gripped her chin gently. "Do you not like her being here?"

She ran her finger around the rim of their mug, considering his question. "I wouldn't say I dislike it. I'd never ask you not to invite her." *Crap*. That wasn't her call to make. "Wait, that came out wrong. I, um, mean. Sorry. I understand I don't get a say in who you invite into your home for the holidays. I overstepped. I apologize."

Asher kissed her, then said, "You're my girlfriend. You're important to me. You have a say, love."

His kind words soothed the pain her own had caused. "Thank you, but what I'd meant to say is it feels weird because I couldn't imagine spending any of my holidays with Marshall. When he and I are in the same room, we suffocate every ounce of good cheer."

"Maybe it's different because I don't have much of a history with Eden." He shrugged. "Good or bad."

Lilith cocked a brow and took a sip of coffee. "You two have a child together."

"Yeah, but we didn't raise her together. Eden lived on the other side of the US. When we talked or she visited, all conversations revolved around Raven. Since she moved to Michigan, it's different, but I wouldn't call her my BFF." He chuckled, kissing Lilith on the nose. "Anyway, you didn't answer me. What do you think of a winter getaway up north?"

After another long beat of loaded silence, she threw aside worries, embracing her desire. She handed him the mug and said, "Sure. It'll be fun."

Asher set the coffee on the counter. He picked her up, spinning her around. "You'll love it. So will the kids. There is a shit-ton to do. The four of us will have such a great time!"

Her heart pounded so hard that the pulse thudded in her ears. She wasn't sure if it was in fear or exhilaration.

CHAPTER THIRTY-EIGHT

Christmas had been the usual mixture of stress and splendor; family, friends, and fun. Lilith had even come to his place after Chloe left with Marshall, staying for dinner and the night. However, the real gift he'd been anticipating had finally arrived this morning—vacationing with Lilith and their girls.

Marshall had dropped Chloe off later than promised, but they'd managed to get organized and on the road by early afternoon. Soft snow fell the entire five-hour drive to Boyne Mountain. The scenery flying by their window was a winter wonderland, and inside his jeep was just as perfect. They laughed, teased, played road-trip games, and argued over the music—like a real family.

He'd always loved his life, but this—with Lilith and Chloe was something else. Down to his soul, he wanted this to be his life all the time, forever. And the forever thoughts didn't even scare him.

"Wow! This place is great," Chloe gushed as Asher parked in the driveway.

"It is," Raven opened her back passenger door, running toward the cabin. "Come on! Let's check it out!"

Asher had to agree. Ryan's A-Frame cabin was damn sweet. His carpenter's critical eye took in the redwood siding and the black metal roof that nearly touched the ground. This home was built with love, care, and skill.

"Let's get the bags later," Lilith said, leaning forward in her seat and gazing at the house. "I want to see the inside as much as the girls."

Grabbing the house key from the truck's center console, he said, "Let's go."

Soon as they were inside, the girls ran up the stairs to the loft. He and Lilith stayed on the main floor. He ignored the kitchen to his right and the bedroom and bathroom behind him. The living room facing the ski slopes held his attention. It boasted floor-to-ceiling windows, arching all the way to the peaked ceiling. In front of him were snow-covered hills with skiers dashing and darting down the slopes. Its edges were scattered with different pines and other trees bare of leaves. It was postcard beautiful.

Lilith pointed to the hallway under the loft. "I'm going to check out the rest of the place."

He nodded, going in the opposite direction. Beyond a set of glass doors, under a foot of snow, sat a good-sized deck with built-in benches surrounding a large firepit. During the day, it was the perfect path to the resort's slopes. At night, it'd be ideal for relaxing and stargazing.

"Dad! It's so cool up here. Come check it out," Raven called.

He turned to find her leaning over the waist-high railing. His heart skipped a few beats.

"Step back, please," he said, holding up both his hands.

She rolled her eyes but did as he asked. He took the stairs two at a time and found the girls lying on a king-size bed in the center of the room. Past them was a window he'd seen when pulling up to the driveway. From this angle, the sunset's blues, pinks, and yellows were visible above the treetops.

Staring at the stunning colors, he nearly missed the conversation between the girls, but the words "bed" and "sides" caught his attention. "What are you two chatting about?" he asked, turning them.

"Which side we'll sleep on," Chloe answered from her spot sprawled on the patchwork quilt.

"You two aren't sharing a room," he said. "Raven, you're with me."

Disappointment clouded their smiles. He wasn't thrilled either, but he and Lilith didn't think this trip was when they should start sharing a room. On the rare occasion she and Chloe visited when renters were at their house, she slept in the guest room. Well, kind of. She'd sneak into his bedroom after the girls were asleep, returning to the guest room in the early morning.

Raven got off the bed, slamming her hands on her hips. "I don't want to share a room with you." Guilt crept into her eyes. "No offense."

Asher chuckled. "Why do people say that when they know their words are going to offend?"

His daughter shrugged. "I dunno. To soften the blow?"

"It doesn't work."

"Dad," she whined, "part of this trip's fun is getting to have a sleepover with my best friend every night."

He hesitated because, damn it, he wanted to have his own slumber party with Lilith.

As if sensing him wavering, Raven persisted. "Please, I swear, we won't stay up all night." She smirked. "Or tell Grandma you shared a room with Lilith."

Asher snorted. "What's she going to do, ground me?"

Raven looked at Chloe. "He says that now, acts tough, because she isn't here."

Chuckling, he stepped closer, looming over his daughter. "Maybe. But remember, you live with me, and I'll ground you until you're grandma's age if you ever share a room with a boy."

"Eew." Raven shivered. "Fine with me. Boys are gross."

"Damn. First, you don't want to share a room with me, and now you call me gross." He clutched his chest as if in pain.

Raven giggled. "You're not a boy. You're a dad."

"I'm leaving. My ego can't take any more," he joked.

As he started for the stairs, the girls asked if he'd let them stay in the loft together. He told them he'd talk with Lilith.

Making his way to the main floor, he wondered how much the girls knew about sex. Raven had begun asking questions lately about what made a person want to be in a relationship or only be friends. He definitely couldn't say the main difference was wanting to have hot, sweaty, fantastic sex with that person.

He called to Lilith, but she didn't answer. She wasn't in the kitchen or living room, so he made his way down the narrow hallway. She was in the other bedroom, staring at the bed. It was a four-poster of a sort. He couldn't blame her fixation. It was a piece of art.

The triangle shape of the house had the outer wall slanted in at a steep angle. The bed's poles were built into the ceiling, so their length depended on the roof's pitch. The wood had been left in its original form, sanded, and polished into a smooth shine. The final result was a tree that seemed to have magically grown into the shape of a bed. It reminded him of Gaudi's artwork.

"Wow," he mumbled.

"Yeah, my thoughts exactly," Lilith replied. "I call dibs on this room."

Asher embraced her from behind, kissing the side of her head. "Works for me. The girls claimed the loft."

She turned slightly. "As in them together? Us together?"

He nodded. "What do you think? They begged, giving me those big imploring eyes."

Something shifted, lightened. He was used to having all parenting concerns solely on his shoulders. Talking with Lilith about them was an unexpected bonus.

She laughed. "I know the look. It is hard to resist."

"I agree. Especially when I want the same thing. I say, let them have their slumber party, and we'll have ours." He gripped her waist, bringing her against him. "We'll have lots of fun."

"I don't doubt it. I mean, look at that bed."

Something in her tone made him pause. "What about it?"

Lilith's cheeks and neck flushed bright red. *Huh*. Now she had all his attention.

Besides its unique design, he tried to find the difference between the ones they had in their homes.

Oh. Anticipation trickled low in his stomach.

"You want me to tie you up?" he whispered in her ear.

"Um. Something like that," she mumbled.

Something like that?

"Mom," Chloe called. "Come see this!"

"I better go." Lilith nearly ran from him.

Asher replayed her words. He dropped onto the bed. *Holy shit.*

She wanted to tie *him* up.

His automatic response was, "hell no." He'd played with light bondage before, but he was always in charge. He'd never handed over the control.

Running his tongue along the back of his teeth, he tasted the idea over in his mind and found he relished it. He trusted her more than any woman he'd ever been with, and her taking charge would be hot. He wanted to discover where she'd take it.

Desire pooled low in him, picturing her playing, finding her pleasure, and taking it. He pressed his palm in his rapidly growing hard-on. Yeah, he liked the idea a lot.

CHAPTER THIRTY-NINE

Raven and Chloe were outside on the patio. Each of them held a shovel in one hand and waved for Lilith to come out with the other. She opened the glass door, and winter kissed her exposed, flushed face.

Pulling her thick sweater tighter, she asked, "What are you two doing?"

"Cleaning off the patio," Chloe said.

"I see that, but why?"

"There's a firepit." Chloe pointed to something covered in the patio's center, then to a neat pile of stacked wood in the far corner. "It'd be fun to sit around it tonight."

Comfy warmth infused Lilith. She hadn't relaxed around a winter fire in years.

"That would be fun. Is there another shovel? I'll help."

"There's a broom next to the ski rack," Raven said. "You could use it to get the last of the snow off. Push it over the side."

"Good idea," Lilith agreed. "I'll go get it. Give me a few minutes."

Like a wuss, she scrambled into her coat, boots, hat, and gloves, lightning quick. She wanted to be outside before Asher left the bedroom, needing to put time between him and her embarrassing admission.

She and the girls made fast work of the patio. By the time he stepped onto it, they'd cleared snow from half of it. They told him their idea, and he was all for it, even offering to run into town to get stuff for s'mores. The girls suggested hotdogs. He agreed and kissed Lilith before leaving.

He returned an hour or so later with two large cloth bags of groceries and four roasting sticks. While he'd shopped, Lilith built a roaring fire in the pit and managed to throw together a healthy dinner..

Asher took an offered sandwich, thanking her. He propped a hip against the kitchen counter, looking toward the patio. "I'm impressed. That's a nice fire." Taking a bite of his food, he moaned. "Damn, this is good."

She warmed with his double praise. "The secret is in the sauce: mayo, garlic, and basil. As for the fire, my dad taught me. He loved having them every weekend the weather permitted. Tate and I are both experts at building and putting them out."

The girls came in from outside and rummaged through the bags. Raven found the pack of hotdogs and held them up in victory. "Got 'em."

"You got the savory. I got the sweet," Chloe said, removing the chocolate bars, marshmallows, and graham crackers from the other bag.

Lilith eyed her daughter. "Sweet and savory, huh?"

Chloe gave a one-shoulder shrug. "I heard it on the cooking show you had on the TV last week."

Raven grabbed the roasting sticks and asked, "Can we get started?"

"Sure, go ahead. We," Asher said, pointing between him and Lilith, "will clean up here, then be out."

Her stomach dipped. Would he mention her earlier admission? She schooled a neutral expression as her heart hammered.

As the patio door shut, he moved to the sink and began loading the dishwasher. "I hope you don't mind. I signed them up for a day of ski lessons for tomorrow. They have to be at the lodge at nine." He nodded with his chin. "It's at the bottom of this hill."

"No, that's perfect. Most of our Colorado ski trips were when Chloe was practically a toddler. I'm sure she could use a refresher course."

"It has been a few years for Raven too. Lately, I've gone with friends. When she was eight, she had a bad fall and ever since hasn't wanted to go. Having Chloe to ski with must have changed her mind." He closed the dishwasher. "I figure a day with an instructor will help."

Lilith finished wiping off the table and counters, nodding in agreement. "Want to head outside?" She went to the door, sliding her feet into her boots.

"Yup. I'll meet you there. I need to get something from the car."

"Did you not unload our bags? Do you need help?"

"Um, no. I got those when you were cleaning off the deck. I forgot something else." He turned in the direction of the driveway. *Were his cheeks pink?*

Whatever he was up to, she didn't have the courage to ask. She'd used it all earlier, hinting at her desires.

She let go of her curiosity and said, "I'll meet you at the fire."

CHAPTER FORTY

The low murmur of the girls and Asher's deep voice woke Lilith. The warmth of the down comforter and last night's late hours lulled her to that sweet spot between sleep and wakefulness. As she considered which way to go, a door clicked shut, followed by absolute silence. Asher must be taking the girls to their ski lessons.

The scent of coffee made its way into her bedroom. She threw back the covers and went to the bathroom to use it and brush her teeth. Then grabbed her laptop and shuffled to the kitchen. Memories of last night's evening under the stars and late hours in Asher's arms added a bounce to her step.

She was standing at the kitchen counter, sipping on her coffee and filling in a form on her laptop, when Asher returned. He came up behind her, kissing her cheek with cold lips. He smelled of snow, soap, and clean man. It was a heady combination.

He must have looked at her computer screen because he asked, "Are you thinking of taking courses?" he asked.

She nodded. "My savings are dwindling. I've been researching jobs that suit me. I think I'd like bookkeeping."

"You don't get alimony from Marshall?"

"I didn't ask for it."

"Why not? Doesn't he want to make sure you and Chloe are secure and safe?"

Annoyance tiptoed through her. It was nice Asher cared and worried about them, but she could take care of her daughter. "I don't need or want his money. Plus, it's not like I'm destitute. I have the lake house rental, and I can work while she's at school."

"True," he conceded. "Also, you'd make a perfect bookkeeper. I've seen your rental ledger. It's impressive."

His compliment quelled her irritation. She clicked a button and then closed her laptop. "Thank you."

Turning, she wrapped her arms around him, her body humming at having the entire morning alone with him. Standing on her toes, she bit lightly on his neck. A soft moan escaped him, and he gripped her hips.

But a second later, he stepped back, taking her hand and entwining their fingers. "Come here."

He led her toward their bedroom. Once inside, he closed the door and told her to sit on the bed. At the dresser, he searched through one of his drawers, his back to her. When he turned, he had something balled in his hands. He set four neckties on her lap. Her gaze flew to his, her pulse thudding with such power it squeezed her throat. She could barely breathe, let alone speak.

"Yesterday, you hinted at something you wanted to try," he said, sitting next to her.

Her cheeks flushed hot. They had to be bright red. She wasn't sure if it was her inhibitions or nervous anticipation causing the blush.

"You'd try it?" she whispered.

"With you. Anything."

"But do you want to?" She stroked the silky fabric between her fingers. "It won't be fun if you're only doing this to make me happy."

He took her hand, a rolled tie unraveled, falling to the floor. They ignored it as he placed her palm on the zipper of his jeans. He was hard as granite.

"I trust you, and knowing you want to do this, you can see how it turns me on."

Warmth pooled between her thighs as her restless heart galloped. She'd gotten better about giving him cues regarding her wants and desires, but taking charge with no direction was completely different.

What if he was bored? Or didn't like it?

Her eyes stared blindly at the floor, her mind racing with everything she could do wrong.

She focused on the fallen tie lying next to her feet. It was bright green with a garish Santa smiling at her. She looked at the ones in her hands and laughed.

"These are hideous. Please tell me these aren't your favorite lucky ties."

He snorted. "No, I bought them last night when I went into town for supplies. I stopped at one of those ten dollar or less stores and grabbed four off the clearance rack, not paying attention to the designs."

He scooped up Santa, handing it to her. "I should have. These are fucking ugly," he said around his laughter.

Their easy banter eased her nervousness enough that she could speak. "Strip," she said.

He followed her order without a word.

She rested on the bed, propped on her elbows, enjoying the show. He peeled off his ski socks, then his Henley. Each thing removed revealed the work of art that was his body. Tight and powerful, with a delightful brushing of hair on his chest and an enticing trail leading into his jeans. Those came off next, as did his boxer briefs.

Her mouth watered to taste him. Still sitting, she gripped his waist, bringing him closer, kissing the length of his arousal lightly before taking him into her mouth. His fingers threaded into her hair as he groaned her name.

She caressed him with her hands and lips until his light touch became rougher and his breathing erratic. She pulled away with a final kiss.

His eyes were fully dilated, and his chest rose and fell with rapid breaths. She loved his desire for her. It made her bolder.

She ordered him to the center of the bed. Like before, he didn't hesitate, even placing his arms and legs in the position to be tied.

After removing her clothes, she fastened his one leg to each post at the end of the bed. Then she crawled up him, running her palms along his muscular legs and wrapping a hand around his erection.

She stroked him until he thrust his hips and cupped her breasts with his free hands. His attention on them was pure bliss but reminded her to finish her task.

"Tsk, tsk," she admonished and repositioned his arms, then scooted up his body to tie his wrists.

She hesitated above him, but before her insecurities took hold, she positioned a knee on either side of his head, lowering herself to his face. He immediately responded. His tongue swirled, and his lips sucked. Her legs shook at the onslaught of pleasure. She gripped the headboard, nails digging into the wood as her climax rushed at her in a matter of minutes.

When his touch became too much, she shifted to his chest, far from done. She wanted him to come apart at the same time as her and when she was calling the shots.

Now that she had the chance, she needed it like air.

Reaching behind, she began stroking him again. When he rocked in her tight fist, and his breathing became uneven, he grated, "Come here. Let me taste you again."

"Even tied up, you're bossy," she teased.

Refusing his command, she swung around, staying in the same area but facing the opposite direction. Then she gave him what he'd demanded while taking his erection into her mouth. She wanted him to drown in bliss, just like her.

He moaned, and it caressed her *everywhere*. For the second time, he drove her wild with his lips and tongue, and another orgasm exploded through her.

Her plans for taking it slow, playing with him, making him beg, evaporated, replaced by the need to have him inside her. She flipped around, facing him. Taking him inside her, she rode him roughly, prolonging her climax while making his detonate. He called her name through gritted teeth as he came, bucking wildly beneath her. They continued until every ounce of pleasure was taken and given.

Exhausted in the most delirious way, she fell onto him, loving the press of her body against his solid warmth. She nestled into him, breathing in his divine scent. They lay, bodies slick, as their heartbeats returned to normal.

"Love," he said quietly. "That was fucking amazing, but could you, um, untie me?"

Resting on her elbows, she smiled at him, satiation and satisfaction blanketing her. "I'd say you earned your freedom."

"Really? All I did was lay here, letting you do the fabulous, erotic work." He shook his wrists. "I take back what I said earlier. These are my lucky, favorite ties. I'm *never* throwing them out, and I'm willing to wear them whenever you want."

Untying him, she noticed red marks. Kissing them, she said, "I'm sorry."

Rubbing his wrists, he chuckled, bringing her against his side. "That was my fault. I yanked on them, forgetting about them when you had me coming so hard I saw stars."

Cuddling into him, she took a deep satisfied breath, tasting his words and the delicious glow from them. She'd taken control, and they'd *both* loved it.

Perhaps she could be strong in a relationship. Asher saw her differently than most men in her life. He could be pushy but wouldn't treat her as someone who had to be managed. She was safe with him. He could make her weak in the knees and needs while allowing her to be a self-reliant woman.

Running a hand up and down his chest, he closed his eyes, sighing. Contentment seeped into her, mixing with lethargic happiness. Her gaze traveled from his pleasure-giving mouth to her exploring hands, moving over his flat stomach. Going lower, she paused as her eyebrows rose.

"Already?" She gripped him gently as heat burned away her sleepiness.

He sucked in a breath, opening his eyes. "What can I say? Your touch is an aphrodisiac."

She rolled on top of him, kissing his perfect mouth. It went from sweet to carnal with a swipe of his tongue and a thrust of his hips.

"Do you need to rest?" he asked.

"After." She shifted, craving their connection, always wanting him—always needing him.

CHAPTER FORTY-ONE

Raven and Chloe tossed a snowball back and forth as they walked along the wide trail. Until one of them overshot their throw, and it sailed into the trees. "How much farther to the falls?" Chloe asked.

"According to the trail marker we just passed, the Upper Tahquamenon Falls is less than half a mile," Asher answered. "Why, are you sluggish after eating that gigantic pasty?"

"No way." As if to prove her point, she took off running.

"Wait up," shouted Raven.

Asher took Lilith's hand, sliding his gloved fingers between hers. "Well, I am. Could you roll me to the falls?"

She squeezed his hand, grinning. "Are you regretting finishing mine?"

"Yeah." He rubbed his stomach. "I might not be hungry for dinner tonight. Or breakfast tomorrow. Maybe even lunch."

They fell into a hushed silence. Everything around them was blanketed in white except for the peaks of greens from the pines, evergreens, and spruces. The only sound was the girls' laughter, the crunch of ice and snow under their feet, and the crash of water from the upper falls. It was a symphony to her ears and a delight to her eyes.

Coming around a soft bend, the enormous rust-colored falls came into view. Chloe and Raven were racing down the wooden stairs.

"Slow down," Asher called.

They grabbed the side rails but kept their pace. She and Asher paused at the top of the stairs, and she took in the stunning sight.

"Wow. This is a winter wonderland," he said.

"It's so beautiful. It almost doesn't seem real." Tahquamenon Falls were even prettier than Lilith remembered as a kid.

Chloe huffed back to the top, bent at the waist, breathing heavily. "Mom, can I borrow your camera?" she wheezed. "There are icicles bigger than me next to the falls!"

"Do you promise to wear the neck strap and *walk* down the stairs?" Lilith asked.

Her daughter's eye sparkled with excitement as she nodded. Lilith unzipped her coat, bringing out the camera. The three of them reached the viewing platform at the same time.

Raven was off to the side, farther from the falls, closer to the enormous icicles. They went to her. Chloe promised to let Raven use the camera after she finished taking her pictures, and they wandered off.

"It's nice how they don't argue much," Lilith said.

"Yeah," Asher agreed, raising his voice over the crash of the water. "She used to have this friend from school. Mandy was her name, I think. Whenever they got together, all those two did was fight. I never got why they hung out and was relieved when it ended."

They stopped at the railing, and she cuddled into his warmth. He put his arm around her, tucking her into his side.

"I love our little lakeside community, but this trip has reminded me of Michigan's rural beauty," Asher said, gazing at the falls. "You know, I've rarely traveled this far north. My dad has family in Oregon. So most of my childhood vacations were spent on the west coast."

"What about as an adult?" Lilith asked. "You mentioned skiing with Raven and also with your friends. Was it never in Michigan?"

Leaning on the railing, he brought her around to snuggle into his front. "We mostly went to Canada. In the British Columbia area. We'd go before or after visiting Oregon. We did ski once where we're staying now and another time at a place outside of Ironwood, but we never left the resort. At most, we'd drive a few miles to a restaurant or bar." He squeezed her waist. "What about you?"

"I was the opposite. I was either flying to Florida to visit my mom or taking camping trips with Dad all over Michigan and Ohio."

"You've never been out west?"

"No, but I've always wanted to go."

"It's beautiful. We should go this summer or the fall."

His words tingled through her—at his self-assurance they'd still be together as the seasons changed. Even though a small part of her was afraid to imagine it, she savored his certainty.

The girls had wandered closer, and after the two of them snapped at least a million photos each, Chloe said, "Mom, can we go to the car? My fingers are getting cold."

"That wouldn't happen if you stop taking them out of your mittens," Lilith replied.

"I have to or I can't take pictures."

"Spreaking of pretty photos. Did you want to watch the sunset on Lake Superior?" Asher asked. "If you do, that's another reason we should head out."

"Good call." Lilith took one last look at the falls before leaving them and his embrace.

Taking his hand, they climbed the stairs. At the top, Chloe hugged Lilith from behind, her head pressing into the middle of her back. "You're so warm, Mom." Fingers of ice gripped Lilith's stomach. She screeched, lurching forward.

Asher pulled her to his chest. "What's wrong?" he asked, wide-eyed.

"My own daughter." Lilith shook her head, trying not to smile.

Chloe innocently had her hands shoved in her coat pockets. She wore a guilty smile. "My fingers were icy. Sorry."

Asher chuckled. "I thought your mom saw a pack of wolves or a bear."

"Nearly as bad," Lilith muttered.

"I dunno," Asher said. "A little cold's not so bad."

"That's because you're a furnace. I swear, you run at a hotter temperature than the rest of us."

Chloe's face lit up. "Can I warm my hands under your coat?"

"Sure." He stopped her with a palm out. "But with the way your mom screamed, I'd like you to keep your icicle fingers above my thermal."

"Deal." She burrowed into his back, wrapping her arm around him and under his coat and sighing. "You *are* warm."

Asher took smaller steps, and Chloe kept pace with him. Raven ran ahead, knocking snow from low-hanging branches, seemingly immune to the cold.

"Are you having a nice time?" Lilith asked Chloe.

Cuddling closer into Asher, she met Lilith's gaze. "Yes. Raven makes the best sister-friend. And Asher is a great step-boyfriend-dad."

Lilith's heart tumbled, free-falling. Her choices and decisions crashed into her, along with her dad's words about shoving Chloe into an insta-family. Did she think Asher would be her stepdad? Lilith pulled on her scarf, finding it difficult to breathe.

What kind of message was she sending to her daughter? The last thing she wanted Chloe to believe was a woman couldn't be single and happy. Or independent.

"Well, you make a great step-friend-daughter," Asher replied, squeezing Chloe's arm that was under his coat.

Thankfully, he didn't look at Lilith. Her expression was probably stormy as her insides turned cold. She wrapped her hands around herself.

"Mom?"

"Hmm?" Lilith stared at the trail ahead of them.

"Can we stay another week? I don't want to leave tomorrow."

"Sorry, kiddo. Christmas vacation is nearly over. School begins on Monday. It's time to go home."

She considered asking if it was the activities or the four of them under one roof, playing house and family, that had her wishing they could stay longer. Never mind. Lilith didn't want to know.

The answer would battle with the question now running fevered, frantic circles inside her head—was she doing right by herself and her daughter?

CHAPTER FORTY-TWO

Entering his bedroom, Asher smiled. Lilith was in his bed, looking like a dream he wouldn't mind having. Her hair was in a messy bun, and she was staring at her laptop, worrying her bottom lip in concentration. Studious Lilith was sexy.

He got under the covers and kissed her neck. "I forgot to mark on my calendar that Raven has Monday off school. Any chance Chloe does too?" he asked.

Things had been hectic since their return from their Christmas trip up north, and they hadn't seen each other in three weeks. Finally getting a weekend together was fantastic, but it was already Saturday night. He wanted more time with Lilith. He was a greedy man when it came to her.

She tilted her head, giving him more access. "I wish, but no, she has school."

Disappointment blanketed him. "Will you leave tomorrow in the morning or afternoon?"

"I was thinking early evening. Chloe swears she has no homework." Lilith ran her fingers along his torso. "It might be weeks before we see each other again, so I want as much time with you as possible."

"Same." He kissed her favorite spot below her ear, then glanced at her computer. She'd been working on her bookkeeping homework. It reminded him of his good news. How had he forgotten? "Will you still be finished with your courses by the end of this month?"

She nodded. "If I can keep putting in the hours I have been, I will. Then I'll begin job hunting at the start of February. I'd like to work from home, but a part-time job in an office will get me experience. I think having it will help build trust and hopefully garner me freelance work."

"That isn't necessary," he said.

"What isn't?"

"Job hunting. You have a job at Crowley Construction."

When he'd seen her signing up for her classes when they were up north, the idea had come to him, and he quickly warmed to it. Hope took care of the books, but it was her least favorite task. And the income would offer Lilith a safety net. As she started her business, she wouldn't be forced to take any and all clients. His mind had kept circling back to her entering some creep's shady store or house, leering at her, licking his greedy lips.

"No," Lilith snapped, slamming shut her laptop and setting it on the night-stand.

Asher's smile fell. "Why not? Hope hates bookkeeping but hasn't found any-one she trusts. I thought you'd like the idea."

"I would have liked you to run it by me. Ask if I am interested. Not micro-man-age my life."

He sat up, gripping the back of his neck. "How is helping you micro-managing your life?"

"Because you didn't *ask* me first. You just went out and did it."

"But it's a perfect solution." His chest tightened. What was the big deal? "My construction company will give you the experience you need and you could do most of the work from home."

Lilith's nostrils flared. "Asher, I can manage my career without you stepping in and running it."

He held up his hand. "Fine, I'll tell my sister you aren't interested."

"I'll do it. I don't need you to talk for me." She shut off the bedside lamp and rolled on her side—facing away from him.

Shit. After tomorrow it could be weeks until they saw each other again. He couldn't let her leave with a rift between them. He rested a hand on her hip. "I'm sorry I upset you."

Lilith drew in a breath, then released it. "It's fine."

She twisted around and snuggled into his chest, running a palm over the worn cotton of his T-shirt. He brought her closer, loving how her soft body molded along his. He kissed her forehead, and she tipped her chin, offering her mouth. He claimed her lips without hesitation, maybe even with a little desperation.

They made love that was closer to fucking–as if she was having a difficult time letting go of her anger at him. There was no talking and not much foreplay. She rode him hard, focusing more on her pleasure than on them. He didn't stop her, let her release her frustrations and desires, but when she began to shake with her climax, he demanded, "Kiss me."

She did, and he devoured her moans and pleasure. After she came, he flipped her. On top, his unrelenting thrusts prolonged her orgasm while chasing his. He slammed into it, gritting his teeth to keep from shouting.

Staying on top of her, he ran his nose along her neck, then collarbone, waiting for the contentment that usually followed. However, it seemed his body was satiated but not his mind. Something was still off.

He shook his head. It was just the stress of being apart so much. "I want to turn back the clock. Go back to summer, when you were my neighbor."

"I'd be happy with returning to our vacation up north."

"Even better. I liked having you in my bed every night," he said.

"Mine is lonely too. And cold." She ran her fingers down his spine. "I miss your heat."

"Then you should stay in mine. All the time." They should forget this long-distance bullshit.

She pressed on his chest. "What do you mean?"

He shifted off of her but draped an arm over her waist. "Stay with me. I hate having you and Chloe two hours away. I worry about you two being alone out there."

Her brows slammed together. "I'm not helpless."

"I never said you were. But bad things happen to strong people all the time," he reasoned. "Plus, I miss you and Chloe. I'd love you both to move in."

"No. Absolutely not."

"Wow, no hesitation." He tried to keep his voice light, but she'd stung him, and his irritation leaked through. "Is it because you don't believe in living together unless we're married, or is it something else? Is it me?"

"I have nothing against it when it's other people. However, for myself, I worry about what example it would set for Chloe and Raven."

"You aren't some woman I just met. What they'd see is that two people who care for each other want to live together."

Rolling onto her back, Lilith didn't meet his gaze. "I disagree. It'd show them it's fine to rush headlong into a relationship without giving it the gravity it deserves."

"Rushing." Resting on his elbows, he studied her. "How are we rushing? We were friends for months before becoming lovers, and we've been a couple even longer."

"We've been together for eight months. People don't move in together after such a short time."

"They do, if they know they're right for each other." Lilith's wide, panicked eyes told him he should shut-the-fuck-up, and he clamped his mouth closed.

"To the kids, it hasn't been even three months." She slapped her leg through the comforter. "Hell, we haven't even said we love each other. So, yes, moving in seems a little impulsive."

"Do I need to say it? Fine. I love—"

She held up a hand. "Don't. You're saying it to win an argument. To get your way."

"No, I'm not." Aggravation crawled through him. "Is the timing the problem? Are you really worried about confusing the kids? Or are these excuses to keep me at a distance, at arm's-length?"

"I don't need an excuse," she said, her voice rising. "You knew going into this, I wouldn't be under the thumb of another man."

"Under my thumb?" he snarled. "I'm not Marshall. Have I ever not treated you like my equal? Ever behaved like him?"

Gathering the blankets around her like a shield, she quietly replied, "No."

"Then don't force his issues, vices, and sins on me." Asher sucked in a breath, letting it out through his nose. "Why are you so sure if we lived together things would change between us.?"

"Because you're smothering me!" she shouted.

He jerked as if slapped. "How?"

"Like this. I mentioned I miss you, and your solution is we movie in together. You see, I'm taking classes, you take it upon yourself to get me job. You keep jumping into my life, trying to solve all my problems."

What the fuck? "Isn't that what people do when they care about each other?" he nearly yelled.

Moisture gathered along her lashes, breaking Asher in half and cooling his anger.

"I love you," he admitted, even if she didn't want to hear it. "Why wouldn't I want to make your life safer, easier?"

"I don't want to be weak anymore, and you make me feel that way. I know a lot of this is my insecurities, my hang-ups, but you make them worse." Her words were a punch to his gut. "It's like you're afraid I'll break. I don't want to be treated like I'm some delicate porcelain doll. I want you to see my value, my strength."

He reached for her. "But I do, Lilith. I do."

"How can you? I'm not even sure I have it!" Her words came fast and hard like bullets, wounding him. "My life is a train wreck. I leave Marshall, and as I'm wondering how I'm going to survive on my own, you swoop to my rescue. You help me with my house, gave my daughter a best friend, hell, you found me friends. Show me how pleasurable sex can be, offer me a job, ask me to move in—"

He threw up his hands. "I don't understand why this makes me a bad person," he choked, finding it difficult to speak. Life seemed to be crashing and burning around him in a pile of confusion.

Tears fell from Lilith's lashes, and she didn't wipe them away. "You aren't, but you're suffocating the independence I swore I'd find. I need space to breathe."

He was gutted. How had he made her feel less than she was? Everything in him wanted to pull her close, into his arms where they were both safe, but that wasn't what she needed. "What do you want?" he asked.

"I think…"—she gulped in air— "I think I need to be alone. Away from you."

His stomach lurched as loss stole his breath. Her eyes pleaded for him to understand. He didn't, but he couldn't turn from her, and she fell into his arms. Her shoulders shook as her tears soaked him, breaking him apart.

"I'm sorry," she mumbled into his neck. "You don't deserve this—"

"Then don't do it."

"I have to," she whispered. "I can't lose myself in another relationship."

His throat and eyes burned as he held her. Everything in him screamed he had to protect her from this pain, but he couldn't—somehow, he was the cause of it.

He swallowed the millions of things he wanted to say to convince her not to leave him. His silence was shards of glass sliding down his throat; he let them cut him and held her until her sobs quieted, and she left his bed for the guest room.

CHAPTER FORTY-THREE

Asher tossed aside his book. Groaning, he rested his head against the back of the couch, rubbing his hands up and down his face. Reading was no match for his restless mind.

It had been nearly a month since Lilith left him, and while he kept busy with work, Raven, and friends, downtime was murder. During the quiet moments, he second-guessed everything. And these weekends, when she was right next door, it nearly killed him. He wanted to go to her house and convince her they were great together.

A heaviness crowded his chest, and he knocked at it absently with his knuckles. Cursing, he stood. He had to burn off his frustrations and disappointments. His punching bag called to him in the basement, but the snap of the cold winter air would be better. The burn in his lungs and the complete concentration required to run on the snow and ice would be perfect.

He found Raven in her room, nose glued to a game on her computer. "I'm going for a run," he said.

She waved a hand in acknowledgment but didn't look at him. He'd encouraged her to stay friends with Chloe, but she'd arrived with Lilith at their lake house this afternoon, yet Raven didn't ask to go over. He was pretty sure she blamed him for the growing distance between them and the loss of Lilith.

Which was fair. He blamed himself.

He was grabbing his outerwear from the foyer closet when the doorbell rang. Leaning back, he glanced through the door's glass and saw Eden. He wasn't surprised. She'd been coming around often, the three of them going out a lot. The distraction was great, but he wished he didn't need it.

"Were you leaving?" Eden asked, gazing at his hat and gloves.

He stepped aside, and she came in. "I was just going for a run. It can wait."

"I was dropping off papers to a colleague on your street, and I saw your car parked out front." She pointed at it. "I took a chance you'd be home."

He slid out of his shoes and tossed his winter gear back in the closet. "Raven's downstairs playing a new online game. I'll tell her you're here, but I hope you aren't in a hurry. She's getting her weekend fix of video games and asking anything of her during a match is next to impossible."

Eden studied him. "How did you become such a good dad?"

"Why? Because I let her binge on electronics on the weekend. According to her, I'd get the Father of the Year award if I let her do the same on weekdays," he chuckled.

"It's a million things, big and small. I've only been back here a short time, but it has been eye-opening. However, even before, when I was living out of state and talked with Raven on the phone, the things she'd say about you, it was obvious you're a great father." She paused, then smiled. "Who would have guessed?"

Asher laughed. "You act like I was a deviant back when we were dating."

"Well, you were on probation when we met," she teased.

He snorted. "Good point."

She play-punched his arm. "And from what I remember, you worked hard at your family's business, but outside, you were fearless with your fun, tipping on the point of recklessness."

He rubbed the scruff on his cheeks. "Yeah, that quality probably had something to do with me becoming a dad a month shy of my nineteenth birthday. I learned to curb it after Raven was born."

Eden quirked a brow. "She told me the summer before this past one, you and a few friends went kayaking over waterfalls."

Ah, yes. That trip to Washington had been fun. He smiled. "I wore a life jacket."

"When I first moved back here, didn't you have a broken leg from dirt biking with Jackson?"

"Fine," He shrugged. "I'm more cautious with love and lust."

"Speaking of that, is it true you and Lilith broke up?"

He nodded and stood, his skin too tight as regret pulsed through him. "I'll go get Raven."

Eden rested a hand on his arm. "I wanted to talk to you without her here first."

That snagged his attention. Hopefully, she wasn't leaving again. It would gut Raven. He nodded toward the living room. He returned to the couch, and she took a seat next to him.

"What's up?" he asked.

Her cheeks reddened, and she focused squarely on his shoulder. What in the world had her so flustered?

"Alright." She rubbed her hands up and down the thighs of her fitted slacks. "I know the timing is terrible, but I've already missed my chance once."

He rested his arms along the back of the couch, waiting her out. If she was the same as when they were dating, she'd take longer getting to the point if he pushed.

"What do you think about me, you, and Raven being a proper family?" she asked.

He froze in shock as confusion lanced through him. "What exactly do you mean?"

"For now, I mean merely the three of us doing stuff together."

What the hell?

"We already do that."

"Yes, but not as a couple."

Raven chose that moment to appear at the top of the stairs. Her gaze ping-ponged from him to Eden. "Mom?"

Christ. What had Raven heard?

"Hey, honey. I was down the street and wanted to stop by to see you. Ask how that science test went."

Raven's face cleared. "Your tutoring really helped." She began talking a mile a minute, lighting up the way she always did around her mother. And Eden's tender smile as she listened to her daughter touched him. They were happy together.

Was Eden's suggestion that crazy? He didn't feel any fire when he looked at her. The last of that had burnt out a long time ago.

However, what good was heat when it only left him cold? The last month proved he was shit at love and relationships. So why not leave love out of the relationship?

His feelings for Eden had shifted. Not in a romantic way, but his resentment had vanished. He could be her friend. Enjoy her company. Then Raven would have her wish and be truly happy.

Would that be enough for him?

CHAPTER FORTY-FOUR

Lilith double-checked the heating and cooling control panel. Yup, it was still blinking that the blower fan was the issue. Changing the heater's filter hadn't made a difference.

Going downstairs, she went inside Chloe's room. She was buried under three blankets. "Do you wish you'd stayed with Uncle Tate?" Lilith asked.

"No way. Then I couldn't see my best friend."

Lilith's heart twisted. They'd arrived yesterday, but Raven never showed up. Usually she was at their house before they were even out of the car.

"I texted her this morning," Chloe said.

"Texted her? She has a cellphone now?"

"You can text people from a phone or tablet using an app." Chloe rolled her eyes, muttering, "Old people."

"Hey, I'm not old," Lilith laughed.

Chloe grinned. "If you say so. Anyway, we're going ice skating when she shovels her driveway."

"I'm glad to hear it." Of course her brave daughter took the initiative to make sure she didn't lose her closest friend. Lilith leaned down, hugging Chloe, hoping to take in some of her strength. She needed it for when she talked to Asher. But first things first. "Wish me luck. I'm going to try to get our heat working."

"You'll fix it," Chloe said without an ounce of doubt in her voice.

"I appreciate your confidence. I hope I earn it." Lilith tapped on the bedroom's doorframe. "But you should head over there now, in case I blow up the house," she joked. Kind of.

Making her way to the utility room, she twisted the gas valve. Her gaze fell on the main water valve. She rubbed her sternum, her lungs and throat suddenly aching.

How had something so disastrous as a broken pipe that nearly flooded her kitchen become a happy memory? Although, at the moment, it hurt like frostbite.

After flipping the power switch, she removed the heater access panel. A flash of neon purple glowed from a little shelf that divided the unit's upper and lower half. She hunched at eye level and laughed. It was a hands-free vibrator.

She'd love to meet the naughty, creative Easter bunny who had left these gifts throughout her house. They'd probably make a great friend. Picking it up with her thumb and index finger, she laughed harder. Change the color and a little of the style, and it would be a twin to the one she'd bought in the fall. Did it also have an app that lets a partner control the setting long-distance?

Damn. She and Asher had had some delightful long-distance phone conversations with that toy. Lilith sighed, muttering, "Great. Now I'm nervous, sad, and horny."

Tossing the vibrator into a nearby garbage can, she returned her attention to the heater. Using the non-contact voltage tester—no half-assing this time—she doubled checked the power.

Nothing dinged. She was good to go. After taking a picture with her phone, she put on safety gloves, then removed the motor wires and control panel. She slid out the blower, setting it on its side.

Leaning close to it, a burst of relief popped in her. Could it be this easy? A tiny piece from a blade had fallen off and was stuck between another one. She removed it, then reassembled the unit. Turning back on the gas and electricity, she ran upstairs to the control panel and hit power.

The heater clicked, hummed, and came to life. Lilith whooped and did a little dance. She'd done it!

She grabbed her cell to call Asher, then stilled, considering her urge. There was nothing she needed from him. She could fix things, or herself, without him. No, the natural urge to speak to him was because she wanted to celebrate this victory, all her victories, with him.

Her partner, her lover. The man she loved.

She rested against the wall, requiring a solid surface as the truth of her feelings sunk into her. She loved him, but her doubts had made her walk away. Yes, he wanted to protect and shelter her, sometimes too much, but she was strong enough to push back.

And with her fears fading, she understood that even with his overprotective ways, he'd always viewed her as an equal, as strong. More importantly, she saw herself this way. He would listen to her. They could work through anything together with love and respect.

She glanced toward her front door. How much longer would she run, letting uncertainty rule her? Embracing the life she wanted was risky. Love could break her heart again, but that was better than letting it freeze in the icy grip of fears, what-ifs, and doubts.

The life she wanted was with Asher.

CHAPTER FORTY-FIVE

"**R**eady to help me with the driveway?" Asher asked Raven when she appeared at the top step from the lower level of their house.

He started toward the door, but Raven stopped in from of him. "Hey, um, Dad, could we talk?She bounced from foot to foot. Her gaze was darting everywhere.

Uh-oh. This couldn't be good. "Did you fail your history test? The one I told you to study more, but you blew me off, saying you were ready?"

Raven jutted her chin. "Uh, no. I got ninety-five percent on it, thank you very much."

"That's great. I'm proud of you." He sat on the couch and motioned for her to do the same "What's up?"

"So, um, the other day I heard you talking with Mom." She held her hands in a "hold-on" gesture. "I swear I wasn't eavesdropping. You two sounded serious. I didn't want to interrupt, so I waited on the stairs."

"Instead of leaving, where you couldn't hear us?" He teased as his heart picked up its pace.

She blushed. "Well, you were talking about me. Sort of."

Shit. She'd heard.

Every time he considered the idea, misery suffocated him, like his heart was shriveling, dying. It felt wrong. But he wanted to give Raven the family she desired and deserved.

He had to choose—his daughter's happiness or his own. It was the first time they weren't one and the same. "Raven—"

"Don't do it," she blurted.

His pulse jolted and skittered, racing to his heart. "You don't want the three of us to be a family?"

She pulled the zipper on her hoodie, running it up and down so fast it was a blur. "I did, but that was because I figured if you guys got back together she'd stay."

Her words cut him. No kid should have to worry about a parent leaving. He opened his mouth to say something. What, he had no idea.

It wasn't necessary. Raven wasn't done talking. "And I get you want me happy. Safe." She rolled her eyes at his often-repeated word. "But what about you?"

"What about me? I'm your parent. Your wellbeing comes first."

She groaned and stomped a foot. "You can't control my happiness. It makes me unhappy when you try."

He jerked, her words knocking into him. He had enough insight about himself to understand his need to protect stemmed from Hope's assault. Hell, when he'd been hauled off in handcuffs and Hope was silently crying into Jackson's chest, Asher had sworn nothing bad would ever touch her—anyone he loved—again.

However, he'd never considered the possibility that his protection might push away those her loved. It could happen with Raven. It had already happened with Lilith.

As if reading his mind, Raven said, "Besides, you're supposed to be with Lilith."

He couldn't help smiling. "Oh, am I?"

"Yeah." She waved a hand. "It's like she said about her parents. Our hearts pick. And she has your heart."

That was true, but she might not want it. She had disappeared into herself close to a month ago. Each day, her absence felt less and less temporary.

"That's it," Raven stood. "That's all I wanted to say. I'm cool with you and Mom just being friends. I want you to be happy, but that's probably not with Mom." In complete adolescent fashion, she crossed her eyes, stuck out her tongue, and laughed. "Now, let's get to shoveling. I'm meeting with Chloe after, to go ice skating. Then Aunt Hope is taking us to the movies."

"Okay. Wait..." he scratched his head. His mind was scattered like the snow falling outside but had he forgotten his sister was coming over, and they had plans?

"You're not going senile." Raven smirked. "Yet. Aunt Hope called right before I came up here to talk to you."

"What? I don't get an invite?" The thought of spending the evening alone with his thoughts held little appeal.

Raven shrugged into her winter coat. "Sorry, girl's night."

He could call the guys. Go to The Hill. He put on his winter gear and followed his daughter outside. He looked toward Lilith's house and her car in the driveway. Or he could go to her place.

Maybe if he explained his past, why he was so overprotective, she'd understand. Then again, it might make her run further from him. He tugged his lips between his teeth. Would talking help or hurt? Did she need more time?

He shoved his hat on his head. Fuck. He didn't know.

CHAPTER FORTY-SIX

Asher watched Raven run up the steps to Lilith's house and barge in as if she belonged there. He also noticed Hope's car was now parked over there. It looked like everyone but him was invited to the movies.

Fuck it, he wouldn't sit home and sulk. He sent a quick text to Jackson, then headed toward his snowmobile, parked next to his garage. As he drove it around, he caught sight of Lilith on her porch.

She smiled, waving at him. Damn, he missed that smile. Something close to happiness warmed his chilly heart. He pulled onto her snowy lawn, stopping next to her. "Want to go for a quick ride?"

A gust of wind pushed against his back and lifted the hair peeking from her hat. She shivered, tugging it further down her forehead. "Sure."

A nervous flutter beat against his ribcage as he patted the seat behind him. "Have you ever been on one?"

"Yes, but not since I was a kid." Her gaze drifted to the cold blue sky, seeming lost in the happy childhood memories. "It was magical."

"Do you want to relive the adventure?" he asked as she straddled the bench seat behind him.

"What do you mean?"

"Let me get us out of the neighborhood, then you take over driving."

"That'd be fantastic. Thank you." She wrapped her arms around his waist, tucking her head against his back, and sighed.

It sounded relaxed, even content. Or was that wishful thinking?

They glided onto the snow-covered road, past houses until they stopped at the end of their street. He made a right onto the ice and cut the engine. "Your turn."

They switched spots, and soon as his gloved hands gripped her waist, they shot forward. He grunted, clutching her tighter, not wanting to fall off. Seconds later, she braked hard. He slammed into her, pushing her forward.

"Sorry. Did you hit the handlebar?" he asked.

"Nope. I'm good. I'll try to be gentler this time."

He laughed, not minding in the least bit. Her body was heaven against his, and he spoke without thinking. "I don't mind, and I love having an excuse to hold you tight."

"Now you're tempting me to continue driving recklessly," she said in a flirty tone that heated him in places more important than his toes and fingers.

"In that case, I won't let go until you ask," he said, a breath away from her cheek, soaking in her soft scent.

She eased the snowmobile's massive skis onto the solid lake. "Ready?"

"Yup. Go for it."

She did, and her whoops of delight were music to his ears. She kept it at near top speed until a gentle, sweeping bend on the lake took them to the section near Hope's house. There they were greeted with the shifting purples, pinks, and blues of a spectacular sunset.

Braking, she asked, "Do you mind if we stop to watch it go down?"

"I was going to suggest it." He'd stretch his time with her until forever, if possible.

After cutting the engine, they shifted to face the lowering sun. They sat in frozen silence as the sun dipped below the horizon, leaving only a soft purple glow. The bold colors and eerie boomerang echoes of the ice, popping and pinging as it shifted, gave the illusion they were alone on a new planet.

He turned from the sky to study her. Her hat was low, covering most of her forehead and ears, her red hair peeking out. The side profile showcased her long lashes, enticing mouth, and straight nose. He'd missed her beautiful face, soft body, quick mind, and perfect heart.

She faced him. Her focus fell to his lips, staying a few beats. When her eyes met his, they reflected determination and desire. She brushed her lips over his. He froze for half a second, then went all in, pressing his mouth to hers with a low, hungry growl. She opened for him, and his tongue tangled with hers, warming him everywhere.

His cell chimed, and reality crashed around him. He moved away to check it wasn't Raven, and get himself under control. The message was from Jackson. Asher didn't reply but also didn't return to Lilith.

He wanted what she might be offering too badly to continue without knowing if she'd made up her mind about them. Searching her face, he looked for the answers to about a million questions. When he didn't find them, he asked the simplest. "What was that for?"

"I missed you." Her gaze traveled over his face. "Should I not have kissed you?"

"Depends. What does it mean? This waiting, not knowing, is purgatory."

And he'd wait a hundred years if that's what she needed, but he wouldn't survive her kissing or making love to him and then walking away. He couldn't return to the grey area where they were friends and lovers. Not when she owned all of his heart.

"I want you back," she whispered. "I was coming over to talk to you when you pulled on this." She patted the snowmobile.

A fierce gust of wind swirled around them, hitting them with ice and snow. Lilith shivered violently in his arms. His question and confessions would have to wait.

"Let's continue this inside a house," he said.

She flexed her fingers. "Will you drive home? My hands are getting cold."

Guilt tugged at him for not noticing, but he stopped himself from commenting. After his talk with Raven, he'd decided to chill–to stop trying to micro-manage people's safety. To trust they could care for themselves.

"Sure," he said, switching seats with her.

He turned on the engine, and her arms slid around him. She held him tight, and it was like a missing piece within him was found.

CHAPTER FORTY-SEVEN

Asher parked the snowmobile in its place next to the garage. As they got off, Lilith suggested, "Let's go to my house. I have soup to thaw us out."

"Sounds good to me." He slid his gloved hand into hers. It was probably her imagination, but his grip warmed her.

Once inside and out of their outdoor gear, she led him to the kitchen. Turning on the stove, she laughed. Earlier, she'd called Hope, asking if she'd take the girls to the movies. Lilith had wanted a good chunk of time alone to talk with Asher. She'd sweetened the last-minute request by offering Hope homemade chicken noodle soup. She'd had taken most of it.

Asher sat at the kitchen table, and she joined him. Tapping her nails on the wood surface, she asked, "Can I unload on you?"

"Of course." He squared his shoulders as if bracing for punches.

She'd done that to him. Guilt and shame clawed at her heart.

Taking a deep breath, she began. "I'd convinced myself I had to be alone. To do things without your support in order to truly be strong and independent. I had this stupid idea that depending on you would lead to dependency, and you'd exploit it."

His gentle eyes were laced with hurt. "Do you still believe this?"

"No. I know in my heart you aren't that kind of man."

He took her hand, kissing her knuckles. "But I did smother you with my fears."

Surprise pinged in Lilith's chest. Asher seemed fearless. "What are you afraid of?"

"Of people I love getting hurt when I could have protected them, prevented their pain."

"Do you think I am weak? Helpless?"

"Not at all, but bad things happen to strong people all the time." His shoulders slumped. "I need to tell you something and not because I'm justifying my actions, but so you understand my overprotectiveness has nothing to do with you being a competent and capable woman. This is my demon, and it might be one you don't want."

His defeated posture and tone had alarm bells clanging through her. She almost didn't want to hear what he had to say, didn't want to risk all they could have together.

That was the old Lilith. This one was strong enough to stay.

"Go on. I'm listening," she said.

"When I was sixteen, I was convicted of involuntary manslaughter for accidentally killing a kid in my high school."

Her mind froze on the word 'kill', then began to race with possibilities and fears. She couldn't connect sweet, kind Asher with a killer.

Before panic could take over, she asked, "What happened?"

"I was at a party with Hope and Jackson. It was a wild one, with lots of alcohol and drugs, and we lost each other for a while. Later, I found Jackson, but not Hope. Those two were dating back then and had gotten into a fight. She'd stomped off. He let her cool off, but then couldn't find her. We split up to search again. He went outside, I went through the house." Asher let go of her hand and grabbed the saltshaker from its stand at the center of the table. He held it so tight the bones in his knuckles strained against his skin. "I found her in the basement on a broken futon with a fucking scumbag from our high school on top of her. She was sobbing, telling him to stop. He was ignoring her. Using her. I didn't think. I acted, yanking him off her by his hair. When he was upright, I hit him with everything in me. He fell back, hitting his head on the corner of an old TV stand, then the concrete. He died before the cops and ambulance arrived."

Lilith's vision blurred, and her chest constricted. She couldn't hold in her tears and didn't try. No wonder he held those he cared for too tightly. He's seen the ugliness the world had to offer at such a young age, and he was trying to keep it from ever touching those he loved again.

She stood and gently pressed his shoulder. He scooted his chair, giving her room, and she crawled onto his lap, wrapping her arms around him.

"I'm sorry. For you and Hope."

He held her tight. "Forget me. Juvie and probation were nothing compared to my sister's hell. She struggled for a long time. I don't want anyone I care about to suffer like that, so I overstep, playing the knight, even knowing the women in my life don't need one."

For a time, they were quiet, holding each other. Then a question occurred to Lilith. "Given the situation, why weren't you acquitted?"

He shrugged. "It was just the fou—three of us in the room. The prosecutor was a dick. He'd convinced the jury that I lost it when I saw Hope and what had happened was no accident." Leaning back, he looked at Lilith. "And I'll be honest. Seeing her helpless and being used by that fucking predator, that's what haunts me. Not the crack of his head hitting the cement floor or his dead eyes."

She couldn't fault him. Ending a life had to leave scars, but at least no one had to worry about being in Hope's place. Not with that guy, anyway.

"I wish you would have told me this sooner." She sighed, remorse heavy in her heart.

"I hate talking about it. People either look at me with pity or fear."

"But I'd made so many wrong assumptions about you. I wish I hadn't viewed you through the eyes of my last relationship. I thought you were trying to control me, that you didn't trust me—like my ex. I didn't see a man wrestling with monsters that had nothing to do with me."

"Now knowing my past—hell, my lack of remorse—you don't feel that way about me?"

"No. Not at all. Neither your past nor our future scares me." She ran a hand up his chest, stopping at his heart. "Our separation made a few things crystal clear."

He tilted his head. "Such as?"

"I now understand the difference between being in love and loving the *idea* of it. I'd experienced the latter with Marshall. I have the first with you." She brushed her lips over his. "I needed some space to realize it. To learn to love and trust myself."

"And do you?" he asked.

"Yes. *Finally*. I also learned that being alone doesn't prove I'm strong." She chuckled. "Just that I'm hard-headed once I latch onto an idea."

He smiled. "You are one of the strongest women I know."

"I believe you," she said, loving how certain they both sounded.

He kissed her. It was soft and sweet.

"Asher, I love you." Her heart jumped and fluttered, light as the wings of a sparrow. "I want to be with you."

He cupped her cheeks. "I love you too. I have from almost the first day I met you."

This time she kissed him. It started out gentle, tasting of devotion and second chances, but she needed more.

She wanted all of him.

He must have felt the same because his lips turned hungry, and he stood, holding her bottom. She wrapped her legs around his waist, her mouth never leaving his, even when he stopped to turn off the stove. When they reached her bedroom, he laid her gently on the bed, his delicious weight covering her.

Slipping a hand under her sweater, he broke the kiss. "Do you want me to keep going?"

"Yes. God, yes."

She shifted, and he removed her top and bra, licking, nipping, and loving her breasts. Pleasure spread through her, her whole body humming.

Untucking his T-shirt, she tugged on the hem. He sat up, bracing his legs between her thighs, removing it and his sweater.

Sliding a hand up his flat stomach, she smoothed her palm over the light dusting of hair, then traced his collarbone, reacquainting herself with his magnificent body. "I've missed you so much," she whispered.

His eyes softened. Rolling to his side, he said against her ear, "Right now, with you in my arms, I can finally breathe. Even as you take away my breath."

She arched her neck, giving him access. He took it, kissing a trail to her lips.

The glorious sound of his zipper and the rustle of his jeans coming off had her reaching for him, needing to touch his velvet hardness.

"Lilith... So good," he groaned as she stroked him.

He pressed his mouth to hers, tracing the seam with his tongue. She tasted his desire.

And wanted more.

Removing her leggings and panties, she pulled him on top of her. He gave her exactly what she craved, entering her. It was slow and soul-shatteringly intense.

Between whispered endearments and gasps of ecstasy, her climax built. From his uneven breaths and powerful thrusts, his would be entangled in hers.

She tilted her hips, and that did it for both of them. Calling out his name, her short nails dug into his back as she fell into bliss. He followed her with a moan that spoke of euphoria.

After, he traced her shoulder with lazy, soft kisses. "Damn, I've missed your taste and scent." He ran the tip of his tongue along her skin, sending a delightful shiver over her.

She hummed with pleasure. "Oh, and what do I smell like?"

He nipped her collarbone. "Femininity." He shifted lower to tease a nipple. "Sensuality."

Bowing into his mouth, she gasped.

He rested his head above her heart. "And love."

Running her fingers into his hair, she massaged his scalp. "Because you own my heart, and I trust you with every vein and fiber of it."

Kissing the spot over her heart, he said, "I love you, and I'll earn and safeguard your trust every damn day."

"I love you too. And you already have."

A serene silence blanketed them. She continued to rub his scalp, letting her mind wander, not thinking about anything, merely enjoying the perfect moment.

Eventually, his breathing evened out as he fell asleep. The sound was a lullaby, and she let sleep take her, knowing the dreams she'd have tonight would never compare to waking in Asher's arms in the morning and all the days that followed.

EPILOGUE

*S*ix months later.

Lilith started to lift the box of books. The strain in her arms and legs had her returning it to the floor. "Want to switch?" she asked Asher.

He straightened from the half-dismantled desk. "Sure."

She rubbed her lower back. "Who knew paperbacks were so heavy."

He hefted the box, then kissed her temple. "How many did you stuff in here?" He grunted, heading to the front door.

"Maybe fifty."

"Feels like a hundred and fifty," he teased.

She admired the flex and bulge of his triceps and biceps. Watching him lift heavy stuff was sexy. Running a hand up his arm, she cooed, "I'll massage all your sore muscles tonight."

He quirked a brow. "*All* of them?"

"Mmm-hmm." Her fingers trailed down his sides to the waist of his jeans.

"Mom," Chloe grumbled. "Stop flirting and help us with the desk."

Lilith laughed, turning to her daughter. "What do you know about flirting?"

She rolled her eyes. "I'm almost twelve. Not two."

"Okay, my wise and ancient daughter, you and Raven get those two long pieces. I'll get the awkward one."

"Why didn't we hire a moving company?" Chloe whined.

It was a show of her willpower that Lilith didn't roll her eyes. "Because we managed it the first two times, we can do it one more time." Because seriously, this would be it. No more moving.

After many phone calls and letters, she'd found someone to rent her condo. Then just as they began boxing up their stuff to move back to her lake house, Tate told her he was leaving his high-profile job to run The Hill—he'd freaking bought it.

After discussing it with Asher, they'd decided to move in together, giving Tate her house. So, on this balmy June morning, she and Chloe were packing up their old life to begin a new chapter with Asher and Raven.

Lilith couldn't be happier. Everything felt possible. Asher was the love of her life. He was her best friend and lover. Whether or not they ever married, he'd be the only man for her.

Tate came into her office. "Your guy told me you needed help with your porn stash."

Lilith swatted her brother on the shoulder. "My romance novels aren't porn." She smirked, pointing to two boxes next to the laundry room. "They are titillating literature. And don't try stealing any of them."

"Don't worry, when it comes to 'titillating' stories, I prefer ones with pictures." He lifted one of the bigger boxes and grunted. "Shit, woman, are you sure these are books and not a dead body?"

"Stop complaining, or I'm going to sew dead fish in the curtains before handing you the keys to my house," she joked, lifting a large piece of her desk.

"You are wicked. Now I see the real reason you insisted I stay there. It was so you could torture me."

"Yup. You figured me out." She followed him outside to the moving van, giddy he'd be her neighbor. They'd even be closer than in the condos. "Oh, wait, I forgot to mark those boxes. These will go into the old guestroom. Asher's turned it into my office." After her online courses ended, she'd picked up accounts quickly. A home office was a must.

"I'm glad you'll have space. You'll need it while working on The Hill's books."

"You seem mighty confident I'll be taking on your restaurant," she joked.

"If you don't, I'm going to egg and toilet paper your house every night until you say yes."

After marking the boxes, Lilith said, "It'd be wise for you to remember, dear brother, you're my neighbor too, and paybacks are a bitch."

"Damn. Fine, you win. But you'll take care of my books, right?" he nearly pleaded.

She patted his cheek. "Of course."

He closed the rolling door of the moving van and muttered, "Putting these boxes in the extra bedroom is a waste of time."

Lilith's brows scrunched together. "What do you mean?"

"Because I'm willing to bet everything in my savings, this room will be a nursery within a few years."

A thrill of excitement raced through Lilith. She'd always wanted a large family, and when they'd first become friends, Asher had mentioned he'd pictured himself with a houseful of kids. Did he still feel this way?

As if summoned by her daydream, he wrapped his arms around her from behind. "It's a good thing we have a finished basement. Plenty of room for an office. Even another bedroom."

Happiness engulfed her, and she leaned into him, practically floating on air. "Yeah? You want more kids?" she asked.

He kissed her. "With you, definitely."

Afterword

Dear Reader,

Whether you're a returning or new, thank you. It is wonderful to write, but a dream to share my stories with you!

When I started this journey, I feared I'd never finish my first story. After I did, I was afraid I couldn't write another one. Now, I'm on my second series – with the second book being released this summer.

I'll let you in on a secret because you've traveled so far with me. The next book—Stormy Waters—will be Eden and Tate's!

If you're not ready to let go of Lilith and Asher, talk to others about them —by suggesting their story to others, leaving a review on Amazon, Goodreads, or whatever book site you love. These sites are great for discussing books. Not only will it let you chat about stories you love, but they help me out immensely. Even a simple sentence would mean the world to me and will keep Lilith and Asher's minds and hearts of other romance readers.

Check out the Opposites Attract series if you'd like to read more of my stories. Keep flipping for the links and more information about each book.

Thank you!

About Author

DK Marie loves to indulge in all things hot. Men, writing, reading, and coffee. The order of importance depends on the day.

Like characters in her books, she lives in Michigan, enjoying her happily ever after with her husband and kids. When not writing, she loves the theater, concerts, and traveling.

DK loves to hear from readers. You can find and connect with her at the links below.

Website: https://dkmarie.com

Twitter: https://twitter.com/DKMarieAuthor

Facebook: https://www.facebook.com/DKMarieRomanceAuthor

Instagram: https://www.instagram.com/dkmarieauthor/

TikTok: https://www.tiktok.com/@dkmarieauthor

Also By DK Marie

She's sweet. He's sexy. Together they might be new kind of fairy tale love....

Greta and Jacob aren't looking for love, but lust and longing strike on a stormy Michigan afternoon, leading to a few torrid hours of passion and pleasure. When the clouds parted, so did they, certain neither would fit into the other's vastly different life.

Weeks later, when they unexpectedly meet again, both believe rekindling the fire will destroy their meticulous plans and dreams. Yet, neither are able to resist the heat.

Jacob wants all of Greta, her heart and body, even though she could destroy the life he's struggled so hard to build for himself. He's also convinced she'll never see him as anything more than a blue-collar nobody—a temporary indulgence who doesn't belong in her world.

Greta agrees. He doesn't fit, and trying for more is a mistake. He'd cause nothing but upheaval and chaos in her orderly life. Yet, for someone so wrong, he feels so right.

As tempers flare and passions deepen, Greta and Jacob will have to decide if they're each other's fairy tale ending. Or nothing more than an erotic chapter.

She sings to the wild side of his heart, strumming his needs against his desires, disrupting his harmony.

Maggie Preswyck carries music in her soul; she lives and breathes melody. Nothing and no one can get in the way of her band's success. Including Tanner Reid— her sexy, temporary guitarist. His talent and quiet humor are irresistible. But mixing business with pleasure could destroy her heart and career.

Every time they rehearse, the chords of passion between them deepen. But Maggie will never give up on her music, and Tanner doesn't want the life of a musician—Her dream is his nightmare. With no middle ground, all that waits for them at the end of his time with the band is heartbreak.

Can Maggie and Tanner adjust their dreams, or will they become another sad love song?

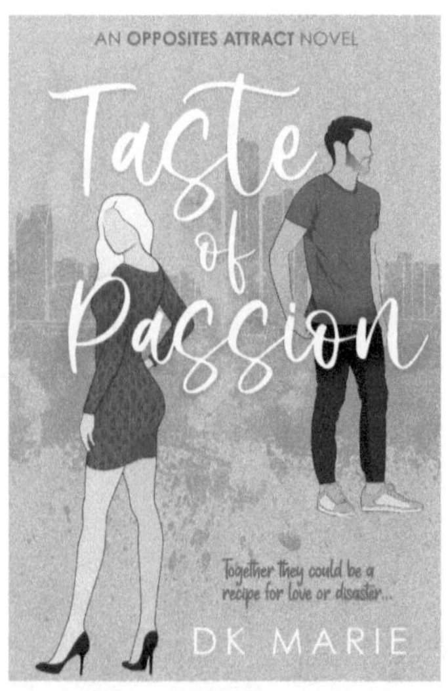

She has a taste for trouble. He craves more than her body. Together they could be a recipe for love or disaster...

Opposites, Cindy Meier and Will Grimm, have two things in common. They love to annoy each other, and their siblings are getting married. *That's it.*

Oh, and they have to plan the weekend wedding party. Will doesn't want to put up with the spoiled socialite who lives in a fantasy world. And Cindy could think of better ways to spend her free time with her hot but grumpy brother-in-law.

The only way to survive the awful chore is with snips, sarcasm, and sparring.

When they're forced together on the sunny beaches of Lake Michigan, their annoyance and amusement morph into something neither expected nor wanted—desire. They give in, agreeing it won't extend past the weekend. *It can't.* Will had finally crawled out of the hell he'd created, and someone like Cindy would send him back into it. And while she might enjoy Will's body and what he does with it, she won't change to fit into his life.

As they struggle to keep their attraction and deepening feelings at bay, they'll have to decide if overcoming their differences is worth the passion they've tasted...

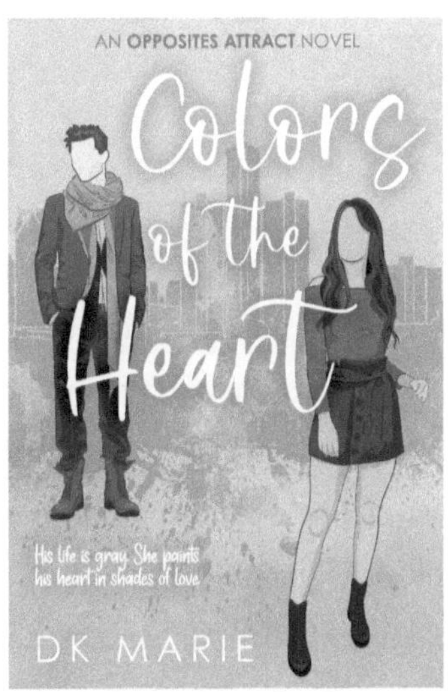

His life has become gray and drab. Her vibrancy paints the dark shadows of his heart, turning them into shades of love.

Harper Marquette pours her passion into her art, not men. But Lucas Genezen had seemed different— her opposite in a way that was refreshing and gentle. Falling for his kind eyes and sensual smile, she landed in bed with him—only to wake to her mistakes and an empty hotel room.

Lucas royally messed up with Harper, and she's better off without his battered heart and life. Yet he can't forget her and wants a second chance. But when she learns he's a young widow, she knows it's foolish to date a man who'll never be able to love her in return—even if it doesn't feel reckless when she's with him. They can't let go of each other or their pasts. Is it possible to embrace both and have a picture-perfect future together, or are they creating endless heartbreak?

Acknowledgments

There are so many people to thank. First is my family, who've supported me, even while they may not always understand my need to disappear with my characters for days, weeks, and months on end. They also remind me to join the real world, and though I grumble sometimes, I appreciate the balance. Love you.

Next to my writer friends, I'd be truly lost without your guidance and chats. They keep me sane. Thank you, Shanna V. Rowena Tisdale, Danielle Ancona, Beth Anderson, Tanna Jenkins, Margaret E., and those in the Inapporate Acres group and other DM groups.

There's also my talented editor, Brenda Margriet. Thank you so much for taking on this story last minute. I knew your insight would make this book shine.

Also, I must send a shout-out to my fantastic cover designer, Avery Kingston. Your eye for making covers fun and artful amazes me.

And to you. With readers, these stories would be only musings in my mind. Thank you for letting me share them with you.